For Amanda, you're alv

Abel's Revenge

This is a story about a city. As with all others, it's a place of violence. There are murderers, and they live among us.

This is also a tale about a couple — sometimes friends, occasionally lovers, but always partners. Dan and Olivia are fighting modern battles; the ones parents have over a lack of money, time or peace.

An escalating serial killer terrifies the streets and homes. The body count rises as their relationship crumbles. Society reveals its dark side, and no one is safe. Dan and Olivia experience this first-hand as danger closes in.

Will Abel's reign of terror ever end?

Who will live and who will die?

THRILLS, KILLS AND SPILLS IN THE SUBURBAN HILLS

Front page headline for the Evening Standard as madness, fear, and murder grip the city.

Chapter 1

Abel

My mother called it the sickness. Those six words sum up my childhood.

First, until I hit eighteen, she insisted I call her mother. That doesn't lend itself to warmth and affection. It's a poor baseline for family life. It may be that I was born damaged, but my upbringing made things worse.

My mother suffered complications after the birth. She experienced excessive bleeding and multiple stitches. They told her to think hard before having another child. In the end, I was it. It's strange to imagine their hopes and dreams resting with me. My destiny was elsewhere from their idle thoughts.

They called me Abel. It's powerful with an element of fear. My mother said she wanted a name people would remember. How right she would prove to be.

Second, my behaviour changed when I started senior school. I don't think anyone notices odd conduct before that unless you're off the scale. Mother found me blasting insects with a magnifying glass, or crucifying teddies on the rockery. Poor Action Man was burnt at the stake for failing to respond to questioning.

They caught me watching a neighbour's house in flames. Instead of making an emergency call, I'd sat on my coat on their lawn and watched the blaze take hold. The police thought they had an easily solvable case. They only exonerated me when the couple confessed they may have fallen asleep with a pan on the stove.

They asked why I didn't tell anyone about the fire. I said I assumed someone else would. I knew that wasn't true, and I simply wanted to see what would happen. After the fuss died down, I realised I was different. Not to everyone, but to most. I felt responsible, and an influential part of me enjoyed that.

I read the bible and came upon the story of Abel. I discovered his brother murdered him and then Abel was forgotten. The focus was on Cain, despite his terrible deed. To my young mind, that felt wrong. I took that lesson to heart. Evil people may commit dark deeds, but it is they who are remembered and is they who have the power.

The next year, a friend and I climbed a wall. He fell. The school found me observing him as opposed to going for help, despite his howling cries of agony. That ended another of my dwindling acquaintances, and the gossip about me pushing him found its way home. I had bursts of crazy behaviour and then spells of normality. My memories of events were hazy afterwards. I decided I didn't want to remember. Try it some time, it's a learned skill.

Thereafter, it was the sickness, as if labelling it made it somehow more acceptable to my mother. Like wrapping a dog shit in birthday paper. My mother wasn't affectionate anyway, so nothing much changed. My understanding was she thought parenthood was a duty you endured until the children left the house and were no longer your responsibility.

My father cross-dressed. She called that the problem. He edited books and worked from home. My memories are of him being in his office with his male friends, laughing and drinking. I recall thinking he had a great job.

I've no idea why my parents didn't split up as they led separate lives from what I could see. Perhaps because, even though she had no empathy, she did have determination, tenacity and her faith. Maybe that's what they'll inscribe on her gravestone. "Here lies Isabella, she persevered". She couldn't have expected things to work out the way they did. Bless her. The sickness and the problem. It's not surprising she wasn't fond of trips to the coast and family meals.

My dad's flamboyance became more noticeable as the years passed. Around the time I was acting oddly, he began to be seen around town. As Lucille. That's a tough thing to explain for any twelve-year-old. As a late-developer, I had little with which to defend myself.

That was a bad year. An impotent rage coursed through my body and a desire for control stamped itself on my personality. The bullies placed a G in front of my name. I became isolated and furious, and I wanted revenge. My parents moved us miles away. I left Abel behind and used my middle name.

I still struggled to connect with others and saw life as a game, the people just pieces — ones to be idly swept from the board when their time came. For unknown reasons, I didn't see children and animals in the same light. Maybe their innocence meant different rules applied. At the beginning, I hoped my parents would notice me. I soon quit that pointless task. Later, I wanted to lash out, to hurt, but I was too weak, and too lonely.

Long years passed. I finished school and applied to a college on the other side of the country, where nobody knew my history. There, I legally changed my surname, too.

I couldn't cope with the routine of academic life. The endless deadlines had me permanently on edge. Sleep eluded me. I remained in touch with my parents, but I discovered girls, drink and drugs. After a night out, Abigail, a girl from the local area, accused me of rape.

I had become interested in dominance and persuasion. I wasn't particularly bothered about having sex with the girls I met, but I was keen to see how far they'd go. It thrilled me to think someone I had met a few hours before, who I might have bought a drink, would later let me insert part of my body into hers.

As with all things, I pushed too much. Many women have no boundaries, but Abigail did. She reported me to the authorities, and it looked bleak. It turned out my dad knew an influential man from a club he attended. To my amazement, the charges were dropped if I agreed never to approach her again. I can only guess money changed hands. That was one of the few gifts my dad gave me. The other was the chat we had afterwards.

He called me to his office on a Sunday morning and stated that we should talk.

'People are different,' he said. 'You may find it better to conceal yourself in plain sight. Society expects us to live a certain way and, even if that's not who you are, it's easier to give people what they want. Eventually, like me, you won't be able to control the impulses from within. What then emerges is the real you. That creature may only be here for a short time. If that's the case, revel in the joy of those moments, and smile at the end.'

I remember nodding. Something inside recognised his words and their coils tightened on my soul.

'Failing that,' he said. 'Stifle it with alcohol. That worked for me.'

He grinned, but that's what I did. I self-medicated with a vast range of substances, and concealed myself amongst those who would reject me.

My mother was rigid, but she showed me right from wrong. My father was the dangerous one, because he taught me how to hide.

Six months later, I drove to Abigail's home to see if I wanted retribution. Her family had little and lived in a labourer's cottage on a farm. I waited behind a tree with a telescope until she appeared. The breeze swirled her dress, and I imagined her giggling as she pushed it down. However, I couldn't see the detail as even with the magnified vision she was still a blur. I wasn't stupid enough to be seen. Should I drive Abel to the deepest part of me, and bury him with shame? Would he leave me? Might Abel die?

Later, I pondered on what I thought about Abigail reporting me to the police as I have a memory of her on top, moaning with pleasure. Then the truth hit. I didn't feel anything at all.

Chapter 2

Judith, the birdwatcher

Judith pulls her large, front door closed and walks down her circular driveway. She stops when she arrives at the pavement and turns to the house. Such a grand building. She never thought she would only live in a few rooms. Raymond's Daimler is still parked outside the double garage. Not being able to drive herself, she wasn't sure what to do with it. The car, and most things, are losing the battle against the elements. She doesn't want to change anything though as this way, sometimes at least, it feels like he might return.

She picks her route along the bulging paving slabs. You need to be careful at this time of the morning. Her closest friend, only friend really, had broken her hip tripping on one. The infection she caught in hospital killed her. She would have been sixty today. Judith's vision blurs with tears as she struggles to remember how many years ago that accident was, and fails to recall why they always laughed together.

Lost in her memories, she bumps into the elbow of Thomas from a few doors away. He was in a trashy magazine she read about thirty-somethings partying in London and she recognised his face. Aftershave fills the air, and she admires his expensive going out clothes. Coming home clothes, perhaps. Thomas is with his new partner with the ridiculous beard. She never did like that particular look. They're necking, as always. Great, big, slavering kisses as though they're sharing the only remaining oxygen in the world.

Is it necessary to do that in the street? All of a sudden, she remembers how she was those first few weeks of love with her husband-to-be, and then she understands. Judith smiles and waits for them to stop so she can apologise. What she gets is a glance around of disdain. The boyfriend often says 'Hi', but he is under the thrall of her neighbour and Thomas refuses to acknowledge Judith. It's one of the few things that still evokes a reaction. It makes her mad. A week must have gone by since she had a chat with anyone.

She walks away considering whether talking to the postman about discarded rubbish constitutes a conversation. The model who lives further down her street approaches. She doesn't know that's the girl's job, it's just a game Judith plays. The woman has the most wondrous, long hair. Biblical brown locks. The kind you want to reach out and touch. It's loose in a Spanish gypsy style and makes her think of wild horses. Maybe her name's Claudia, and she does shampoo commercials. Judith waits for their eyes to meet so they can hail each other.

The beautiful lady breezes past and, as usual, ignores her as well. Where do they all go until five in the morning? No one else greets her on the way. Judith enters the park. There are street lamps on the path but they don't have the power of the ones on the road. Strange shadows stretch from bins and benches. Judith doesn't fear the dark anymore. She knows the worst things that happen to you occur while you're in bed.

That's how it's been since Raymond died. Every day, sometimes hourly, she recalls those final few months. A year has passed, and she still exists in a pea-souper of grief. And of guilt. He was the poor man choking on his last breaths. The one whose mucus caused those horrifying sounds from the back of his throat. However, she often felt like the victim. He was leaving her alone, so it was Judith's tragedy.

There's a field at the edge of the park. It's wasteland mostly. Kids have pulled two fence panels loose. If you are small it is possible to squeeze through. Once, four boys saw her from a distance, but they fled as if they had seen a ghost. She doesn't worry about meeting anyone with evil intent. She has little to lose and may even appreciate the drama. It would be good to know her heart still beats.

A pond in the middle of the field attracts the wildlife. The dawn chorus builds as first light appears on the horizon. A fallen log on the far side makes a comfortable seat to let the birds distract her from the pain, so she steps through the long grass. There's little breeze. What there is keeps her hood on her head. She feels it shift and swirl, and that's when her nostrils flare.

Judith believes that the sense of smell is the final one to depart at the dreadful end. The only way she seemed to be able to settle Raymond in those awful, relentless, last few days, was to cuddle his skeletal frame into her body. Let him draw in her comforting fragrance. Obviously, he smelled of death by then, but there was a time when his scent close by was all she needed. Is that why she allowed the rest of her life to slip away and is that the reason she has nothing to live for?

This stench though is something completely different. She knew it over forty years ago, and the vivid recollection surprises her. In the distance, she sees a thin trail of smoke. Removing her pocket binoculars, she scans the area and watches the wisps drift through a large tree. There can be nothing good over there. To her surprise, she strides towards it with purpose.

She's subconsciously aware of absent birdsong. She hears an animal scurry away through the undergrowth. Other than the ever-present hum of traffic, this world is nearly silent. The wind has changed back but there's no need of a reminder. She felt the whoosh as the car went up that day. It had driven into a skip, not even that fast, but the resulting explosion could have been from any number of war films.

Judith and others had stood close by and watched. There was nothing anyone could have done. She understood instantly it was the aroma of human flesh cooking that had caused her tongue to fold against the roof of her mouth as if to block her airwaves. A strange smell. Sweet and sickly charcoal was the closest description she could give when eager children probed her experience later. It registered in her brain as something never to be forgotten.

In the clearing under the tree is the metal-spring frame of a single bed. There is no avoiding the reek so close but Judith doesn't care. The bed on its own isn't surprising. She's seen many a hammock or tent in that spot, even a fridge once. It's the contorted black body that grabs her attention. On approaching, she sees used, disposable, barbecue trays under the bed. Judith also clocks the twisted wire that secures the wrists and ankles to the four corners.

Whatever clothing there had been is burnt and unrecognisable, yet the face is untouched except for a few bruises and marks. On close inspection, the face belongs to a woman free from pain. Not old either, as her skin is freckled and clear, but in life she'd have been painfully thin. What had this person done to be treated in such a way? Did she deserve it? Maybe she was a drug addict and a prostitute. Judith had watched the torture of Raymond by a relentless cancer that knew no mercy. At least this one's demise would have been over relatively fast.

Judith wonders why she doesn't feel for this girl's plight. Has she become a monster herself? The emotion bubbling away in her body is not sorrow or shock; it is anger. It's resentment of the model and the gay lovers who ignored her earlier. They know nothing of suffering and what Judith has been through. They're too self-obsessed and arrogant to consider other's feelings. Judith wants noticing, but the thought of getting involved with the police is unappealing. She checks her mobile and notes there is a reasonable signal. There's no escape from the twenty-first century here. An anonymous payphone from the street will do instead.

She turns to leave. She'll need to find somewhere else to watch the birds. A trickle of sweat rolls down her back as a creaking sound comes from behind her. She's too old to run and looks back at the body. All is quiet. Even the cars are silent. She edges closer, looking down at the face. Is that a twitch she can see? Judith peers down and suddenly the girl's eyes ping open. They scream in unison.

Chapter 3

Dan Flood

'Dan, can you come here before you leave?'

It's an order, not an invitation. I'd hoped to slip out, like a pimpernel with a quest for mid-strength lager. Olivia has collapsed on the sofa with the dog. Her eyes droop and she absent-mindedly fiddles with her shoulder-length blonde hair. The Labrador, Bailey, looks far more pleased to see me than she does.

Bailey loves me more than the rest. That's because I'm the one who walks him. Perhaps in his own canine way he hopes to even up the affection in the house. I resisted the terrible names my daughter, Grace, came up with for him. Plank, Donut, and Peanuts being the memorably poor ones. Bailey was reasonable in comparison. Of course, he doesn't respond to that now.

Life likes to mess with me. Our son, Charlie, couldn't pronounce Bailey when he was young, so he called him Baby. We all thought that was hilarious, so we called him the same. Therefore, if you hear the plaintive cries of a spurned lover on the common at dawn shouting 'Baby, come here', that's me. Only Peanuts was worse.

'God, can you believe this?' She gestures to the TV.

The screen fills with smoke, debris, and running people.

'Where is that? Greece?'

She shoots me a disdainful glare. 'It's our city centre.'

'Wow.'

'Wow? You say wow? A gang stabbed an immigrant to death in the street yesterday.'

'I apologise. Wasn't I shocked enough for you? I didn't realise we have acceptable comments to make for that sort of thing.'

She gives me a small shake of her head so I know I'm wrong, but a smile sneaks out.

'Sorry I snapped. I've had a draining day.' Tiredness hangs heavy on her face.

'You wanted to live here.' Heaven knows why I thought it necessary to slip in that blade. That argument is old and weary.

'Have you seen Charlie?' she asks.

Is it a question or a demand?

'Yeah. Chucky is in the kitchen trying to hammer something square into something round. Like the fridge into the washing machine.'

'I wish you wouldn't call him that.'

'You wanted to call him Charles.'

'I wouldn't have done if I knew you'd keep calling him Chucky.'

'I didn't know the devil possessed him back then.'

'He's a normal three-year-old boy.'

The wreckage of our house indicates otherwise, but I can see when I'm beaten.

'What's Grace doing?'

'God knows. I've not seen her for hours.'

A final dirty glance lets me understand any more banter wouldn't be appreciated.

'She's in her room, lining up those plastic things that cost more pound for pound than gold.'

'Are you meeting Ian?'

She knows I am. Why do I feel guilty? I nod with caution.

'Don't get too pissed.'

'Of course not.'

I turn to leave and consider if I should kiss her goodbye. Bailey's stomach gurgles which is a regular occurrence, unless it was Olivia's. Either way, I give it a miss. She barks another comment at my back.

'Remember what I said.'

Are there any worse words a woman can say to a man? I have no idea what she's on about. Since having children, my memory has become a piece of wood left in water — a heavy, useless thing that absorbs little. I forget the names of everything. Those plastic things, the names of other people's kids and any date of importance to make sure I'm always on the back foot.

Our goldfish even stare at me as if to say, 'Nice to see you again, Dan', and I can't remember what they're called. Their bowl is in the hall. Cleaning it is one of my jobs. I peer into their murky world and note they're still relaxing on the surface.

My shoes aren't where I left them. I swear she moves them to further mess with the little confidence I have in my ability to recall even the most basic of information. My dog walking boots will do. I hope the mud and grass will fall off on the way. She marches out of the lounge as I put my hand out to close the front door, and I think she's come to kiss me goodbye after all. Instead she climbs the stairs, adding a closing directive.

'Don't forget.'

The door shuts, and a chill wind buffets my nervous eyes.

Chapter 4

Olivia Jones

I climb the stairs, picking up a tie on the way, and step over his shoes at the top. I toss his work shirt into the wash basket. Why does he leave them next to it? Surely it can't be that much more effort to stick things inside. I trip over a pair of trainers in the bedroom and wonder again if he has early onset Alzheimer's.

I must try not to nag him. When did we become a couple that didn't kiss each other when one left the house? He is trying and I know he struggles to live in such a busy city after growing up in a little town and the life he later led. I brought him here. Responsibility lies with me.

We met in Vietnam. Initially, on a bus. There were many shocking twelve-hour rides when you backpack through a place like that. We didn't talk the first time we saw each other. Every seat was taken, and he had to ask a man to move a box so he could sit down. After many hours of stern silence, the man growled at him in terrible English that the box contained his wife's ashes. Poor old Dan. Those never-ending journeys along damaged roads on broken seats are rarely easy but that took some beating.

We sat ten seats away but caught each other's eye. He gave me a small grin as though he'd known me his whole life. It still makes me smile now when I remember. I was approaching forty and yet I stuck my tongue out at him in the manner of a naughty schoolgirl. He laughed, bold and loud, like he didn't care what anyone thought. He held my stare for a few seconds, then winked, and a shimmer ran through me. I somehow knew he would be important in my life and a sense of calm came over me that had been missing for a long, long, time.

I do what I've often done since he moved into my house, even though it's been many years. With stealth, I slip to the window to watch him walk down the street. He usually saunters along, smiling at people, and it always makes me relax. I hate that we argue as I love him so much. Things will get better when the kids are older. Then we'll have more time for each other. He hasn't come into view yet, so I wave at our neighbour cleaning his fabulous car. He's a nice guy. We're lucky to have friendly people around us.

I adore where we live. I bought this house over a decade ago before prices went crazy. It's so peaceful. We couldn't afford to buy here now, with me being part-time and Dan's salary. I try to make him think it's both our homes, but I know it can be difficult to move to a place where someone has lived a life before you met.

The leaves are turning in the long tree-lined street. It's as though we live in a village as opposed to the suburbs of London, and I know we'll be okay. Soon we'll marry, and then he'll belong.

Chapter 5

Dan

I rest my head on the front door for a minute. Olivia and I are drifting further apart. Will we ever get it back? On cue, to sour my mood, I hear the idiot next door whistling. I can't sneak out the rear of the house as the railway line runs along there, so I have to walk out the same way every time. He will be in his drive, cleaning that monstrosity of a car. If I hustle he might not notice.

The *Chariots of Fire* theme tune powers my legs as I pace past him.

'Hey, Dan.'

His posh New York accent stops me in my steps as if a border guard shouted freeze.

'Mike, good to see you. Washing your car?' *Again.*

It's getting late in the year and the air has a nip at this hour, yet he wears a tight T-shirt. I'm a pansy in my three layers. His car looks like it cost more than our house. It's a flame red behemoth with an enormous bonnet. He cleans it with long, languid strokes as though he's stroking his penis. Being British, I'm too polite to comment. Instead, I admire his rippling muscles and squint at the flash from his megawatt smile.

He's a doctor or surgeon or something. He has told me before but I couldn't concentrate due to the rubbing.

'Car looks great.'

Our ride sits embarrassed next to his and is far from great. We have a sensible people carrier, and it's brown. Yes, that's right. Try to think of the last brown vehicle you saw. Why make a car in that colour? We, for obvious reasons, bought it cheap. I didn't think driving a shit-coloured car would bother me. Yet, every time I get in it, a piece of me dies.

It's not even well made. The seats at the back are, in effect, a crumple zone for when you are rear-ended by any of the plethora of uninsured cars around here. If we have to give other people's kids a lift along with ours, I always shove theirs in the back. Is that normal? Or should I share the risk? When I'm driving them, I have visions of a squashed tin of sardines with the tomato sauce oozing out.

Not only is it an eyesore, but it's also a total money pit. The thieving sharks at my local garage grin when I turn up. I'm practically paying their pensions with their exorbitant demands. Every time I've arrived to collect my car the mechanic has been sitting on a tyre, smoking. Even Mike says he'd like to teach them a lesson. He calls the manager Thieving Terry. We still use the garage as we suspect they're all like that and at least Thieving Terry's is situated nearby.

Mike nods in agreement at my car compliment, and taps the wing mirror next to him as though it's his dog.

'Thanks, man. I love this car. When you coming over for a few beers? I have my own theatre. We could watch the game or a movie.'

Never. There's no way I'm going in there. I'll bet he preys on men such as me. Beaten down by life, so we're too weak to fight him off.

'Soon, buddy.'

He makes me say words like buddy, too. I disappoint myself. I deliver a rictus grin, hunch my back, and shuffle away.

Chapter 6

Abel

I scare myself. The venom is building.

Each fresh insult from the people in this city drags me back in time to those slow months after I quit college. I returned to my parent's home a failure, and wallowed in pity on my bed. Anger coursed through me, but instead of going mad, I let the darkness loose.

There was only one victim. The shadowy path by the river was a place I knew well. Only a few ventured there at night even though it was a shortcut to the housing estates from popular pubs. I cared not about the gloom and cycled without lights. I bumped into the man and knocked him to the floor. He was a target selected and drowned due to his lonely, drunken vulnerability.

I awoke next morning in soaking clothes and remembered something; not much, but an intoxicating taste of power.

Mother avoided my bedroom, so I concealed the evidence. That said, part of me wanted to be caught. The headlines called it a tragic drowning. The newspapers wrote of the perils of drink. That made me laugh because I was the danger. In my mind, I had cleansed him with the silence of eternity. I considered handing myself in and owning up because everyone should know my name. I lusted for recognition.

But living at home was like existing in a vacuum. There was no joy or pain, no highs or lows, and more importantly, no stress. We had regular, healthy meals and trips to church. The Abel who watched the fire he set after turning the neighbours stove on, the boy who shoved his friend off a wall, the student who abused that girl, and the man who did that terrible deed, departed. The urges died as the memories faded. I decided I wouldn't become that which we fear when we glance over our shoulder. With a vow of no more sickness, I would be a person who respected others. One who forgave their foolish ways.

My mother gave me money, I suspect to get rid of me, and I left to float around and enjoy life. I took jobs for little reward and even less responsibility. Days melted into months of an alcohol-filled haze with no concerns. I lived cheaply and saved hard, knowing I could always just leave before any pressure came to bear. The slightest stir from the sleeping demon had me packing my bags. Soon, he was completely forgotten. Many years went happily by.

How foolish am I? Of course, Abel attempts to return. I ignore him, but time weakens all. I trained myself to never look back and to never give in. There were to be no more regrets. Nevertheless, I fear he takes control. Already, there are huge holes in my memory. What do I do? Or is it already too late, and should I be asking myself what have I done?

I could see a psychiatrist but, as you can imagine, it's hard to tell someone you possess a murderous part you struggle to control. Besides, I'd hate to peer too deeply inside my soul and see what lurks at the bottom. I don't want or need analysing because I know Abel wants to be recognised. He yearns to be known and feared. Would more people die? I doubt that is his true purpose. However, if he breaks free, nothing remains sacred, and in his pursuit of notoriety, no one is safe.

Chapter 7

Dan

It should only be a ten-minute stroll to the pub, but it's dusk and I'll have to walk around the park instead of through. Strange things happen in there. This city is brimming with CCTV cameras, but not in that place. It's like a different world in there.

The junkies hang about near the entrance. Got any spare change, guv? I might as well give them a can of cider and cut out the middleman. The beggar couple I often see outside the railway station is there. Sores weep on her face. I chuck them my coins and tell them to buy vegetables. He has the good grace to laugh, and stands to chat.

'Thank you. Some people actually spit at us.'

'There are a lot of pricks about.'

'You know, I hate them. I despise my existence enough without that. One day, I'll have my revenge. By the way, I accept notes.'

'Perhaps you wouldn't be in this position if you accepted jobs?'

I leave chuckling as he shouts after me to offer him one.

Like that man, I never expected, or wanted, to end up in a place like this. My job destroys me. It's worse than being a battery hen. At least they don't have to go out for lunch. My salary seems reasonable, but here it's minimum wage. A fantastic salary in Cannon Ball, North Dakota is a poor one in Los Angeles. The same amount gets you nice things in Bitchfield, Lincolnshire, but little in London. Yes, these places do exist.

The only ones lower in the food chain than me are the Australians crammed four to a room. At least they're all high. What I'm saying is only rich people have a good time here. These big, urban areas are places with no emotion. Make a mistake and crack a smile, then a huge hand comes from the heavens and two fingers pop your head.

Only a few streets from our road, the houses deteriorate in quality, and passing faces admire the pavement or their latest phone. I regularly see an old man wearing an ancient three-piece suit in his bay window, the paint peeling from the frames. Today, he stares. I raise my hand in greeting but his gaze goes right through me and his expression remains the same. Ignorant sod.

I'm looking forward to seeing Ian, though. Apart from work *friends*, he is the only one I can meet for a no-pressure beer. He's mad, but keeps me anchored. I think I'd go insane myself without Ian. He reminds me of the fun person I used to be.

I lengthen my stride, fantasising that I'm on my way to a country pub. I'll find large comfortable chairs and open fires. The barman will greet me by name and have a pint of chilled, frothing lager ready without even having to ask for it. Next to my drink? A big bowl of home cooked crisps, unfettered by anyone's piss-covered fingers. Ian will be waiting, waving, as the jukebox quietly plays a selection of my favourite tunes.

Instead, I stand outside Café Bleu, and groan. It looks as inviting as a dentist from the front, and the only thing that will be blue is me when I pay their eye-watering prices. Glossy, disinterested teenagers staff this anaemic shell. They serve me as though I've inconvenienced them. Every time I arrive, I stare at their blank faces and it's clear I'm unwelcome.

There used to be loads of good pubs and bars, but over time they closed due to the double-edged axe of the smoking ban and ridiculously cheap supermarket alcohol. In the UK now, it's cheaper to buy a can of lager in those shops than a bottle of water. Not here though. We could meet elsewhere, but Ian is happy to come here, and it means I don't have the depressing experience of waiting for, and then getting on, a city bus.

The place, as always, is empty. Ian is nowhere to be seen. I stand at the bar and attempt to burn the back of the barmaid with my Superman X-ray vision. It doesn't work. She must have heard the door go, but tenderly slides a finger over the screen of her iPhone.

On every other occasion I've been here it has resembled an arctic winter, but tonight it's boiling. My many layers cook me like a microwave meal. By the time she graces me with her presence, sweat stings my eyes.

She's the one Ian calls 'The Russian'. She is chillingly beautiful. Azure glare, platinum hair, make-up three or four inches thick, and a face that never smiles. Not for me anyway. She looks twelve years older than my daughter which is a sobering start to my evening. I admire her slim figure in haute couture clothes, and glance at my filthy shoes. I feel like the vagrants in the park I've just been pitying.

Ian always describes her as being 'so clean'. As though she's different from someone else who is fresh out the shower. One reason I enjoy his company is that he has amusing low-moral fibre. He says she's so hot she could poo on him if she wanted. She is pretty, but I'd probably draw the line at that.

My pint looks like a glass of urine. She doesn't even ask for the money, only holds out her hand and gestures at the till. I take a note from my wallet, reach in my pocket for coins, and remember I gave them to those blood-sucking tramps. She plucks the note from my fingers as though she's removing a hair from a slice of cake. Ian arrives as she slams my change on the bar.

'Make that two, please.'

There is a pause, a glance to her phone indicates she wants to say no, then a scowl as she pours.

Ian looks me up and down.

'Have you been hiking?'

Chapter 8

The squat

Barry Butler loves his job. Not his actual profession of course. That's a mind-numbing role where he watches the minutes and his life tick by while advising people on the best deal to save money on their energy provider. It's a pointless self-defeating existence. They've even brought in hot desking, so he has to sit at a different terminal each day. He can often smell whoever had the misfortune to have finished their miserable eight hours on the phone before him.

After his girlfriend dumped him for their boss, he's stopped bothering to pin his photographs up at the start of a shift. However, the money is good. He upgraded his wheels and bought new Under Armour tactical boots. As soon as he put them on, he gritted his teeth. He wears them tonight, and he feels pretty damn good.

That's because, for thirty-two hours a month, he is Special Constable Butler — a man with power. Admittedly, they don't pay him, but he loves it so much, he does it for free. He knows he walks taller in the uniform. He doesn't belong in a suit. Sometimes Barry lets his imagination run wild and imagines himself as Judge Dredd. He growls to himself, 'I am the law.'

A surge of adrenalin flows through him and he pedals faster. A member of the public rang in and explained that the front door of a house in their road has been open wide all night. He knows the area well. In fact, he is sure he's been to that property before. A twinge of fear unsettles his stomach.

Turpin Street is always gloomy. The streetlamps flicker here and normal people rarely venture out after dark. It's strange as the surrounding areas are lovely. Detective Constable Jordan told him that a rich sheikh owned many of the houses along here, but he'd disappeared a year ago in suspicious circumstances. The buildings were mortgage free though, so they remained unloved and empty. They were gradually going to ruin.

Mrs Jordan is a fantastic officer. Barry looks up to her. With luck, he will be a real policeman, not a plastic copper like the newspapers kept calling people such as him. Just think, he could work with professionals every day. It's a shame he keeps failing the entrance tests.

The homeless took notice of the opportunity that the vacant dwellings provide. Like rats, they have swarmed into the buildings. Barry hates these bastards, but he also secretly admires them. He wished he had the balls to jack his job in and live off the grid. Maybe one day, but he needs a reference for his next police application, so there's no escape at the moment.

He arrives at his destination and props his push-bike again the wall. Music blares out of the window opposite. He recognises it as the place he came to last time. A female squatter said a man raped her. They arrested the person she described but the victim then disappeared and the case collapsed. Three youths walk into the small garden from the house facing him and jeer. They've made a fire in a bin and it lights them up like devils. The rapist is one of them. Barry can see his glinting, gold front tooth in his grinning mouth from where he stands.

When he becomes a real policeman, he will come back here and arrest them. The sweet stench of marijuana wafts over to him. That's a reason right there for him to confront them. It's a shame they aren't given guns. In the meantime, he'll take the bike inside or they'll steal it. He knows he should wait for the other officer sent to join him, but hanging around outside with these idiots is unappealing. He wheels his bike through the small garden and up the steps. The door the neighbour said was open is almost closed, so he nudges it wide with his front tyre.

'Police! Is anyone there?'

He hears the men behind him mimic his shout. There is no reply from inside. He leans the bike against the first closed door on the right. There is a light on in a room at the bottom of the corridor. It seems like a long way to the end of the house. They designed them narrow back when this was built. Barry wonders if it was a stupid idea then, too.

He isn't Judge Dredd anymore. His steps through the dusty surface feeling inadequate. Shards of glass tinkle on the tiled floor. The stairs lead up to total darkness. There's no way he will go up there. Barry considers the glow from the far room. There shouldn't be any lights working in here. All the services including electricity would have been disconnected long ago. As he gets closer, the light ahead draws him in. He doesn't think he could stop even if he wanted to.

The galley kitchen is filthy. The surfaces appear to have had full bins emptied upon them. He tries the switch as the bulb is still present but only a click is his reward. It's colder as he approaches the final half-open door. Again, he cries out. 'Police, make yourself known.'

Barry hears nothing, there is only a build-up of pressure between his ears — an increasing roar that loosens his bowels.

Slow, deep breaths echo in the silence. Barry reminds himself, he is the law. If he can't handle something as mundane as this, he isn't worthy of the uniform. With a final sharp inhale, he draws his baton, and nudges the door back. There is no one there. The light is a big torch on a stool pointing at the ceiling. The only other thing in the room is an open freezer cabinet. There's a cable running to the window and a slight hum indicating it's turned on.

Barry leans over the cabinet and notes the chill from within. There are lumps inside, covered in a thick layer of frost from the lid not having been shut for some time. A familiar item sticks up, he reaches in and pulls the piece of metal, and a pair of spectacles comes away. There are eight frozen masses in the freezer and Barry knows what they are. He decides he doesn't want confirmation and backs out of the room.

He walks, then runs down the corridor, slipping and sliding on the trash. A banana peel has him careering over, but he corrects himself and snatches at his bike. The door it was leaning against swings open, and there they are. Eight chairs in a circle. The bodies face each other — a blood stained chainsaw on a table at their centre. There's no talking though, because they're headless. Written in large red letters on the long mirror are the words 'PARDONED'.

Chapter 9

Dan
At Café Bleu

Ian lowers himself into his seat in the same way a crane driver puts a fifty-ton block of concrete in place. I repeat the manoeuvre.

'Man, we are getting old,' I say.

'You're full of the joys of spring.'

'It's autumn, that's why.'

'Let me guess, job doing your pip in?'

Ian works for a top investment bank. Despite our years of travelling together, he still managed to pass his exams. He's a natural, so companies ignore his flaky CV. He has a habit of jacking in his job, without giving notice, for any better offer — commercial or leisure. They disregard this. Therefore, his wage is immoral. That said, he insists on paying more than his fair share, and if I'm skint he's happy to pay for everything. I often blame my destructive relationship with alcohol on him.

My salary of course sucks. It's time to complain.

'Yeah, it's getting worse. We're so short-staffed, I can't cope, yet they expect us team leaders still to hit the ever-increasing targets. I'm so stressed by leaving time I've started having a beer on the train on the way home. That's fine on a Friday, but you get odd looks on a Monday.'

I take two big gulps of my now lukewarm piss and grimace. 'I'm worried I'm becoming a closet alky.'

'You're hiding it well.'

The barmaid distracts Ian by marching past to pick up an empty. I grin as she doesn't smile at him either.

'I don't know where the years have gone. One minute I'm chasing chicks through nightclubs, now, given the choice, I'd rather watch someone else do the gruesome, tiring deed, than do it myself.'

Ian laughs. 'No way. I'd still have a go myself.'

'My metabolism is so slow, I only need to glimpse at a donut and my moobs expand a cup size.'

'Rubbish, you're still slim compared to most of our peers.'

For the record, Ian weighs much less than I do.

'I'm so tired, the default expression on my face is similar to that dog, that famous one. Damn, what's his name?'

'K9.'

'You tool, that's a robot.'

'Lassie.'

'Jesus, why the hell would I look like Lassie?'

'Droopy?'

'Yes, that's it. Hang-dog, that's me.'

'Well, you've got two young kids, so it's not surprising.'

I examine Ian. He could pass for thirty-five. Not that his age concerns women if he's able to slip his vulgar salary into the conversation. Not for the first time, I think his total antipathy towards having children was the right call.

'Yeah, I suppose. I'm washed out.'

'You're only forty-two, you moaning old git. We could get some coke!'

Ian's face opens up as though he's discovered the cure for male pattern baldness, which is something else I'm too far gone for.

'Yes, brilliant idea. That's your solution for everything.'

Nevertheless, a treacherous growl echoes through my innards.

'Well, it is the answer for tiredness.'

He has a point, but there's more than the price to pay.

'I can do without the life-shortening paranoia that tomorrow would bring, thank you very much. That last stuff you got wasn't even coke.'

'That was good shit.'

'No, it wasn't. It was blatantly Chinese compound X. I spent the next week feeling like my neck was a metre long. Let's just have a few beers. I said I was only popping out for a couple. I'm already in enough trouble.'

'Missus still giving you earache?'

'Yes, I can't do anything right, no matter how hard I try.'

'That's women for you.'

'I'm not entirely blameless. We both irritate each other.'

'Well, I can imagine how you would infuriate someone. Olivia's a great girl. What does she do that winds you up?'

I search the recesses of my battered brain for a suitable example. 'I keep washing the old Chinese food tubs, and she keeps throwing random parts away. So, we have a drawer full of mismatched bottoms or lids. When I said why do you keep chucking them out, she said I didn't know you wanted to keep them.' I pause for dramatic effect, then deliver the coup de grâce. 'Then, why the hell am I putting them in the dishwasher?'

Ian shakes his head and gets another round of drinks. He realises he's in for a moaning session that might not make any sense. He plonks my drink in front of me, and says, 'Carry on. It's good to get your feelings off your chest.'

I continue because I've got more. 'She drove home with a flat. Knackered the tyre and the wheel.

She said she thought something felt wrong. Why the heck didn't she stop and check?'

'You aren't getting on well, your girlfriend has no common sense, and your drawers are full of useless plastic. Why don't you leave?'

I pause to contemplate this. It isn't as though the thought hasn't crossed my mind on a continuous loop lately. 'It's the kids.'

'You can't stay together for the kids.'

'Why not? My parents did.'

'Yes, and look what a rounded fellow you've turned out to be.'

I snort lager through my nose.

'Would you be together if you had no kids?'

'No way. I'd be free.'

'There you go then.'

I take a large sip of my latest drink and am pleased to find it has fizz in it on this occasion. Maybe she does like him more. I consider his words as Ian plays the devil's advocate well.

If we didn't have kids would we argue? It's parent-related shit that causes problems. The never having enough sleep. The fact they can be insanely irrational, and hassling until you explode. We have so little time for each other now, when we're not arguing about fast food containers. When you have children, it often appears as though the other person is taking advantage. The reality of it is you're both having a crap time. Might we be fine if we were childless?

'So, what are you going to do?' His inquiry drags my mind back from those pointless questions.

'I'll suck it up until the good times roll.'

He gives me an exasperated look. 'I thought you were getting married?'

'Yeah, we are. We were. I've since realised that marriage is what you do before you have children to stop you splitting up when they arrive. Then when you want to bale, it's much more inconvenient. After you have kids, you struggle to be nice to each other for any length of time without having a barney. That's not conducive to planning a white wedding. Besides, she isn't bothered either.'

'You reckon? I remember when you first met. It was sickening. Like being with a pair of teenagers, slobbering over each other.'

'It was brilliant. I impressed her with my witty repartee. Although, we were different people back then. I must say, it was a surprise when she said she was pregnant.'

'You chose to move to London afterwards. You could have told her you weren't interested. There's no point moaning now. You need to get on and make the most of it. Remember somebody somewhere is praying for the things you take for granted.'

Oh God, he must be drunk. It's horrible to hear sensible reason from my dearest friend. The shock on my face makes him smile.

'You sure you don't want any cocaine?'

I give him the finger and check to see if they've put any crisps out yet. If I get there first, they'll still be okay.

Much later, I skip home — pleased I've resisted my evil pal's illegal thoughts. My stomach rumbles and I wonder if Olivia wants a burger.

Chapter 10

Olivia

The doorbell sounds and I let my closest friend Rachel in. She's keen to enter and beams at me.

'Who's the beefcake next door?'

'Nice to see you too.'

'Priorities over pleasantries. Is he single?'

'Mike? I'm not sure. Dan thinks he's a dangerous pervert.'

'Takes one to know one.'

I'd gone travelling with Rachel when I met Dan. She never warmed to him. It's a shame as I feel stuck between them. The first time I had a proper conversation with Dan was in a bar in Saigon called The Heart of Darkness. Rachel and I had decided to spend three months backpacking around Asia as a fond farewell to our thirties. We were both single, childless, and had spent our whole lives concentrating on our careers. We both wanted kids, but suspected it was too late.

It's possible Rachel is jealous. Although I don't believe that's the case. I'm sure she wants the best for me. We're both forty-seven now so her motherhood ship has sailed and sunk. She is godmother to both our kids. When she moved to California last year with work, I lost a good friend and a brilliant babysitter. I think those "couple-nights" she freed up for Dan and me, kept us together in the early days.

She comes over and kisses me, with a worried expression in her eyes. 'You look tired.'

'I am.'

'Dan not pulling his weight again?'

I hate mouthing off to her as I know there are two sides to every argument. But I can sense the pressure building in my head over our struggles. If I don't release it soon, a pair of horns will burst out of my forehead.

'He tries.'

Rachel chuckles.

'They all do. You come and have a glass of wine with Auntie Rach and tell her his shortcomings.'

'Okay, but alcohol always makes me fall asleep next to Grace when she reads me her story.'

'Go on, live a little.'

Rachel is from Dublin, and has thick, sexy, long, black hair. She likes a few glasses of wine. She says she finds it hard to lose weight, seemingly unaware that alcohol is full of sugar.

We settle on the sofa and I vent. 'He's so messy. He can walk into a room which a tornado has ripped through, step around the debris, and sit and read in the middle of it. I finish work and come home to two hours of housework.'

'Give him the talk.'

'I'd love to, but we aren't getting on well, so I don't want to pester him. He's trying and he will do the jobs if I ask him, but I have to be specific: empty the washing machine before lunch, hang it out properly, fill the dishwasher, press the button to turn it on, remove when finished, pick up children. Like a robot giving orders. If I don't, he doesn't do it, or says he'll do it later.'

We're interrupted by my son coming out of the lounge. He's grinning.

'Mummy, I've done a poo in my big boy pants.'

I put him to bed and tonight *I* read to Grace to keep me awake. There's no rush as I hear Rachel doing the washing-up downstairs. I leave Grace snuggled up and content. My daughter insists on having the light on after Dan made a *Gremlins in the wardrobe* joke. I don't mind so much. I love that she falls asleep so fast and then I can see her dreaming. Young children have such perfect skin. Even now, I still check for her rising chest.

'Isn't he a bit big for shitting himself?'

'What a charming phrase. You're right though. He's okay for number ones but reckons he can't tell when the nasty business is arriving. He farts like a sailor too. The male of the species is a filthy beast.'

'Here, listen. These men never grow out of it. I have a funny but horrible story for you.'

'I don't want to hear a sordid tale full of sex. It'll remind me of what I'm missing.'

'No, it's worse than that. You've got to hear this. I met Graham through Internet dating. He seemed fantastic. He was wealthy, bright, and fit. We had a few meals and things progressed so he came around my house to watch a movie, and I made a curry. I wasn't sure he was ready for Rachel's Ass Scorcher, but I thought if it's meant to be, he'll cope. You know I enjoy a small kick.'

What Rachel means by small kick is a sizzling hellfire blast that will leave you dabbing your rear end with wet cotton wool for twenty-four hours afterwards.

'Anyway, after the meal, we were getting down and dirty on the carpet when he leaps up and says he needs to use the bathroom. He's in there for ages, so he is. I'd finished the wine and was almost asleep by the time he came out, said he had to go, and left like he'd found a ticking package. I'd heard him flushing the toilet many times, so I wandered in there.'

She laughs and snot comes out of her nose. I join in. She's so much fun.

'It stinks to hell. I lift the lid and there's a huge ball of toilet paper in the pan. Every flush spins it around as though it has a heavy nucleus. So, I prod it with a pen and it's weighty. Like a hedgehog has fallen in. Two days later it's still there.'

I stop myself analysing why someone would leave it there for that long.

'Did you have to ring a plumber?'

'I wasn't going to call for one of those thieving feckers.'

'What did you do?'

'I crushed it with my hands. Broke it up that way. I imagined it was his head.'

'Gross! Why not scoop it up and whack it in a bin bag?'

Her eyes narrow in thought, and she whistles through her teeth.

'Damn, I didn't think of that.'

'So, I don't need a hat.'

'Not yet.'

I consider whether I should say what's popped into my head. Dan wouldn't be happy, but the wine has loosened my bonds. She is my closest friend.

I whisper to her. 'Don't tell Dan, but I've a worse story. One morning, after he'd gone to work, Charlie called me and said there was something in the toilet. It looked like a doll or toy wrapped in tissue? Before I could stop him, he pressed the flusher. The paper and water vanished in an instant, leaving the biggest turd I've ever seen in my life, lying there, like a crocodile on a bank. It was incredible and not possible it came from a human. Charlie's expression was amusing. His woeful face crumpled. With shock he said, "Daddy did that".'

'My God. Men are so disgusting. What are they like? Did you have to squash it?'

'It was huge. I was scared to touch it. I thought I might get bitten, or dragged in. After a long think, I popped to the kitchen and fetched a pair of scissors.'

This time we spray each other with wine.

'My lord. It's not surprising you don't have sex anymore.'

'I know! Where's the mystery?'

Once we calmed ourselves, I tried to explain.

'He's a good person. I brought him to this steel prison, as he calls it. Made him conform. He needs to get used to the idea, that's all. I still have butterflies when I look at him, like on that bus.'

I didn't discuss my inner fears back then with anyone. Not the ones that woke me at four o'clock in the morning, forcing me to take deep breaths. Even with Rachel. Each day was the same. I had money, holidays and no one. I loved him straight away. He was bright, flawed, crazy, and a free spirit. I see how this place is overwhelming him. I wonder if we hadn't had children together, might we have gone our separate ways?

Rachel drags me back to the present.

'I know. I remember meeting him as though it was yesterday. It was awful. He weaved his way over and asked your name. You told him, and he replied, "Well, I can be Popeye then". What the hell? I'm staring at a dimwit and preparing to tell him to feck off. When I glance over, you have a face like Cinderella's when the shoe fit.'

'It was loud in there. He thought I said Olive.'

'Yeah, whatever. I bet the slippery sod had a list of lines for any eventuality. How random are those events though? To find someone on a bus all those miles away, have kids, and then learn to hate each other. It's perfect.'

She smiles, but I can tell she's about to be serious.

'You don't have to be with each other you know, just because you have children together.'

'We just need some breathing space.'

'Look, I'm moving to California for good. We've only got six months to transfer our side of the business over, and there's so much work to be done. We want you there, Olivia. In the meanwhile, I'll fly backwards and forwards a lot as I need to sell my house, and I'll babysit whenever you want for as long as I can when I'm here. Take Popeye bowling or something.'

'That's brilliant. Thank you. We only have my parents nearby now for that. They will childmind but they're approaching eighty and my dad's a total liability. The last time we visited I found ant powder in the four corners of the play room and Grace came in saying, "What's this?", while carrying a loaded mouse trap. My mum has her moments too. She'd been cleaning knives at the kitchen table and left them there to go to church. I managed to stop Chucky dissecting their cat. They don't see the dangers.'

'Chucky?'

'Bloody hell. Dan has me doing it now. I mean Charlie.'

'Come here to me, you can't stay together for twenty years if you're not happy.'

'I'm not sure you understand how it is for couples when they have children. Breaking up damages their lives. You'd do anything to protect them.'

Her face falls and it's too late to take the words back. I think she wanted babies more than I did. Her next question is barbed.

'You aren't still getting married?'

I don't answer straight away even though it's what I want. I'd love to have the same surname as Grace and Charlie. For Dan and I to commit to each other. I wish he'd be more enthusiastic about it though. I'm so sick of people saying, "I talked to your husband," or, "where's your husband?" that I've given up correcting them. But are they the right reasons to get married? Rachel waits for my response.

'Dan sent flowers to the office for me. The note only said "Surprise", and I really was, but I've been so busy, I forgot to say thank you. Modern life with children is hard work. We'll get there.'

'So, you are going to get married?'

'Definitely. We just need to find the time.'

Chapter 11

Dan
The next day

I'm woken by the sound of ripping cardboard. Only one of my eyes opens straight away, the other peels like separating Velcro. Within the blurry landscape, I see Bailey with a burger in his drooling mouth. My salivary glands appear to be broken.

My arm is stuck under my body and even when I sit up, it feels like a prosthetic. I try to grab the fast food as it will give the dog the violent runs. He's not happy at that idea and races to the kitchen. I have to bribe him with bad language and a digestive biscuit to get him to release it.

All the lights are on, so I stagger back to the lounge, grab the container and hide it outside in the bin. It's always best to dispose of the evidence. Olivia has said nothing about my weight gain, but the truth stares her in the face and me in the mirror.

I'm limping on with the work shirts, but every now and again, a button flies off in the same way a clipped toenail does. Once it happened at a bus stop as I yawned. It hit the Perspex roof like a bullet and the guy next to me dropped to the floor. Unfortunately for him, the bus arrived and everyone got on and left him. It's another reason to hate this place. I was sitting by the window, staring at him as he tried to compose himself. He peered at me through tears and pulled himself off the damp pavement. Everything good in me brought me to my feet to dismount and help him, but when I looked up, the bus was full. I left with the rest and stared the other way.

Sneaking back into the lounge, I tidy up at high speed so it doesn't resemble an epileptic manatee's love shack. I bump into Olivia as she descends the stairs carrying the container I'd just placed in the bin, and I give her a puzzled glance.

'That's the look I had on my face. I didn't fancy a burger at midnight. Thanks for waking me up though to check.'

I rummage around in my mind for recollection and remember buying three burgers. One for her, one for me, one for the walk home.

'At least I slept on the sofa.'

She reckons after drinking I thrash my legs in the bed, kick her and swear in my sleep. I try not to think why.

With a nod, she reluctantly agrees. 'Yes, I should be thankful for that.'

She gives me a look of pity as I flop back on a chair. The kids barrel into the room. Grace mastered the remote control quicker than Olivia, who still treats it like a magic wand. One that she doesn't have the instructions for. As per usual a horrifying sense of déjà vu comes over me as the jaunty theme music of soul-crushing, repeated cartoons begin. Charlie pulls all the toys from every shelf and box.

'You need to get a move on, or you'll be late for work.'

Oh no. What was I thinking? Now I recall saying to myself 'three drinks maximum'. The thought of eight hours at my desk with a hangover is the equivalent of ten years in Turkey's grimmest jail. I can't handle it. My core body temperature rises in panic and I scrabble for an escape route.

'I'm not going. I feel ... ill.'

She's heard it all before. She knows it's not illness, only me being lame.

'Fair enough.'

Olivia hasn't said that in the past. She usually chides me to leave. Gives me the same rubbish your mother used to say when you tried to miss school. Gems such as, "Go in for the morning," or, "Get dressed and have breakfast and we'll see." This time, her face is blank, and she leaves the room. A train crammed with worry trundles towards the platform. I trail after her.

'You don't mind?'

'Look, Dan. I know your job sucks and I also understand it's unlikely you can get a new one with the same family-friendly hours. But we need the money unless I go back full-time. I thought you didn't want that. He offered again last week.'

The horror of being a stay-at-home father looms large before me. Now it's an intercity train, brakes failed, driver screaming, that comes into view.

'I think what your boss would prefer is you moving in with him. I'm sure he could find a few chores in the bedroom for which you're suitable.'

She ignores my taunt. 'Actually, it is helpful if you don't work today. I have tons to do. You can pitch in. There are three loads of washing, and you can start with brushing Grace and Charlie's teeth. I'll go into town this afternoon, so you do the playschool drop and the school run. Cook them a healthy dinner because they had chips last night. Two of Grace's friends have birthdays next week, so pop on the Internet and buy something suitable.'

So many blows in quick succession. I reel from side-to-side. The kids demand fried eggs. Judging by the smell in the kitchen, something unpleasant has occurred. It could be Charlie. He does his wees in the toilet, but still thinks big jobs belong in his pants. I remember Olivia saying potty training Grace was the most stressful period for her. I missed that as it was before they changed my hours, and with hindsight, I'm glad I was out of it because it's proving a trying time.

'The dishwasher is playing up, too.'

'Am I a plumber?'

She dodges the weak parry from a beaten opponent. She impales me with her final strike.

'Am I? Use Trust-a-trader.com. Get rid of that box of Star Wars toys in our bedroom as well. They've been there years. If I see them again, I will move them myself. Forever.'

It's terrible. I know I'm being played, but I'm not bright enough to counter-attack. My brain folds in on itself. Minimal sleep, dehydration, and a general lack of understanding of the rules give her a flawless victory.

'Maybe I'll go in after all.'

Chapter 12

Olivia

I resist the urge to tell him to stop swearing as he searches for the things he needs for work that he carelessly discarded yesterday. It's not a good time to inform him of our plans for the weekend, but if I want that to register he'll need advising at least three times.

'My mum wants everyone to go to church on Sunday.'

He recoils in fake shock, like Dracula stepping into the light.

'No way. After my sinful existence, going into that place is climbing into the crosshairs of God's sniper rifle.'

He still makes me laugh. He rolls his eyes and knows what Grandma wants, Grandma gets. My mother always frightens my boyfriends. It's one of my favourite things about her. I admire her no-nonsense regard to relationships. My poor father would never have stood a chance.

At the moment, I only work three days a week. The time that Dan moans about with the kids is the time I love. Watching their little interactions in the bath, or reading them stories is all I hoped it would be. To me, that's what being a parent is. Sure, it's hard at times, and I'm often tired, but nothing worthwhile is easy.

I worry that if we split up, he'd leave the country and go travelling again. I want my family to have a father. Maybe we need to separate though, so he can realise what he's missing. Before I had children, I used to be great at finding solutions. Now there are long searches for compromises.

I'm not sure if his head is wet from the shower as he leaves for work, or it's beer sweat. I get a waft of aftershave and smile, knowing he will be paranoid about smelling like a brewery. He doesn't kiss me or the kids and leaves the front door wide open. Although, at the gate, he stops and turns around, remembering only an arsehole would not lock the door. He sees me grinning and gives me a double thumbs-up. The smile he gives is better than a kiss. It tells our story.

Nevertheless, it may be coming to an end. Over the last few months, it would have been easier if he didn't live here. Dan never takes the kids out to give me a break, and he creates as much mess as they do. He spends hours trawling the internet, looking at strange sites. I'm forever cleaning up after he's shaved or even made a sandwich. I can tell everything he ate that day, because the evidence will still be on the work surfaces or, if I'm lucky, thrown in the sink.

I thought those stories where women stay married for years because they don't want to upset the children was madness when I was younger. Now I have my own, I understand. At least he isn't negligent with the kids. I think any evidence of that would be the end of the road.

He needs to buck his ideas up though. Cut back on the drinking, and get exercising. He'd better remember what I said as we are playing my boss and his girlfriend at badminton soon.

Grace and Charlie amaze me by brushing their own teeth, going to the toilet when prompted and not complaining when the TV is turned off. I'm gobsmacked when they get into our car for the school run without a word. We got a great deal on the car which meant we could have a nice holiday that year.

I check Grace's seatbelt as she now insists on doing it herself, and notice Mike, the neighbour, leaving his house for work. I reach over and click in Charlie's seatbelt. Mike's charming voice is heard.

'Morning, fantastic day.'

I have a short denim skirt on and realise that leaning into the car will have given him a reasonably good chance of a glimpse of my underwear. I decide I don't care and pause for a second longer in the hope I'll turn around and see him beaming. I'm not disappointed.

'Yes, it is. How are you? The kids are behaving, but the dishwasher's playing up.'

He removes his sunglasses and frowns in concern.

'That's too bad. Dan gonna fix it?'

'Unlikely, he's not great with his hands.'

That statement gets my second big smile of the day. The roof is down on his car and he takes his jacket off and leaves it on the back seat. Despite being under pressure from strong shoulders, his shirt has the full complement of buttons.

'No problem. I'm away for two days, then I'll come over after work, say around seven. I'm great at that sort of thing.'

He winks as he leaves. My tummy turns over in an unfaithful way. I remember a time when Dan looked at me like that, and I'd have to fight his roaming hands from under my skirt.

'Mummy, Charlie has done a poo.'

Chapter 13

Dan

I had to queue to enter the railway station this morning, never mind to get on the platform. I then waited for four trains to go through before I shoved myself onboard. It's not a warm day, but the carriage is a cauldron. Tempers bubble beneath the surface and eyes tighten. I'm an animal on a big lorry. Wedged in, having a poor time, and on the way to the slaughterhouse.

There are too many people, and they're too close. I want to take my suit jacket off, but my shirt is sodden with sweat and I know it will be see-through. At the next stop, more harried commuters try to get on, but we're already rammed. Sliding doors silence angry words and scared cries. Hot breath and pointed elbows rock me as we swing through the tunnels. My heart races, and my chest heaves.

A slim girl next to me tries to move away as I pant damp air onto her. The motion knocks her off balance and we meet like lovers. I stare at the ceiling so as not to see the disgust in her face. The sweat on my hand makes the bar I cling to slippery. The girl has somehow gone. I look around and vivid faces with blurred surroundings buzz at me. It's a roundabout, going too fast. I'm dying. My hands are useless. They have no strength. I lose my grip and collapse.

The doors open again and clean, chilly air pours into the carriage. I crawl through the legs, onto the platform, and curl up next to a bench. If anyone notices, they say nothing. A shriek as the doors shut grabs people's attention. I know I can't get on another train. I stand and struggle towards the exit and lurch into the daylight. There's a stall selling water and my breathing slows.

I reel into the office, passing the security guard who gives me a disapproving glare. He's anal about seeing my pass, even though I've worked here for five years. A crying man has his attention this morning. It's one of the guys from IT who they laid off last week. To my relief, the lift is empty. I am late, after all. The stranger in the mirror looks sick. Heavy bags and furtive eyes avoid my stare.

I'm on a 10:00 a.m. until 6:00 p.m. shift, which means I'll leave at seven at the earliest. I work noon until 8:00 p.m. shifts on alternate days and get out after nine on the late ones. They call it family-friendly hours.

That's the term they use enabling you to do the dreaded school run. Of course, there are many arguments to be had before you exit the house — toothbrushing, hair, dressing, fighting. I could go on. Then, at the office, I'm shattered and have a full shift ahead of me. When I get home after the commute, it's late and I go to bed, only to arise and start again at ten. It's no surprise my mind is slipping.

The route to my desk is via my boss's. Kenneth, or Ken as he prefers, isn't a terrible guy, but he's gullible and pervy. I'm unsure how he keeps his job when so many are losing theirs. Perhaps it's his titanium optimism. Fresh problems are new challenges as opposed to further rungs on the eternal ladder. He annoys me.

'Nice of you to pop in, Daniel.'

'There was a problem with the trains.'

'Yeah? Everyone else got in on time.'

I close my sore eyes and repeat in my head, 'I won't hit him today'. I'm not entirely sure of his motivation with calling me Daniel. There is another Dan in the department and maybe he's too stupid to differentiate between me and a seven-foot-tall Jewish man. It always feels like a slight, though.

'We have a meeting in ten minutes, Daniel.'

'What for, Kenneth? No one told me.'

'We've had two more guys from the blue team call in with this virus. They're struggling and are way behind target.'

'That's because their team leader thinks the only method to motivate them is to continuously feed them chocolate. Coaching, training, monitoring? No chance! Shovel in more sweets, lollies, and ice creams like a demented fireman on a steam train. That will do the trick. They aren't ill, they're sick. Anyone would be. Either that or too fat to get through the entrance doors. Tell him less carrot is needed and more stick. Better still, make them eat carrots, give me the stick, and I'll educate him.'

My right eye squints as I finish the rant.

'Are you okay, Daniel? You seem a little highly strung. We can cope, it's not a problem. We'll move some staff around until they've caught up.'

His spotty neck reddens and the master plan is revealed.

'Ah, I see. By some staff, you mean my staff.'

He grins at me. My heart speeds up again.

'Well, yes, in a word.'

'Then, I'll be behind.'

'You'll catch up. You're a performer. We rate you, Daniel. You never let us down.'

'Fabulous.'

I give him what I hope is a dirty scowl, but most likely looks like I need the toilet, and carry on to my desk. The air-conditioning in our office is always on, it just doesn't work. The team leaders bought fans. Mine has been stolen as usual. I check the rota to see who's on the late shift and then steal hers.

She has sweetly written her name in correction fluid on the base, so I'll need to use a coin to wipe that off before she gets to work. In the summer, it's an incinerator in here, and people are less forgiving. Today, she will laugh it off and steal someone else's when they go to lunch.

I glance at my emails and find there are surprisingly few. Sometimes it's lunchtime before I've actioned them. I swivel in my chair. Celebrating small wins is necessary in this hell. There's a posh Parker pen dropped on the floor near my desk. They must want me to have it. Double result.

Olivia thanked me for sending her flowers this morning. I had no idea what she was on about. I sign in to online banking and check the payment history for my credit card. There's no floral entries at all, just the usual recreational items for my own needs. I smiled when she mentioned it. It was weird as the way she laughed made me think it wasn't the first time. Hopefully she'll never find out who's been sending them and I'll be able to retain the brownie points.

Ken pops his head out of the sea of desks.

'Daniel. The meeting is cancelled.'

'Excellent.'

'Blue team leader has rung in sick. You'll need to cover his guys as well as your own.'

Chapter 14

Abel
The next day

My father died a long time ago. He seemed pleased to be going. I realised over the following years I missed him. I should have spoken to him when I had the chance. Did he know the black dog of depression or did he have issues like mine?

I don't have shadowed thoughts because during bad times I feel absent. We live amongst millions of people, yet I'm isolated. I walk the streets at night or first thing in the morning, and I see others who have had enough. We never acknowledge one another as that would be the same as facing the truth.

The sickness I repressed all that time ago, is stronger. For many years it was only a memory. However, now, it pulses. Without treatment, it has grown and multiplied. A cancer needs no observation to blossom. Although what was there has been corrupted further by the dark.

I'm not sure what will happen. Does it now need to kill? I understand it wants control and action. I'm too weak to withstand its desires, and I will gradually cave.

I smile with a shrug. I am the sickness. Why do I resist? Ultimately, unequivocally, and with dread, the world will remember me.

Another jogger runs past. They look so similar they might as well have a uniform. They neither nod nor smile. I'm beginning to wonder if I'm invisible. Is this a dream?

In this stone place, we are a rotten race. We do evil things to each other seemingly without consequence. Royal families, the politicians, the rich, they keep us so repressed that I doubt they know we're alive. We could be robots, made to serve them. They need us to pump their petrol, mix their drinks and serve their food. We are necessary, but unequal.

With these thoughts, I recognise my task. As the sun climbs, my role becomes obvious. I will rise up. They will acknowledge Abel, and those like me. They too must know fear. Gone will be the days when their main concern was vacancies at their favourite restaurants. This city is criminal already, they need to be made aware. All shall suffer. It's the start of something different; an age of dread and suspicion.

I slow down in the location I selected. An unlucky woman with poor timing and a bouncing ponytail strides around a steep bend in the path. The streets are hushed and empty. The arrogant cow has sunglasses on despite the early hour.

She edges to her side of the track as she approaches. Does she suspect in that cocoon of music and Spandex? Are her eyes straight ahead, dreaming of her fat promotion, or are they darting for escape routes? Is she aware her life will be different now?

At the last second, I step into her path. Both her hands come up to prevent us colliding. I grip both wrists and smile.

Chapter 15

Barbara, the jogger
Two days later

Barbara recalls as soon as she steps into the police station that she hasn't been in one since a school visit fifteen years ago. She's nervous, and has been for two days. It's a pleasant morning, yet she pulls her coat around her. With a shudder, she approaches the counter. The floor behind is raised and the big man peers down, giving her a tired smile that fails to animate his face.

'I'm here to report a crime.'

'Okay, what sort of crime is it?'

She realises she doesn't know, and feels foolish.

'I rang earlier. Detective Constable Sharpe said to come in and speak to him.'

The desk sergeant picks up a phone and makes a call, gesturing for Barbara to wait on a row of wooden seats attached to a wall. A man younger than Barbara's twenty-nine years comes out of a door and gestures for her to follow him through a detector. It beeps, but he ignores it. They enter a bright room with sharp furniture and both take a seat. A lady enters the room and sits next to him.

'Barbara Evans, I'm Detective Sharpe and this is Detective Inspector Yvonne Jordan. You said on the phone you wanted to inform us of a crime. A man attacked you.'

'That's right. It happened a few mornings ago.'

'Why did you wait to report it?'

The details of the incident have furred up in her memory, but the shock of seeing the police tape in the park on the way home that night is vivid.

'I heard another girl in the same place was tripped up and beaten. I thought they may be connected. That park is near where I live, and I use it most days.'

The inspector interrupts.

'Do you want a coffee or a glass of water? I'm sorry for the harsh room. We have other places to talk but they're busy.'

'It's okay. My incident wasn't as horrible as hers.'

The police officers frown. The older woman takes control. 'Please tell us what happened. Give as much detail as you can.'

He opens his notepad, and Barbara looks up and begins.

'As I said. I jog there most mornings. Lots of people do. I'm a lawyer and it helps clear my head. I was near the end of the route and a man I ran past stepped in front of me at the last second.'

'Go on.'

'I placed my hands on his chest and pushed to get him to move, but he didn't. Then, he grabbed my wrists.'

'Okay, can you describe him?'

'Not well. He was approximately my height, five ten, fairly average build. It was still dark, and we were under trees, so I couldn't see him. He wore a sweatshirt with the hood pulled down over his face and a black snood, and I think he had a beard.'

'What's a snood?'

'Like a scarf.'

Sharpe stops himself rolling his eyes. He wonders why Barbara didn't say scarf.

'What happened after he grabbed your wrists? Did he hurt you?'

'No, he held them firmly but not painfully. He stood in front of me and mumbled a few words. Then, I kneed him in the groin. Hard. I kickbox. I know what I'm doing.'

'Good for you. Then what did you do?'

'I ran away. He toppled over as you'd expect.'

'Did you see anyone else at the time? Other joggers you knew?'

'You understand how it is living here. It's best not to talk to strangers, so I listen to music and avoid eye contact.'

'In summary.' Sharpe checks his notes. 'A man of average height, weight and build, and of indeterminate race, stepped in front of you. He wore dark clothes, and probably had a beard, but the snood made it unclear. He grabbed you resolutely on the arm but not hard enough to bruise. You incapacitated him and ran away.'

'That's right.'

'You haven't given us much to go on, and he hardly sounds like Jack the Ripper.'

'If you weren't going to do anything or take me seriously, why am I wasting my time?'

DI Jordan looks as angry as Barbara feels. She addresses Sharpe.

'Get me a coffee if she doesn't want one.'

When he's left, she speaks in a quieter tone.

'He didn't mean to criticise your comments. We're always short-staffed, and today we're struggling to cope. The jogger assaulted in the same place as you is still in intensive care, and another woman was punched in the face this morning in a different park.

'Sharpe is frustrated and at the back end of a long shift. We have no witnesses, or any idea what the perpetrator looks like. The last girl said the same as you. Average, non-descript, we don't even know his skin tone. Can you recall his eye colour?'

'No, but that's what stayed with me. They were dark and emotionless. You recognise if someone means you harm, and he did. The adrenalin got me through the experience, but now I'm afraid. I'm too scared to go jogging, and I hate being alone. Even though I fought him off, it's affected me.'

'I understand. You feel helpless and vulnerable. Sadly, this type of crime is common. We get at least one a week. You said he mumbled something to you.'

'Yes, but the last four words stayed with me.'

'What were they?'

'My name is Abel.'

Chapter 16

Olivia
Two days later

I see why Dan hates the school run. It's a mile journey that regularly takes over half an hour in the car. It'll be easier when Charlie's older. Then, he can go on his scooter with Grace, and I'll walk. It will take the same time but be healthier.

A lorry belches diesel fumes into my window as it passes by, and my love for this place weakens. I've never been to California, but in my mind's eye it's blue skies and open spaces. I can't desert my parents though. They have no one else to care for them.

The squawking from the back seats is still below jet fighter level, so I leave them to it. My deceitful mind wanders to seeing Mike at seven o'clock. I don't want anything to happen, but it will be nice to flirt. He's the type of guy I always used to fall for. Blond hair, good-looking, generous. The first six months were often amazing, but as soon as we made it over that hump and I saw a future, they went nuts.

It was as if they sought a new version of me. Some of them wanted someone younger as the years passed, but most missed the buzz of enjoyment from the mutual fantasy of having found one's soul mate. When that ends, as it must, they crave the "high" and start the search again. That's hard to take, when your clock ticks.

One relationship lasted two years until I caught him in my make-up. I wouldn't have minded, but he ruined my favourite lipstick and did a terrible job. Maybe Dan's right, and all men are confused. Although, I imagine Mike would look good in drag.

He knocks at seven sharp. I knew he would. I've spent an hour worrying what to wear. It's a minefield. Something too tarty gives him the idea to do me over the range cooker. That might be okay as long as the oven isn't on.

Saying that, I'd prefer notice, so I could give it a quick clean. Otherwise, I could end up glued to it. That would take some explaining when Dan came home. I settle for the denim skirt he liked and one of Dan's shirts. Even though he is taller than me, with my big boobs, they fit just right. It will be a barrier between us, and should keep me faithful.

Strolling in, Mike resembles a mechanic from a washing powder advert. White T-shirt, blue jeans, and a dirty smear on his chest, that surely, he must have done himself. He has a fancy tool box too which is battered so it looks well used. I'm treated to a smile, and he waves at the kids. They shrink from his stare, as though a hungry dinosaur wandered in for supper. In his defence, they do that to most visitors. He rolls two kinder eggs across the floor to them.

'Is the broken thing in the kitchen?'

I'm tempted to say Dan's at work, but instead I nod. Mike is slippery. Did I tell him those eggs are the best treat for kids because there's only a small amount of chocolate, but also a toy. I hope he hasn't drilled a hole through our connecting walls and been listening. I shut the door to the lounge to block out that bloody pig theme tune, and conclude that if he had overheard us, he'd not have come in. More likely, he would have moved house.

I watch him attack the washer as if he is Grace tackling a twelve-piece jigsaw. There are a few squirts, hisses, and taps. A couple of beeps and an 'Ahhh'. It reminds me of Dan having a beer and a ready meal.

'Whoever topped the salt up didn't screw the lid back on correctly.'

Neither of us need to acknowledge who that was.

'I should think that caused it to fizz up inside and then fluid will have gone in the overflow at the bottom of the machine. Too much water in there and it stops. It's a safety feature.'

'Can you fix it?'

'I have. I've drained the pan. It might work straight away or give it a day to dry out and you'll be good as new. I'm more than happy to pop over, Olivia. Don't forget that.'

There is something thrilling about a handy handyman.

'Can I get you a drink? Tea, beer?'

'I'd love a glass of vino?'

My eyes stray to our empty wine rack. It used to be full. Dan emptied it as fast as I could fill it up, as if it was an unwritten challenge, so I don't even try anymore. Perhaps Mike has been listening through the walls. He clicks his fingers.

'You know, I have a few bottles already cool in my fridge. You enjoy char-do-nay?'

The way he says it makes me think I would love chardonnay.

I grab my oversized glasses and hand them to Mike when he returns. He pours me a judgement-dismantling measure and reveals a charming story of where the wine originated. I flick the radio on to a local channel and take a sip. He has good taste.

Time flies. We're only interrupted by a call from Grace's school saying we had six items in the lost property box. It's not surprising. Dan loses at least one thing a trip when he picks up or drops off the kids. Mike laughs when I tell him. He says he used to adore the school run, and the only way to do it is to count the items off when the children come out. I'd said the same to Dan.

He tells me he's a dentist. He mentions his family, why he left New York, and even the odd bit about an ex-wife and a boy he rarely sees. Reading between the now blurred lines, I can see he's still bitter.

I don't hear a peep from the kids and, with trepidation, go to check they haven't set up a meth lab. They're quietly playing teachers and pupils. That's unusual, maybe they smoked the meth. The house is peaceful and relaxed in a way I can't ever remember since we had children.

Nevertheless, the bedtime routine beckons, and I break the news to Mike. With his usual daintiness, an exhausted looking Dan chooses that moment to arrive home from work. He trips over the school shoes and falls on the carpet. My bad. I chuckle as I repeat Mike's Americanisms. For a few seconds, Dan contemplates not getting up. He pulls himself to his feet with a disorientated expression. I have a vision of him stepping from an upturned vehicle in the same way.

He shouldn't be back for hours and I can't help frowning at my watch, or the guilty glance I give to the two empty wine bottles on the table. Mike's innocent easy-going visage has changed to one of challenge.

'You're home early, love.'

'Not a moment too soon it appears.'

Chapter 17

Dan

What a nasty sight to greet my eyes. It's lucky I don't wear slippers, or I'd be tempted to peek under the kitchen table to see if Mike was wearing them. Knowing him, he's brought his own. Her shirt has a button missing too, and you get an eyeful from any side-on vantage point. No wonder Mike's grinning.

Now I look closer, his face has a sneer on it. It's a challenging alpha male glare I have neither the energy nor the inclination to challenge. I explain my arrival as the silence roars in our ears.

'Ken let me go home early as I fell asleep at my desk. I had a weird, long, mostly shit day.'

'Mike's leaving so I can put the kids to bed. Are they still in the lounge?'

'They were both playing outside on the driveway when I arrived.'

Olivia flies away as the children aren't allowed out the front unsupervised. She's gullible too. Mike stands next to me. His teeth smile, but his eyes glint.

'You have an amazing wife.'

It's not a compliment. He's delivered a threat.

When Mike's gone, and the kids are bathed and in bed, I don't have the enthusiasm for a full-on row. I settle for a few low blows while we watch TV.

'Very cosy. I'll wait in the garden next time. You could put a deckchair out so I have somewhere to sit. Cotton wool as well for my ears, please. Or shall I call you when I leave the office, then you can get rid of him, and clean up with a mop and bucket before I arrive.'

'You're funny.'

'What was Doctor Death doing sampling my wares?'

'He came to fix the dishwasher.'

'Is that what the kids are calling it nowadays? Seems to me he came to drink our wine and interfere with the maid.'

'You drank all our wine. He brought his own. And I'm not *the maid*, as you so nicely state. He isn't a doctor either.'

That statement disarms me. She's far from repentant. I hear the dishwasher gurgle in confirmation through the open door to the kitchen. Olivia's phone rings. She gives it a strange look and lets it go to voicemail. Then, she listens to the message.

'Why didn't you answer it?' I ask.

'I keep getting weird calls. I can hear them breathing and then they hang up.'

'It will be those dodgy lawyer's calls, wanting you to sue for an accident you had five years ago.'

'One kind of growled my name. He sounded like the Gruffalo.'

'Maybe it was the Gruffalo. Did he offer to come over and *fix your dishwasher?*'

'Very funny.' She is smiling though.

'What does Mike do then, assuming he isn't Superman?'

'He's a dentist.'

I perk up, as even though The Dentist of Death doesn't work, there's potential. It makes sense too, what with all that unsettling grinning.

'A dentist, eh? I bet many a young lady, or gentleman, has woken up after his hastily administered gas to find they had a sore bottom or teeth marks in their underwear.'

'Do you see the best in anyone?'

I pause to think.

'Do you mean famous people, or people we know?'

I'm not sure why I do it. It's as though the only method of communication I can manage is sarcasm. The news headlines come on and save me digging a bigger hole.

'The police are warning everyone to be cautious after three different women were assaulted at parks in the suburbs. Joggers in the early morning should be particularly vigilant and go with a friend if possible. They want to speak to a man approximately five feet ten with an average build. They suspect the man's name may be Abel. If anyone has any information, or believes they could help the police, please ring this number.'

Olivia reaches over for my hand and squeezes it. 'I'm starting to feel unsafe here. I've never thought like that in my life. Those silent phone calls aren't helping. That drunk girl who wandered off from her friends and was found burnt and tortured in a field has now died. Who would do such an evil thing? I can't even begin to imagine what her family is going through. The awful fact is someone committed that act and you might be sitting next to them on the bus the next morning.'

'There do seem to be a lot of sick and angry people living here.'

'Do you know the cleaner at our place had her handbag snatched off her shoulder while walking on the pavement. She'd just left our office and a moped went past and then it was gone. Poor girl. Obviously, there was no police anywhere. She was on the way to pay a deposit for her holiday. We all chipped in to get her the money back. I'm sure it didn't used to be like that here.'

'Why don't we move with your business to California? Screw this place. I always wanted to learn how to surf.'

'You know I can't leave my parents. I'm worried for them as well.'

'That's a shame. In that case, try not to worry too much, those incidents were miles from here.'

'That's true, but it isn't only that. Since we've had the kids, there are dangers everywhere.'

'Isn't that just part of being a parent? Besides, Abel is after the joggers. So as long as you knock that on the head, you'll be fine.'

She gives me a filthy frown, and drops my hand.

'You mustn't change your life for the sake of these bastards. He won't stop me running.'

'You're mad. They'll catch him soon. Can't you go on your rowing machine until then?'

'You broke that remember. I'll take my pepper spray. He'll pity the day if he ever messes with me or my family.'

She turns to glower at me. There's a ridge of fire to her I never experienced until we had Grace and Charlie. There isn't anything she wouldn't do to keep them from harm. Do not come between a mother and her children. Her eyes search mine and the arguments and mindless routines of our lives are, for the moment, forgotten.

'Worried about me, are you?' she says.

'Always, although I'm concerned for him too if he leapt out at you.'

She shuffles over to my side of the sofa, and puts her head on my shoulder. After a pause, she reaches up to kiss my cheek. I turn so her lips touch mine and, as often happens, that's all it takes. The planets align, and our problems melt away.

Chapter 18

Abel
A month later

I do my best to hide my gift under my massive raincoat. It isn't raining or even cold, so I look unusual, but you don't bump into anyone normal at this time of night on Turpin Street. The important thing is the absence of wind. I hear the music before I see them. What is wrong with these people? The three youths sit in deckchairs in the small front garden passing a joint between them. I cough so they notice me.

'Heh, man. What are you, a clown?' They jeer as I pull the balloon from under my coat. One of them falls off his chair as he struggles for breath from laughing. The other two bump fists.

'Kind of. It's for you. I brought you a present.'

'Get out of here. We don't need a fucking balloon.'

'This is a special balloon though. I filled it with super-strength marijuana smoke.'

In their befuddled state, they're interested. That is enough. Apart from the parked cars, the street is empty. This will only take a minute so that's fine. Stepping towards them with a smile, I consider popping the balloon on the fire, but stick with the plan. I've practised many times.

It's a latex balloon twice the size of a football. That gave the best results under optimum conditions. With a flourish, I hold it in the air. The one with the golden tooth notices my latex gloves and looks at my face. Dim recognition opens his eyes. Too late, my friend.

I deliver the message. 'You are weak, and I am mighty.'

With the large hood over my head, I slide the goggles down and pull up my scarf — in case there is a mist. I dip under the balloon facing down, and with a sharpened nail from my pocket, jab up and pop it. It's easy to get acid. I didn't need much.

The three of them clutch their faces and thrash around. They are surprisingly quiet, considering. Agony, I expect, after the initial shock. I considered using a sledge hammer. I like their finality, but they are heavy and cumbersome. The club hammer fits in my belt though, and will do the job.

It's a tricky technique to master. You need to swing with your hips. One blow each stops the screaming. I roll gold tooth over and decide a trophy is in order. With concrete behind his head, his face collapses with the impact.

Now, who's next?

Chapter 19

Dan

As per usual when I leave the railway station and start the walk home, I lurch like I've been in a wrestling ring for an hour and a half. I pass the pub that Ian and I frequent and note the beautiful people at the bar. The staff, that is. It's still empty.

I haven't seen Ian for four weeks, which is unusual. The reason for that was the thawing of relations at home. We had sex twelve times in that period. A fair effort I reckon. More than we managed when we tried for Charlie. I found necessity an effective contraception.

My job still sucks. People are quitting in droves. A joker started leaving toy rats near the doors and windows, but even they've gone. Few serve their notice. The sales targets though, stay the same. It's a collective insanity. We plough on in a march to the death. The end is nigh, and that will be a release. I for one shall be thankful. Perhaps I can headbutt Ken on the way out.

If I'm lucky, it will open a new door to a better future. Saying that, I've been looking online at jobs for a guy with my experience and they are spread thinly. Knowing my luck, I'd get a shittier job, further away, for less money, and Ken would still be my boss. Maybe a role where I'd have to share a desk with him.

I stand outside our home and sigh. The truce is forgotten. The same rows are re-surfacing. Those of moving from this place, who created the mess, and other bollocks I don't understand. Each day leaches more energy from my depleted resilience.

The main argument, which will never go away, is the fact I'm happy to reside in a reasonably clean sty. Olivia, on the other hand, isn't. Her madness is thinking she can tidy for respectability and it will stay that way. She does after all live with three pigs, and I suspect even Bailey is a porker in a furry overcoat.

I can't see the point of hoovering twice a day, or tidying the toys up if Charlie's only going to pull them out a few minutes later. Fair enough, I can understand if we have visitors. Each time the doorbell rings, Olivia imagines it's the film crew from 'Clean House'. The cameramen would burst past while the host commented, 'What is wrong with these people?', and, 'Who could live in this?'

Our sex drives returning was the lull before the end of the world. Now all the arguments we have ever had climb out of their graves like zombies. They wander around the house, attacking us at will. Such as, her excessive use of Fairy Liquid, shampoo, washing powder, bin bags, soap, and her infuriating habit of eating the fresh stuff first. The slightly older things; bread, yoghurts, milk, fruit and so on spoil, edging me closer to insanity. I hurl those facts at her like I'm in the front row at a stoning.

She shields herself with her own grievances, of which there are many. She has reserves, too, as my shortcomings are legion. The battle ebbs and flows, with no one winning a clear advantage. That's a good thing, or the vanquished, in a rush of spite, is liable to drop the atom bombs of weight gain, money, or marriage into the melee. Could we survive the fallout from that?

Mike's lounge curtain twitches as I walk up our drive, but he pulls his head away before I can give him the finger. I'm a western gunfighter with nerves shot through drink. I'm not alone; the whole city's nerves are on edge. There was a terrorist attack in the centre again which fuelled the fears. The news is all negative at the moment.

Another woman was raped in a park north of us. They suspect Abel is casting his net further afield. A stadium collapsed in South America killing thousands. A dam burst in China wiping out entire towns. Our world is becoming a sinister place.

I was invited to leaving drinks after work for two of the admin staff. They planned to travel together. The state of affairs at the company meant the choice for them became easy. I could barely stand to acknowledge the lucky gits. I declined. Instead, I came home hoping for a thawing of relations and maybe some action.

I've always found sex was one of those things if you don't have it for a while, you forget about it. I'd been awakened and therefore it dominated my thoughts. So, I bought a bottle of that red wine with the little bull attached for Olivia, even though it's drain cleaner to me. There's a new Thai place opened nearby that delivers.

I take a deep breath at the door. No bickering tonight, Daniel. Remember, knobheads don't get nooky. I walk into the hall with a smile. Olivia glides past me in a long, black dress that makes jackpot bells ring in my head. My grin widens. Has she had the same idea? The light perfume she wears fills the house, and I gaze at her as she throws a bone to Bailey. He stares at it and wishes for younger teeth.

I present to her the wine!

'Ah, the bottle with the bull attached. Isn't that expensive, or was it on offer? Don't save me any, I'll be late.'

'Eh?'

'Did you forget?' She squeezes my cheek as though I'm an errant child.

'Do I need to get ready?'

'No, silly. It's a work thing, remember. Beau won a new contract. A big one. We're celebrating. There's a busy French place in town getting rave reviews. Beau's paying for everything. The prosecco will flow tonight.'

Beau is Beaumont Arundel. Her super-successful young boss. He's good-looking in a private schoolboy way. You know the type; loafers, untucked shirts, and chinos. The same outfit for work, funerals, parties and for sleeping.

I hate his name. It's the kind of thing you see on the bars of soaps in posh hotels. He, too, has fallen for Olivia's charms, despite there being a ten-year age gap. He often comes to pick her up in his latest BMW even though it is miles out of his way.

Olivia denies his interest, and says he's a wonderful man. The only pleasing part of the sorry saga is that Beau occasionally bumps into Mike. That makes me smile. They are like a pair of toffs about to tussle. I should leave duelling swords on the front lawn.

'Why doesn't Beautastic invite partners as well if he's so great?'

'They are welcome. I said you'd have to look after the kids.'

No way. I'm missing out on a posh meal at the latest swanky restaurant. Dare I ask what her idle-backed parents are up to this evening? Grace and Charlie love it in their massive house.

'Mother and father busy, were they?'

'You know I don't want to use them too much.'

Olivia looks stunning in the mirror as she checks her lipstick next to me. Her flowing black dress is an off-the-shoulder number. It's classic and classy. I'm sweaty and dishevelled in comparison. A little bonkers-looking too. I need to shave my head again soon, or I'll resemble Jack Nicholson in *The Shining*. My face has blotches on it which no doubt is a reflection of my poor diet of late.

'The children are in bed and sorted, so you have a night to yourself.'

A car horn beeps outside the house. She puts her highest heels on which make her legs resemble the finest lollies, and air kisses me so as not to smudge her lippy. Her tiny jacket top, which makes me think of toys from my youth, is pulled on and she skips down the path. I follow her and wave. Damn him.

He opens the door for her like a scruffy chauffeur, and shoots me a toothy grin. I involuntarily run my tongue over my own inadequate teeth. I bet he uses Mike as his dentist. I doubt Beau wears pants so he won't see the bite marks. And his arse is most likely always sore from sitting on his massive pile of uncomfortable cash.

They burn off, leaving a trail of smoke. A sense of doom comes over me as I turn to go back inside. Mike's curtain twitches and this time I have the reflexes to insult him.

I can't be bothered to eat. I stick the wine in the freezer — I can drink it with a straw later if it's cold enough — and clamber the stairs. Bailey pulls himself up the steps with equal energy. The bed gives reassuringly as I crawl under the duvet. The hound lies heavy over my feet. I'm exhausted.

I remember the two of us staying at a hotel on the banks of the Mekong River in Phnom Penh, Cambodia. We'd travelled there together as a group after meeting in Vietnam. Ian had tried it on with Rachel who'd politely declined, but everything remained amicable. The hotel restaurant had a terrace on stilts which made you believe you were sitting on water. We bought chilled beers and sat looking at the moon.

No doubt dead water buffalo and human poops floated past, but we couldn't see or smell them, so it was extremely romantic. She told me she worked in Fintech. It sounded so cutting edge, mysterious and dramatic. It still does to be honest as I can't remember what she said. I should look it up.

There are vast sums of money, looking for the right investments, circulating around the world. She whispered of expensive hotels and beautiful parties.

I imagined myself in a tuxedo on her arm. Tonight, is one of those times I dreamt of.

A small trump drags me into the present and Bailey rolls over onto his back. We were up early together, pounding the streets after he'd surprised me by bringing me his lead, so he's shattered, too. He is usually such a lazy dog. I should force Bailey downstairs as he isn't allowed to sleep up here.

The room is stifling, so I get up and open the window. I prefer sleeping with it pushed wide. She'll shut it when she returns. I ponder, for the thousandth time, about our compatibility. Bailey's presence is comforting though, so I slide back under the covers, and nod off with my memories.

Chapter 20

Olivia

The interior of Beau's car reminds me of science fiction films. The whooshing sound is not dissimilar either. I adore Beau. He's so one dimensional in his affection and love for people that it's pleasant being around him. My eggs drying up made me want to do something radical. He agreed to me having three months off without a thought to the hamstringing it gave his department at our old jobs. When he started his own business, he wanted me with him.

I recommended Rachel to him when I left on maternity and she seamlessly took over. They make a good team too, although he's scared of her. Many men are. She's bold. The main difference between us is I'm not as forthright but I have a feel for the market which few others do. I'm not naïve enough to believe Beau hasn't tried to replace me, but I know now he's failed.

'Exciting times, Oli?'

I forgot to say, he calls me Oli. Dan says he's given me a sex name, and he rolls around in his damp satin sheets dreaming of me and shouting it.

'Very much so. You've done brilliantly, Beau. It's a wonderful achievement.'

'We will have to ramp it up in Cali now. Are you onboard?'

'I'm tempted, Beau. I really am. But my parents are old, and my kids would miss them. It's an upheaval for everyone, never mind the fact it's another country.'

'What about that rascal, Dan? What's his views? You guys still getting on well?'

Dan has been distant of late. I've caught him pacing outside on the phone. When questioned, he was furtive and defensive. He said it was just a work call.

'He wants to go because he hates it here. I haven't got his hopes up by discussing it with him. Children make choices complicated and it's another busy place for him to get used to. I think he's lonely.'

'We're fixing that, remember? Badders in a few days. We'll have a drink after the game at the bar. He'll meet most of the team as they're playing badminton that night as well. Dan's a good guy, isn't he? Call centre fellow, yes? We'll look after him.'

I've spent a large proportion of time and effort keeping Dan and my boss apart. On better days, I hope their respective positive and negative outlook on life would meld like yin and yang. I pray they will complement each other. The realistic me knows Dan would be sarcastic and Beau confused. At best.

The restaurant is heaving when we arrive. The owner hugs Beau as if he's welcoming him back from the trenches. He kisses me three times, extremely fast. I can only manage one and am left pouting in the air like a surprised duck.

He ushers us through the throng to an enclosed terrace at the rear. The big cheeses from the business are here and most of the little ones. Rachel has saved me a space, but Beau guides me into a seat next to him. I notice his girlfriend, Felicity, isn't here. Excellent. Compared to that glamorous amazon I always feel like the cleaner.

Rachel looks perturbed until Herman the German from marketing folds his impressive frame into the seat on her right. He must be eighteen stone of weight-lifting fury. Rachel pours him a large wine and flutters her false eyelashes at him. Even from where I am at the table, I can see one of them is loose. She winks at me, and I doubt Herman will survive the experience.

We are essentially a start-up company, but progress has been impressive. Beau is struggling for the staff he needs out in California, hence Rachel's transfer. This big win means he needs many others there soon. It's a fantastic opportunity. I must talk to my parents. I thought it was them and my friends here that stops me leaving. Instead, Dan is the reason.

There is no way I could leave without the children, and without him it doesn't work. Unless I use childcare. Dan can be useless at times, but it's still preferable to someone else looking after them.

The problem is, where are we as a couple? His drinking is increasing again. We had a few weeks of relative soberness and the resulting sex reminded me of happier times. Not so frantic, of course; it was ten years ago. Then, as his sobriety slipped, we had a few sessions where I might as well have jumped on one of the winos from the park. I suspect they wouldn't have passed out so fast afterwards either.

However, what Beau says is true. This is everything I've worked towards. It might be the big opportunity of my professional life. I'll give Dan a month under the spotlight. See if he's responsible enough to prove he can raise our children in a new place while I'm at work. The question is, do I tell him he's being tested, or not? It's probably best I say nothing. Like with that bloody awful wine he keeps bringing home.

Chapter 21

Dan
Two days later

I finally have time to myself. After the school run at least. There's a big company meeting at my work to which I wasn't invited, and everyone got the day off. Brilliant. If that doesn't bellow, 'Game Over', I don't know what does. The best we can hope for is enhanced redundancy or an extended consultancy period. Both of which mean more cash for doing nothing.

Relationships at home are icy. She tripped over the box of Star Wars toys I promised to sort out. In all honesty, they were in our bedroom for months. I've brought them down to the front door, so I can't forget my one and only job today.

Then, I'm going to eat salty snacks, guzzle beer, and watch Star Wars the movie. Maybe all of them. Olivia is picking the kids up after work, then taking them to Old MacDonald's, as Grace calls it, for a Happy Meal. I don't even need to worry about picking them up later.

'Okay, small people, do we have everything?'

They can't hear me over the squabbling. Today, I won't shout.

'Sweets, anyone?'

The snakes both chant, 'Me me me.'

'You should answer me first time, children. And there are no sweets.'

They groan, but it's one-nil to yours truly.

Five minutes into the journey, Grace equalises.

'Daddy, where's my drink beaker for school?'

Cursing and sweating in the rush hour traffic, I turn around in someone's drive. They glare at me through the window as though I'm about to park it there for the day. I pull up in front of our house, jump out, run in, grab the bottle, get back in the car, and do up my seatbelt.

'Charlie's done a poo.'

That's two-one. Enough of the score analogy. I always lose. Rain patters on the windscreen, too, in case I'm in any doubt whose side God is on.

It will be a close call to reach school on time. We arrive with seconds to spare, but the bitch at the gate shuts it as we run up and I have to go to main reception and register as being late. I've got a free day, so I manage not to swear at anyone. I hum the theme tune to The Empire Strikes Back on the way home.

**

At our front door, the postman, Pete, is bent double staring through our letterbox. Pete resembles a greasy tapir. He is someone else I try to avoid.

'Greetings, Pete. Can you see Olivia in there?'

There's a strange sound as he jerks upright. Him and Bailey would get on well.

'Erm, no, no. It's empty.'

'Better luck next time, eh? If you'd rather, I'll give you a few photos. No money shot I'm afraid, but a couple of good sunbathing pictures. Save you the bother of having to come over here.'

He looks frightened. And weird. He also has muddy feet and trousers, like he's been delivering to scarecrows.

'I had a parcel.'

I wait for the parcel. He blinks at me. I haven't the energy for this. So, I let myself in, and say goodbye.

'I used to collect them.'

For a minute, I think he's talking about photos of Olivia, until I realise his little black eyes are staring at the Star Wars figures. I exhale and decide I'll give him a few minutes. He can't be completely worthless if he likes science fiction.

'Great, aren't they? Olivia wants rid of them, but I don't want to throw them away. Every time I pick one up, it reminds me of the excitement I used to feel.'

'Yeah, me too. We could do swaps.'

It's immediately obvious Pete has absent listening skills. And that's one of his more minor problems. I bet he was the type of kid who jammed the figures up their noses the moment they got home from school.

'I need to get rid of them, Pete. Not disguise them by changing them into similar ones. Even Olivia won't fall for that.'

'I can make money at a car boot sale I go to with them. Good money. I swapped a Darth Vader for a burger last time.'

I analyse his expression to see if he's joking or not.

'That doesn't sound like the deal of the century.'

'He was missing his cape, and the burgers were expensive.'

I gently close the door on Pete's face. Manners are unnecessary when dealing with subspecies. Note to self: avoid Pete at all costs. If contact is absolutely necessary, ensure the police are present.

Pete has ruined *Star Wars* for me, so I watch *Aliens*. My phone ringing wakes me from a fitful dream where a critter has hold of my groin by mistake.

'Dan, it's Olivia. I'm running late, can you do the school run?'

Shit. My sluggish brain tells me there's little left of the eight pack of beers I bought.

'Can't your parents go?'

'No, they can't. You're not doing anything today, so you do it.'

I distinctly remember her telling me to enjoy my free day. Why the hell did I answer? I'm not drunk enough to tell her the truth.

'Okay, I'll go.'

'Good and don't forget we have badminton tonight.'

I drop the phone in shock. Badminton? With who? My brain wobbles like poorly set jelly, and I recall something about playing against Beau and his girlfriend. I recall joking his girlfriend's name is Rupert. I have more pressing problems. I'll have to walk to pick the kids up which I hope will sober me up. That means they'll moan all the way home. Unless I take chocolate.

While walking, I experience a moment of clarity and remember what she told me not to forget the night I went out with Ian. It was to ask for my badminton racquet back. I'll have to hire one.

I arrive five minutes late at preschool, so the other mothers are long gone. Cue dirty looks all around from the staff. Charlie is crying because he thinks I've forgotten him. He dawdles the four hundred metres to infant school and we are the last there as well.

'Can you come in a minute, Mr Flood?'

What! No thanks. Ten-nil to God. I try to keep as much space as possible between the teacher and me, but she walks into a small treatment room. I follow her in, and they hand me an injury form. Grace fell over in the playground and has a grazed knee. She jumps off the bed with a smile. The teacher's face is impassive. I thank her. We can both smell beer.

Chapter 22

Olivia

Mike is rubbing his car when I get home from work. He loves that vehicle. Unusually, he doesn't look super-pleased to see me. He must be freezing in those clothes this time of year though. Stick a jumper on, man.

'Thanks for changing those bathroom bulbs, Mike. We struggle with that fitting.'

When he stands, I see why he is distracted. There is a long, silver mark down the side of his car. I can almost hear his teeth grinding.

'The garage quoted me eight hundred to fix it.'

Before I can reply, the sound of a hippo being dropped into a blender comes from our lounge window. Mike has a *shall I ring the police?* expression on his face.

'It's only Charlie. I'll catch you later.'

'Mummy, Daddy won't take us to Old MacDonald's.'

My patience dwindles further. He knew I'd promised them that. He has a vacant air about him which makes me think he's been drinking. I go to kiss him hello and have to chase him around the kitchen table. He smells strongly of mint.

After I've taken the children to McDonald's, my parents arrive to babysit before I have time to get the thumbscrews out. Once they're settled in, I race upstairs to change, calling down to Dan.

'Tell me you got your racquet back from Ian.'

'He promised to drop it around yesterday, but recalled he'd lent it to someone else.'

That is annoying. Although I'm amazed he remembered to ask in the first place. He'll regret hiring one of their shit loan racquets. Dan comes up the stairs and leans against the door. I hope it isn't to hold him upright. I don't want him embarrassing me later.

'Olivia, have you spoken to Pete before?'

'Pete who?'

'Pete the postman. I caught him looking through our letter box. He had really muddy shoes, too.'

'Ah, him. I've seen him taking a short cut through the allotments. I'm not sure his name is Pete. He's harmless.'

'You reckon? He was creepy as hell. Pete the deviant is more appropriate. He wanted to buy naked pictures of you.'

'Shut up. It's you that's the degenerate.'

He shoots me an exasperated look. We can't even agree if we like the postman or not. I walk towards him and he clatters down the stairs. He is avoiding me. As he disappears out of view, I see that box of toys next to the door. I asked him to get rid of them, not move them to a new place. Choose your battles, Olivia, or you'll be fighting the whole time.

I pull on my Shock Absorber bra. We don't want any black eyes tonight, and I thank Joseph Shivers for inventing Spandex, or Lycra, or whatever this supportive stuff is called. I now have the buttocks of a twenty-five-year-old. Badminton is the only chink in Beau's armour. He is massively competitive with it. I've played him before and he isn't that good.

I'm similar. I hate losing and believe you should give your all at sport, even if it means thrashing your opponent. Unless it's your boss, of course. I let him win the odd one, to keep him happy but I walk a fine line. If he knew I wasn't giving it everything, he'd be angry. If I spanked his arse though, he'd be humiliated.

I doubt Dan will be any good, especially at doubles, which is a shame. The bitch is coming tonight. And, like Rachel's hedgehog, she must be crushed.

I can't wait to get out of the car when we arrive at the company sports club. Dan has overdone it on the aftershave. Beau has paid for the court, so we only need to hire a racquet for Dan. He swings it around as though he is limbering up for Wimbledon. I flinch as he misses a light fitting by millimetres. We wander into our respective changing rooms. Him whistling, and me with feelings of despair.

We come out at the same time and walk towards the hall. Dan moaning as usual.

'Gyms are weird places. You have to find one that's on your level, or you can't relax. This one's unsuitable for me. Mine would be called The Fatness Centre. Only people with a BMI over twenty-five allowed, and to enter the pool you need to have over forty percent of your body covered in hair. There'd be none of these pecker-heads hanging around at the water cooler. I mean, who wants a three-hour conversation about how many protein bars you wedged up your ass that morning.'

'Sounds more like a watering hole, than a gym.'

'Can't we play in a community centre or something?'

I have to shut him up, or he'll go on forever.

'Would you prefer we played in a church hall? We can pretend it's 1970.'

'Very funny. No need to take the piss if I'm uncomfortable. Look around you, most of the people in here are so slim and fit they don't even have a BMI. The last place I want to be is somewhere filled full of lantern-jawed women who could kick my ass.'

'You should appreciate they let you in here. You will be by far the hairiest and smelliest beast they've ever allowed in these premises. The moment you leave they'll get a hoover out and feed anti-bacterial spray through the sprinkler system. I suspect they'll dispose of everything you sat on, touched, or looked at. Staff included.'

I stick one more dagger in at the hall doors. Just for fun.

'Please don't go near the pool, or you'll shut the place.'

Beau and Felicity are warming up on the court. She's a lovely girl. Sweet, kind, a little monotone perhaps, and I hate her. It feels as though someone has slipped a lead coat on me as we approach them. Whereas my Spandex grips my faults together like cling film, hers is necessary to hold everything down. Even her calves are so high and buoyant they could do with cover. I don't want to look at Dan's face, but I must...

Chapter 23

Dan

Momma. I stumble into the gym in a trance. A simple person's smile droops on my face. I thought Jessica Rabbit was a cartoon, but she's real. I can hear her talking. Olivia is saying something as well, but it's not on my frequency. I turn around but only her eyes are in focus. That's a nasty scowl. A warning sound beeps in my deep, deep subconscious.

'Are you going to shake her hand, Dan?'

'Oh, sorry. Sure. The lights are a bit bright for me in here.'

Damn. I could have worn sunglasses. That would have been better for sneaky reasons.

'Hi, Felicity. Beau.'

They both pump my hand and are pleased to see me.

'Shall we warm up?'

Beau hits it too hard for me to return easily and I have to backpedal. I give it a huge swing of my arm, and it lands on the sweet spot of my racquet. I'm disappointed with how far it goes. It hovers politely in front of Beau who hammers it into my dicky knee. I can't stop a squawk coming out of my mouth.

Felicity rushes over, full of concern. Pain, what pain? Up close, she has skin like a butterfly's wings. It even moves in a similar fashion. I can hear the Spandex losing the battle for her breasts. We warm up for another minute and, for obvious reasons, I underperform.

'What are you playing at?' Olivia snarls in my ear as we walk to begin serve for the first game.

'What do you mean? Do we want to win? Don't forget he's your boss.'

'She isn't. We will triumph, Dan. Remember that. You understand the rules, don't you? Over the net, not through it.'

'I'm just getting going.'

'You'd perform better if you didn't have to drag your chin around on the floor after you.'

Ah. She noticed my subtle glances. We play the first game and get thrashed. I ignore Olivia's tuts, try to ignore Felicity's tits, and the atmosphere remains cordial. I am improving though. The main problem I have is the hire racquet strings have the tensile strength of a teabag. They're playing badminton, I might as well be playing lacrosse. I'm almost catching the shuttlecock and hurling it back with brute strength.

We play another game and I rally, but I'm still distracted by the vision of loveliness opposite. I can describe her outfit to the nearest stitch. Yet, I can't tell you if Beau is clothed or not.

I focus on her teeth. They are magnificent, white, powerful things. I best keep the shuttlecocks away from those bad boys or she'd shred them to pieces like a pigeon through a combine harvester. I bet the shuttlecocks are expensive here. Maybe they're made from pigeon's feathers.

The strings on my racquet can't handle the pace, and slide off defeated. I get a replacement and note it's as taut as Felicity's stomach. Olivia's face is a furious red. It isn't through exertion. Her and Felicity are equal, my pathetic efforts are dictating the score. If I don't want to attend the emergency ward to remove Olivia's racquet from my body cavity, I need to find form.

The difference with a normal racquet is incredible. My arm still strains as though I have the old one, causing my shots to blister through their defence. We sneak ahead. Olivia ups her game too. I sting Felicity's nipple with a blazing overhead and get my revenge on Beau's testicles with a slam. Both give me a small buzz of sexual pleasure.

Olivia's gone mad — stamping across the court. She's started high-fiving me when we win a point. Beau growls the scores. They draw level. I'm tiring, and a glance at Felicity is worrying. There's not a drip of sweat on her, whereas I look and feel as though I've been skipping in a sauna.

She is breathing heavier. Her front teeth protrude further and she has a small snarl at the side of her mouth. Both features send a bolt of electricity through my genitalia. Stay on target, Dan. I focus on Beau and detect a slight limp. We take the third game.

I catch a guy in the next court checking out Olivia's butt cheeks. I have to say, she looks hot as well. She's panting, too. I wasn't expecting this to be such a sexual experience. We slip behind in the 'deciding set', even though we are 2-1 down. I can tell Olivia wants this as she whispers to herself at the start of each point. Beau's limp is affecting his backhand. Every shot from me goes to that side.

It is me that's now unhinged. I am relentless and dominate the court. I froth and pound and spit us to the brink of victory. Beau's cool withers and dies as he loses his team another point. A small trickle of sweat finally falls between Felicity's heavenly bosom. I'm wilting, in every department. Beau is a cornered rat. I'm too weary to make a joke about where Mr Nice Guy has gone.

We have a serve to win. Olivia elbows me aside as a loose return comes over. Her racquet flashes past my face like the blade from a samurai sword and the shuttlecock scrapes the line at the back of their court. Olivia roars her victory cheer. Every other court stops playing. Beau shouts, 'Out.'

Felicity and I look at each other with wide-eyed apprehension. Olivia replies.

'It was in.'

Time draws out like a blade. My right leg jiggles of its own accord. I'm unsure if it's through tiredness or nervousness.

Beau opens his angry, pinched mouth infinitesimally to deny her, when the staff member behind him who was walking by says, 'Yeah, it was good.'

I manage to stop myself collapsing to the floor. We shake hands again. There is little eye contact. Any talk of a few drinks afterwards is forgotten. I'm too tired to get changed, so slump and steam in the passenger seat while Olivia drives. We approach her parents', but then I'm surprised when she takes the turn for our house.

'Aren't we picking the kids up now?'

'Later. I said I'd collect them at nine.'

I manage a confused, exhausted nod.

'First, we're going to bed. You've earned a reward.'

Momma.

Chapter 24

Abel
A week later

This will need to be the last park 'attack', as the authorities are patrolling them. They are changed places. Only the brave, foolish, or homeless wander through them in the dark. All sober up as their footsteps echo around them. In true city style, they fear the night, but dawn is when it's quieter. That's where they'll meet me.

I've enjoyed watching the news and seeing my name mentioned. I love that I'm in control despite insane actions on my part. An inch to the left and that bloody kickboxer could have turned me into a post-op trans person. As it was, I could only hobble. I tripped up the other runner as she laughed at me when I limped past. How was I to expect the clumsy cow would dive onto a concrete kerb? I'm not sure who punched the other girl because it wasn't me. Nevertheless, it gave me a good idea.

I require one defining moment. This morning is it. Everyone will know my name after this day is over, but I need to choose my victim with care. Another knee to the balls would be the finish of me. I'm familiar with this park, and it's perfect. There's a tight bunch of trees next to the summit of a small hill. I broke the streetlights a few mornings back, so when you get to the top there is a plunge into near darkness. It will be unexpected. That's where I'll be.

The person whose attention I want to grab lives near here. She will be unaware of the coming storm. She needs to feel my presence. Although it would be a shock if it was her who grafted up this incline and came into view. The first girl who runs past is unsuitable. She skitters by like a flighty deer. I couldn't run that fast downhill.

I'm ready to give up for the morning when the ideal candidate creaks into view. She must be a size twenty, minimum. I imagine her ankles groaning as she grinds to the top. She is trundling so slow at the peak I can walk up behind her. I grab her shoulder and spin her to face me.

Her terror fires my resolve. She knows who I am. I clutch her arm and pull her along a path deep into a tight copse. She falls over a felled tree. She is exhausted but pushes herself upright. I hope she isn't going to fight as I only wanted to scare her. I wait for her to turn around, but she doesn't. She whimpers.

'I don't want to die. My name is Dorothy. I have two children.'

'Be quiet.'

'My name is Dorothy, don't kill me. I have two children.'

'I said shut up.'

She reaches behind her and pulls her jogging bottoms and thong down in one quick movement and leans forward again. Still crying, she offers me everything.

'Do what you want, please don't hurt me. I have two children.'

Her large white bottom glows in the moonlight resembling perfect orbs. Her mantra is irritating. Satanic thoughts swirl around my mind. I care about the kids, but do I give a shit about her? Lucky I didn't bring a weapon, or Dorothy would be silent. There is a thick stick next to her foot and the twisted part of me yearns to grab it. A vision of a bloody battering flickers through my head like a film from an old cine camera.

Dorothy isn't my target. Judging by the grimace on her face as she came up the hill, she's suffering more than I am. Her task is futile. She'll never fit into this world of vanity. However, she will be a messenger. Beware, people. Abel is coming.

'You want to live?'

'Yes, yes, please.'

'What's my name?'

'Your name is Abel.'

An impulse makes me slap her arse. It's humiliating, and that is ideal. She squeaks but otherwise remains silent.

'Say it again.'

I slap her behind on the word Abel.

'Who do you fear?'

'Abel.' She cries. She must try harder.

'Say it again.'

A muffled sound.

'Shout. Or you die. Who am I?'

'Your name is Abel!'

Smack.

'Who do you fear?'

'Abel!'

'Preach it.'

'Abel!'

'Fear me.'

'Abel!'

'Know me...'

Chapter 25

The police station

Detective Inspector Jordan is having a bad day. Recently, a psychopath sprayed three lads with acid and bludgeoned them with a hammer. There would be no more normal for those men. This morning, one of them died. His mother came straight from the hospital in total fury. She wanted justice. What had the police done, who had they arrested? Jordan knew they'd made no progress. They had no suspects and no witnesses. She sent the woman on her way with lies about DNA tests and profiling. The lady didn't hope for a prosecution anyway, she wanted revenge.

Jordan had little sympathy. The lads had been squatting in the house opposite where eight homeless men were decapitated. They said they'd noticed a man leaving and entering on numerous occasions but couldn't describe him. One of them said he'd thrown a beer can at him for a laugh but he'd just ignored it. Told them they were too stoned to remember faces. They found the whole process amusing, and kept saying "they weren't no snitches".

It was likely to be the same person who'd attacked them and her team were clueless. A serial killer was the last thing she needed right now with resources stretched to breaking. On top of that, there was some lunatic going around assaulting women. A shitstorm gathered over the lack of progress. If none was made soon, a drenching would occur.

Jordan looks at the dishevelled woman in front of her and regrets having to question her so soon. Anything she could tell them might make a difference though. Detective Constable Sharpe nods he is ready.

'Okay, Dorothy, in your own words, start from the beginning.'

Dorothy takes a deep breath.

'I was near the end of my jog, and I'm not a fit person. I was knackered, and he came out of nowhere. He grabbed my hand and pulled me into a clearing. He pushed me over a log.'

'Was he violent, out of control? Did he hurt you?'

'No, not really. I was so scared, he more guided me.'

'So, he wasn't rough. Did you try to get away?'

'I knew who he was, and I froze. I didn't want to die.'

'Why do you think it was Abel?'

'He dressed in black with a scarf, moustache above it and a hooded top.'

'Did you scream?'

'No, I have two children.'

'Then he ordered you to pull down your jogging bottoms?'

Dorothy weeps. She takes a full minute to calm herself.

'No. I pulled them down.'

Sharpe looks at Jordan.

'Without him asking? Why did you do that?'

'I heard he's raped and killed loads of women. I thought if I let him do what he wanted, he would allow me to live. I'm divorced. My children don't have anyone else. They are more important than my discomfort.'

'Then what happened?'

She breaks down, but continues through heaving shoulders.

'I think I annoyed him because I wouldn't stop talking. He asked me who he was.'

'And?'

'I said, "Your name is Abel". Then he smacked my bum.'

Jordan squints at Sharpe.

'Hard? With a weapon?'

'No, his hand. I suppose firmly best describes it.'

'Do you have bruise marks?'

'I shouldn't think so. It didn't hurt. He kept asking me to say his name and then he spanked me.'

'Then what happened.'

'He whispered in my ear to not move a muscle, and he left.'

'Could you describe him? Anything, his skin or eye colour?'

'No, I faced the wrong way.'

'There's nothing you can tell us to help identify him?'

'He did remind me a bit of a vicar.'

'Pardon? Explain, please.'

'He was almost preaching to me. As though he was delivering a sermon or a message.'

'What do you think the message was?'

'That this is just the beginning.'

'How long did you stay there?'

'I'm not sure. Quarter of an hour I should think. He was so powerful and calm. A dog walker found me while he was looking for his spaniel who was sniffing my groin. I thought for a minute Abel had come back. It was an embarrassing experience.'

'He didn't return?'

'No. I heard his shouted warnings as he ran through the woods.'

'What did he say?'

'Tell the city. I'm coming for you all.'

Chapter 26

Dan

Sunday used to be a day for lazy pub crawls. Now we reserve them for arguing. Well, bickering is more accurate. By nine in the morning, the kids have needled us for hours. Olivia has been following me around, barking orders at me. I nurse a hangover and don't care whose turn it is to hoover up the dog hair.

The small shed at the bottom of the garden is my escape. I've lit a cigarette, turned the radio on, and sunk into my deckchair when she arrives.

'I thought you gave up smoking?'

'I did. I started again.'

'It's cosy in here. I love what you've done with the place.'

The shed is empty apart from the deckchair and a spade. My radio hangs on a nail. I decide not to mention she only allowed me a small shed so the kids wouldn't lose too much garden. It is depressing. I bought myself a wooden cell. I allow myself a few seconds to imagine using the spade as a whacking device while she talks.

'Beau wants to play badminton again. Shall we see if Mum will babysit for us?'

'You're joking, aren't you? I barely survived that night. I'd rather dry hump a beehive.'

'Well, that's a nice vision.'

I smile back at her. I know this isn't what she's here for. These skirmishes are just that. There's something else eating her up inside. She will consider it important and believe I don't. She'll be right. As opposed to mentioning it ages ago, it's festered and now it's ready to leap out and bite me. I'm cornered, too.

We're both distracted by the breaking news on the radio. Abel is everywhere.

'Police reiterate their cautionary advice to women. There were two more park attacks but what is concerning them now is that Abel's escalating intentions are murderous. In the early hours of yesterday morning, a couple were mowed down by a car on the pavement. They died. There were no eyewitnesses. However, the police received a letter with the time, date and place of the incident and the words, 'My name is Abel'.

'I hope they catch this man soon, Dan. I keep getting a bad feeling about him.'

'About Abel? Why him in particular? London is full of pyschos.'

'I don't know. Just that he'll ruin our lives. I'm jittery on public transport now. I swear a bloke followed me to the station when I left the office, and then he was in the same carriage and kept staring at me.'

'Did he get off at the same stop?'

'No, but I felt his eyes on me as I walked past him.'

'I'm sure it was just a coincidence. Come here.'

I pull her onto my lap and she winds her arm around my neck. The chair complains, but holds. Her hair smells the same as I remember. I miss what we had.

'Are you aware if you're going to get murdered, it's most likely that it will be by someone you know?'

'Who'd want to murder me?'

I push the spade idea out of my mind.

'Probably no one. After all, it's the kind of thing that happens to other people.'

'You'd be on HotNorwegianNanny.com before my body had cooled.'

'Funny you should say that, I've been on it for ages. Just in case, obviously. Seriously, though. I reckon it's your boss, Beau. The space between his nose and lips is too thin. My mother always said that makes someone untrustworthy.'

'Beau doesn't have an evil bone in his body.'

'I saw a glint of the beast the other night when he was losing at badminton. It's the quiet ones you have to be wary of. Have you been around his house?'

'No.'

Hmm. She looked shifty and answered too fast. I'll let that go for the minute.

'I bet he spends every evening drawing faces on watermelons and then making love to them.'

'Dan, you don't have a good word to say about anyone.'

With that she gets off and the truce is finished.

'While I have your attention. We need to discuss Grace's birthday party.'

Ah! It's that which has been riling her. I've been frantically avoiding the topic hoping Mr Masturbater gets booked up and is unavailable.

'You know my views on the clown.'

'Mr Mystery Maker is not a clown, he's an entertainer.'

'Why is he so expensive then? He costs two days wages and I don't even get to laugh.'

'I checked, and he's still available. There's a twenty percent booking fee on top of the price as well.'

'What?! He needs to blow me before and after for that to be in any way acceptable.'

'That's another nice image. I've booked it. You need to go to their website and pay for it.'

'Why don't you use your card?'

'Shall I do everything?'

'Of course.'

'Happy?'

'No.'

'Grace will be, and that's what counts.'

She frowns but then her eyes open with interest. Reaching around me, she picks up a square, flat, wooden box that was in the corner.

'What's this?'

I have no idea. 'Open it.'

She passes it to me. It's well used and grimy, yet inside is an immaculate chess set. As they say on the Antiques Roadshow, it's a nice thing — like the prized possession of a filthy beggar. A brief flicker of recognition is there and disappears. I show her the open box. 'Is it yours?'

'That's right, Dan. I play chess in your shed.'

'Weird. Perhaps, one of those blokes who put the shed up dropped it.'

We recall the pair of hairy knuckle-draggers together and laugh.

Olivia gives me a serious look. 'This party is important to Grace. What would you rather spend your money on?'

The shed door slams after she leaves, and unsettles the spade. It falls over and the handle lands straight on my sore knee.

Chapter 27

Dan
A month later

Christmas is over for another year. We had our usual big day row but otherwise we emerged unscathed. Somebody peed on the tree. Blame was thrown around like confetti, but the jury (Olivia and Grace) was unable to convict any of the accused (Charlie, Bailey and Me) due to the fact it could have been any of us. Two of my presents were soggy but I daren't complain.

I was so hungover boxing day, that I went to take the dog for a walk, but left without him. I came back in a panic to find him on my side of the bed. As always, the holiday passes in a blur, and before I know it, the dreaded commute is here again.

I have the misfortune to bump into the milkman as I leave for work. I go out of my way to avoid him as well, but am trapped for the second time at my front door. Olivia has been using him for years and says it makes the area homely. The supermarket is miles cheaper, but she reckons if we cancel as well, then the old people around here will lose a service and a friendly face. That's a reasonable argument apart from the fact he is, to put it lightly, angry.

He has enormous arms above a narrow waist and a nasty habit of leaning towards you in a threatening manner when he speaks. Olivia tells me his hairstyle is a top-knot in the fashion footballers have. Acceptable for them, maybe, but our guy is older than I am. His thick Scottish accent adds to his menacing demeanour as he questions me.

'Did you hear there's been another hit and run? A poor sod on a bike was ridden into from behind.'

'Did they say it was Abel?'

'Aye.'

'You're up early, aren't you? Haven't you seen him on your travels?'

'There's many strange folk up in the wee hours. It's best to keep to myself.'

'I see.' I do a theatrical look at my watch. 'Well, I don't want to be late.'

'My missus is making me demented. She's a cruel woman.'

He's standing in my way and I start to feel uneasy. We don't have the kind of relationship where we moan about our other halves.

'She said, and these are her words, "If you fail to give a man what he wants, he'll go elsewhere". I'm not getting any off her, so what does that mean? Is that a green light for an affair? Or is she accusing me of one?'

'Hmmm.' What is he going on about? 'Don't you milkmen get loads of offers from bored housewives?'

'Sure, we do. I say no though. It will ruin wee Jonny's life if his mother and me broke up.'

If that makes any sense to you, then you're brighter than me. I settle for an attempt at lightening the tone.

'All women are crazy. They're more interested in their child's happiness than ours. What's that madness, eh?'

'You're not wrong. You're a smart guy. My name is...'

He waves a hand around at what I hope is a wasp, or I'm in trouble. I wait for the word Abel to arrive, but instead he says Malcolm. I'm so relieved I make a joke.

'We can call you The Malkman.'

Wild eyes zoom in. Jaw muscles bunch.

'You will call me Malc.'

Clouds darken and the earth cracks before he smiles.

'You're Dan, aren't you? Your wife told me. Lovely woman.'

With that, he walks away. I watch as he picks up a massive crate of milk with one hand as though lifting a dropped handkerchief. Any conversation with him is intense, and I want to drink afterwards. Even if it's only eight in the morning. I wait until he's out of sight before I leave.

Chapter 28

Olivia

We stand over the body of the father of my children. Dan perspires and twitches. His eyelids fight to keep his eyes in their sockets.

'Why is he sweating so much?' Rachel says.

Her nostrils flare as she leans over the sofa to get a better look, as though she is expecting there to be a terrible smell. I suppose that wouldn't be unexpected.

'I'm not sure. Perhaps he's ill.'

Bailey cuddles up beside him, so they resemble a couple in love. One being slightly hairier than the other. The multitude of beer cans in the vicinity implies it's a self-inflicted condition.

'You must be so proud.'

'Now, none of that.' Nevertheless, I still laugh. 'I'm worried about him. He was ashen-faced when he came home from work. He talks in his sleep, and I've even caught him sleepwalking. They're cranking up the pressure because a company are looking over the accounts to see if they want to take it over. Otherwise, it will go into administration.'

I reach over and pull two crisp wrappers from between the cushions. Next, I peel a half-eaten lolly off the armrest. Rachel raises her eyebrows.

'The crisp packets are his. He doesn't like getting up while watching the box, so he leaves them there with the thought of getting them later. Charlie has much the same idea with the lolly.'

'Then, being pebble-minded males of the species, they forget?'

Rachel pulls the curtains back to let in light and reveals two empty cans of cider. I pick up the used folded-up nappy he left on the fireplace. It only has wee in it, and no doubt he'd move it in the next twenty-four to forty-eight hours, but it still annoys me.

'What if someone dropped in unexpectedly? Apart from the obvious burgling jokes, I'd be mortified if people thought we lived like this.'

'But you do?'

Horrible, but true.

'Correct. I pity whoever ends up marrying Charlie. And he's only three.'

The 'M' word stops either of us laughing.

'So, have you considered the move to California? It will be brilliant. They have amazing nurseries there. I can show you everything.'

'Is it how I imagine? I want to live in a lighter place than here.'

'I suppose. It's still another city though. Skyscrapers, traffic, bullshit. Same useless men. Talking of which, have you revisited the topic with Sleeping Beauty here?'

'We're not getting on well enough to make such a trip. Maybe we need space and time apart. I'm worried he'll have a mental collapse. We have the kids and Bailey to consider, too.'

'Why not leave without him? The dog can see past his foibles. They stay here, and you see how you get on. Give it six months or so. Maybe he'll find someone else.'

'Stop that. He's been having a lot of furtive phone calls lately. He says it's just work stuff, but I'm not so sure.'

'Weird. I can't imagine anyone else liking him?'

'Rachel! I decided not to go because I don't want to desert my parents, but this Abel madness has unsettled me. I know it's irrational, but Grace is on a trip to the zoo next week, and I'm worried.'

'It is frightening. There's loads of weird stuff happening. To my surprise, I'm looking forward to leaving.'

Rachel gives me a hug and pushes my nose up to make me look like a pig. She's been doing that since we were four years old, and it never fails to lift my spirits. She still finds it as funny now as she did back then.

'Come on, cheer up. Where's your chocolate hiding?'

She holds my hand as she leads me through to the kitchen. I miss my best friend so much. She makes me feel normal, and that is something I haven't been feeling of late.

She opens the cupboard door under the sink and removes the row of cleaning bottles lined up at the front. The treasure is exposed. She lifts the Dairy Milk bar up in the air as though it's Simba, being presented to the animals in The Lion King. I have to hide the chocolate in the house. Dan complains if I leave any in the fridge because he's supposed to be on a diet. If he finds any, much like the wine, his brain short-circuits and he has to eat the lot in one sitting. Charlie and Grace will help if they are quick enough.

Ten minutes later, we both give each other a disgusted smile. Bailey places his paws on the table and gloomily sniffs the empty packet. With an air of dejection, he picks his Bonio up and accepts there's nothing else.

Rachel groans. 'It's the devil's delight, all right. Look at that. One thousand calories and I wasn't even hungry.'

'We have as much control as Dan. So lovely, but I feel weak-willed and worthless.'

'Same here. Now where's your secret, secret stash?

Chapter 29

Dan
A month later

It's Saturday morning and the kids are at Olivia's mum's. Olivia is still going to work though. I was looking forward to last night as we had the place to ourselves. The plan was a few drinks, then the steaks I'd bought with a nice bottle of red, and maybe jiggery-pokery.

Olivia left at 7:30 p.m. to drop the children off. The prep for dinner was finished, so I had a beer and a few peanuts, and watched the Friday evening game. Olivia returned at 9:45 p.m. By that time, the alcohol was gone, and I was having sleepy-slobbery. I woke up on the sofa with Bailey's breath on my face at 3:00 a.m. We're both still there.

Nothing's been said so far, apart from 'good morning' when she came downstairs and brought me a cup of tea. If we had any flowers or plants in the house, they would have died instantly with the unbreathable atmosphere.

The argument is coming but oddly I'm not up for it. I don't feel myself. I'm even more dopey, lethargic, and stressed than usual. Last night's five hours sleep is the longest I've managed since that company started auditing the books. Although I'm unsure if alcohol-induced passing out counts. I feel like I spent the whole night running. It's over four weeks since we had sex, too. That was the purpose of losing the kids for the evening, unless that's another sign I misread.

I can tell Olivia is in the shower because I hear the pump. It's been whirring for ages. I daren't mention it again, but she can't be washing herself for that long. If she's doing her hair, why not turn the bloody water off for that bit? The chance of my shower being better than lukewarm is zero.

As she strides into the lounge, I note her weekend casual is smarter than my weekday best. She must have covered me with a blanket last night. I have an urge to pull it over my head to protect myself from the hail of criticism which is ready to descend.

'Dan, I'm sorry about yesterday.'

I swear I can sense Bailey relax at the same time as I do.

'When I arrived at my parents, they asked me to stay for a drink. We ended up having an important, long chat.'

This is going much better than I expected.

'I told them about California. They told me to go. They thought I should take the opportunity. I argued, but they said they'll be fine, and wouldn't forgive themselves if I stayed because of them. Mum even offered to travel out on holiday for the first month or two to help me settle in.'

'Great news. Sun, sand, and surf, here we come.'

It's only as I try to untangle the dog and me from the blanket, that my slothful brain recognises the word 'me'.

'That's why I was late. I drank too much and walked back to clear my head.'

'What?! That nutcase is roaming the streets, and you're wandering half-cut in the drizzle.'

'My dad said something similar, but you can't let one man scare you from doing things in a city this size. He'd be getting what he wants.'

'You are bonkers. Why don't you start a running club? Call it Deathwish Joggers. You can leave at thirty second intervals so the killer surprises you in turn.'

'You could come with me?'

'To California, or for a run?'

I receive half a sad smile.

'I was talking about a run.'

'Oh great. I can be at the front, no, the back would be far worse. I'd have a sore neck to match my aching legs from looking behind me. It'd force me to keep up even though the last time I ran anywhere was ten years ago when you told me my favourite lager was on offer at the shop.'

My knees creak as I stand, adding weight to my argument. She attempts to lighten the tone.

'I'll cut a hole in the back of my shorts, so you have something to distract and motivate you.'

'Nice. Let's hope you aren't on his list. Do you need to go to your parents' and fetch the car?'

'No, I haven't time. Beau is coming to collect me from here.'

She goes before I can see the expression on her face. Would Beau make a good serial killer? Unlikely, although I've heard it's possible to kill people with kindness. My heart is still in my mouth, and I follow her to the door.

'Is Beau here already?'

'No, I'm taking Bailey for a walk.'

'Wait up, I'll join you.'

I'm dressed in last night's clothes, so slip my trainers on and catch up with her outside the house. We stride together, Bailey in between us, looking from one to the other as though all his wishes have been granted. We face forwards as we talk. The things we are ready to discuss won't be easy to say, or hear.

'Are you going to go to California without me?'

'I'm thinking that way.'

'And the kids?'

'Yes, they'll come with me.'

I feel weightless. As though I could drift away. My hangover doesn't allow me to present any reasonable counter-proposals. Is it for the best?

We step aside to let an old couple pass. They are healthy and relaxed. They're clad head to foot in the latest hiking clothes. The papers are always writing about poor old pensioners who have to choose between heating and eating, and are then found slumped over their two-bar fires six months after starving to death.

Who knows where those people are because I never see them here. Even the retired folk here in this city make me think I don't belong. This place is full of good-looking people – young and old. Clad in designer gear. I rub against their world like scrunched-up newspaper against glass. Grandma has the audacity to wink at me as she ambles past.

'Is there anything I can do to change your mind?'

She stops, and turns. Her eyes are clearer today.

'I'm not sure.'

At the park, uniforms are everywhere. A pulsing crowd lines up at some police tape. I hand the lead to Olivia and walk over to the scene. I don't even need to ask what's going on because there's a conversation in front of me, audible to everyone.

'Someone stabbed him in the neck while he sat in his car. The knife was sticking out when they found him.'

'I know the guy who died.'

'Who was he?'

'Alf's son, the one who was always in and out of prison.'

'He was never going to make old bones.'

I jump up to look over the people and see the milkman, Malcolm, being shoved into the back of a police car. As his head is guided in, I'm sure our eyes meet. I turn to check where Olivia is, but she's gone.

She must have set off home, so I do a kind of half-run and walk that I realise I've seen other middle-aged folk do. When did I stop running? Olivia has stopped further along the road and is talking to Pete the postman. I should be able to catch up, and then we can chat more before she leaves. I need to tell her I want us to go to California together.

Chapter 30

Olivia

On the way back to the house, I collide with the postman as he steps from behind a hedge, and we both tumble to the floor. I know he could have been delivering a letter, but the look on his face indicates he was doing something weird. The surprise makes me drop the lead and I watch Bailey as he runs off home. I'm not too worried as he should wait at the front door. Pete lifts me up with a surprisingly strong grip.

'Sorry, Pete. I didn't see you there.'

'Sorry, Mrs Flood. I didn't see you either.'

That annoys me when he calls me that like the rest. He delivers my bloody mail, so he knows my surname is Jones. He stares at me as if he wants to say something of importance. I nod to encourage him.

'My name isn't Pete.'

'You don't say. Dan's always called you Pete. Have you told him?'

'No, Dan's a great guy. I think, you know, him and me could be friends, so I thought maybe it was a joke. Postman Pete!'

I see. Dan is finally right about something; our postman is crackers.

'What's your real name?'

'Joseph. Joseph Wickmeyer.'

That sounds like the name of a Nazi war criminal hiding in Argentina. Now, I'm not sure if he's taking the piss or not.

'Really? You aren't one of those people who are always changing their name by deed poll? You know, yesterday, you were Strawberry Cupcake, and next month, you'll be Bernard Cat Killer.'

He grins at me, in an unnerving way. Note to self, no more jokes with Pete.

'Anyway...' What do I call him? 'Sorry again, I was distracted by whatever occurred at the park. It's as though crime has rocketed. Did you hear what happened?'

'Yeah, the guy was stabbed to death.'

It's the first time his face lights up to show he's human. A sick one excited by murder.

'They found another identical kill a mile away. They say it's Abel.'

'Oh my God. When are they going to catch him?'

'I hear a few of the residents around here are thinking of setting up a security posse. You know, patrol the streets. I will sign up to it. I am skilled at taekwondo.'

He isn't smiling, so he must be serious. I step back as he looks as though he wants to show me a move. That's brilliant. I recall the animal that Dan says he resembles. Instead of Kung Fu Panda making our neighbourhood safer, we'd have The Taekwondo Tapir. Everyone will sleep well tonight.

I've never been so pleased to see Beau as he pulls up next to us. I love that he always opens the car door for me. He gives the postman a look that says keep away from my expensive vehicle. I turn and note Dan scuttling towards me in a geriatric bus-missing fashion. I consider waiting, but Bernard Cat Killer is hanging around like a bad smell, so I wave to Dan, get in, and we zoom off up the street.

I remember the dog but presume Dan will let him in. Beau smiles at me in the way he often does. He's such a handsome man. Even so, I try to stop myself looking, but it's impossible, and my eyes glance at the space between his top lip and nose. It is small. I shake my head. Dan has me doubting everyone around me, including myself. We're both going doolally.

Chapter 31

The model with no name and beautiful hair who ignores Judith

The girl trudges along the street just before dawn. Tiredness and sadness fight for dominance in her brain. She keeps her head down in this scary land. The other girls whisper of bad men and missing friends. If they are to be believed, killers and rapists lurk at every corner. She comes from a tiny village by the seaside where things like that are unheard of. Sadly, nothing else exciting occurred either.

Little tourism and even fewer jobs meant most youngsters left. She managed to get a student visa although she planned to work. Tears roll down her face as she thinks of the many hours she wasted before leaving. All that time daydreaming of being noticed and signing up to a modelling agency, or meeting a rich businessman.

Back home, everyone knew who she was — The Prom Queen — and treated her with respect but also affection. Even at the airport her father had begged her not to go, while her boyfriend sobbed behind him. That was a year ago. She writes but dare not ring. Her mother would see through her strained voice during the first sentence.

They promised her a live-in vacancy at a five-star hotel. No stars would be closer. The rundown flop-house where she works is infested with every kind of vermin possible; cockroaches right through to prisoners on the run. Her reception job studying the nuances of the English language is, in reality, a laundry role in the bowels of the building. She sweats and uses sign language to communicate with the Chinese madam who runs the show. No one cares what her name is.

All she'd learnt was how to fend off unwanted advances whenever she was ordered to service the rooms. She doesn't want to be a failure, yet she can take little more. To her amazement, the money she receives is poor by her own country's standards. Even the animals back home aren't worked so hard. The cash they take for her tiny room is so extortionate, there'll never be spare to save. But, still she hopes for a miracle. Gold coins are available but she won't do that.

This morning she lingered by the hotel kitchen as she left. The smell of freshly cooked bread transported her back home. One of the chefs had walked up to her and given her a brown bag and a wink. The rolls under her arm make her skin sweat, and her mouth waters as she imagines them slathered with butter. She keeps her shopping in her room now as it lasted hours in the communal fridge of the rambling house where she stays. She lives with thieves.

She hates these split shifts. Finishing at five a.m. and then having to go back at noon. At least it's quiet at this time of the day and she has a place to sleep by herself. Others live in bunk beds. The back door is propped open as usual to release the stench of marijuana and fried food. She never feels safe here. Anyone could walk in and take, or do, whatever they wanted. No one knows her and she knows nobody. What kind of a life is this?

The trap at the bottom of the stairs holds its brown victim for the fourth day. She can't bare to move the mouse herself, so like the rest, she steps over it. The lock on her door has never worked, so she shuts herself in and rests a chair against the handle. The bread rolls are thrown on the bed. Struggling out of her ill-fitting uniform, she bends over and picks up the plastic container to locate her butter.

As she removes the cutlery, she shivers, sensing someone else in the room. The man stands in the darkest corner. Mostly in shadow. He's dressed in black but the full moon has no curtains to war with, so his profile is visible beneath the hood. Even she, living like this, has heard of Abel. He puts his fingers to his lips. She understands immediately, if she resists there'll be no mercy.

Slowly, he guides her to be seated on the bed. Then, he pushes her back and sits astride her and looks down. Now his face is in darkness. The scissors glint in the pale light. Her neck tenses as her raging mind pictures vampires from nanna's stories. She closes her eyes.

The first cut is painless, and then so are the rest. It's her hair he is taking as opposed to her life. His manner is brisk but efficient. Time flees while it has the chance. She lies on the bed long after he's gone. Neither crying nor tearful. She isn't surprised. Nothing in this sinful place could do that. She almost expected it.

Eventually, she rises and looks in her compact mirror. A petrified rag doll blinks back. An easy decision is made. She lifts the bedside table off the floor to retrieve her passport and money, only to find an empty space. She shrieks for five full minutes before anyone knocks on her door.

Chapter 32

Dan
The next day

I lost my temper at work today and shouted at a young girl. She left crying. Then, they ordered me into a meeting room with the sales director and the HR manager. I had to walk the entire length of the office. Everyone knew as their eyes followed me along the route. The only thing missing was a solitary drum beat.

I expected to be at best, suspended, and at worst, fired. They asked me why I'd done it. Instead of explaining that she had too much work and struggled to prioritise, I told them she kept making the same mistakes. They said they understood and not to worry, and they'd tell her not to come back. I didn't realise she was in her probation period because she worked on the blue team. I should have explained, but accepted the easy way out.

They allowed me to leave early, so I walked for an hour to Ian's office and sat outside until he'd finished. I tried not to think of how that girl is feeling. We're now in a hotel nearby, Ian paying a ridiculous price for our drinks. Even so, I need to forget.

'You don't look good, mate. Are you pining for something?'

I've caught sight of myself in the multitude of mirrors in this strange place, and I'm well aware of that fact. While sitting outside, I had a searing white light go off in my brain. My temperature levels soared and dipped for no reason, and my heart strained to leave my chest. Like a fool, I looked the symptoms up on Google. They match those of someone bitten by a deadly spider. That's unlikely but I did look behind me just in case.

'I miss what I can't have. I want carefree travelling, man. I want to pack my bags and go. Everything's too complicated here. Do you remember when we were at university?'

'Birds and mates.'

'Yep, girlfriends are for Christmas. Mates are for life. When you get past your teens, it's good to have a bird at that time of year, or your presents are rubbish. Then, after the hot chestnut eating and mistletoe action, you set her free. Saves you the thankless bullshit of Valentine's Day.'

'Correct. Ruthless, but true. What's your point?'

'Well, it turns out kids are for life too, and the snarling monster that jettisoned them for you.'

'You talk as though you moved in with a witch. I saw Olivia a few weeks back, she looked cracking.'

'Would you shag her, given the opportunity?'

His long pause is disconcerting.

'Possibly. She is rather feisty for my liking. I prefer my women to have less ambition, or at the least be drunk most of the time. The problem with your missus is she's a shark masquerading as a dolphin. She appears sweet and playful, but the real truth is your life's in danger.'

'Yeah, if you piss her off, threaten the offspring or if she's hungry, she'll rip off your head.'

'Although, I recall you two used to be at it all the time. Once, in Thailand, I thought you would rattle the hotel off its foundations.'

I remember that night. We stayed in a wooden guesthouse near a beach. It was a marathon session, and we ran out of bottled water. I was so dehydrated from the alcohol and frantic action that I drank out of the toilet tap because I wanted to stay in bed as opposed to locating a shop. Four days of the shits was my reward for that foolishness.

I decide the best way to explain it is to use the biscuit analogy.

'Olivia is a chocolate biscuit. The finest money can buy. When you first get a packet of these biscuits, you can't believe your luck. Everyone wants one and is jealous because you have an inexhaustible supply. You show your mates to annoy them. The world is wonderful.

'To start with, you eat them everywhere. You grab one in the shower, have a couple while gardening, perhaps even sneak down an alleyway on a night out for some. In fact, they are so tasty, you don't care if someone sees you. You get chocolately in your cinema seat, and you come home from work early, or nip back at lunch, just to have a quick bite. It's the only thing on your mind.

'Then, it fades. If the biscuit barrel is always full, then where's the fun in biscuits. You think about crisps. If you fancy a biscuit, you'd prefer a different type. Something plain maybe, or one you haven't tried before. Possibly even two of those at once. Like a multipack.'

'Ha ha. So true. Sometimes you only want a cheap snack although you'd prefer not to be seen with one.' Ian beams. 'I take it you've not discussed this phenomenon with Olivia.'

'Hell, no. She thinks I'm avoiding her, and keeps dropping heavy hints. The more she does, the more resistant I find myself. I can't be right in the head. There's a smoking hot woman chasing me around the bed, and I'm pretending I've got a migraine. The only time I feel up for it is after drinking, and then she's never keen.'

Ian leans back in his seat. 'Ah, I know what the problem is. The technical explanation is you're old and past your best. Women in their forties go through a renaissance. They want more, just as us men are capable of less. They want quality sex, like they read in those ridiculous magazines. Three hours of massaging, followed by sixteen of foreplay. Even talking afterwards. Basically, she's gone shagging mad, and if you aren't delivering, she will be doing everyone else she meets.'

'What a smashing thought. Let me guess, her boss, the neighbour?'

'Everybody. Your milkman, postman, this Abel guy, definitely all of her female friends, even those homeless dudes you keep moaning about.'

'Wow. No wonder she's tired. Chafed, I expect, too.'

'You need to get out of this place. This city has gone rotten. All the guys at work say it. I've had enough as well. It's time to move on. This is the longest I've ever worked for the same company. I'm stale. This Abel set fire to a rehab centre near me. The one where I always thought I'd end up visiting. The police received a business card with, 'This is the beginning,' on it.'

'You're going travelling without me? Jesus, Ian, that's just what I need. You sending me pictures relaxing on a Greek beach, surrounded by tanned delights.'

It's monumentally depressing. I made my bed though, or sofa in my case, and have no choice but to lie on it. 'Any ideas where you'll go?'

'A plan will turn up, it always does. Once you open yourself up to the idea, then life finds a way.'

'Hmm. Are you sure you're not quoting Jurassic Park? Please feel free to send me a picture of you gored somewhere painful by something unpleasant.'

'What's the latest with your job? Olivia loves hers, and you hate yours?'

'Yes. Her company sneaked into *The Top 100 Independent Companies* to work for. Great benefits, excellent salary, and unlimited potential. My company came nowhere and my role is right at the bottom of the list, between sewage worker and street prostitute. I have to deal with tons of shit and get paid little for being shafted on a regular basis.'

'Is Olivia still not keen on California?'

'No, she's considering it now. We're going to chat to her parents. This Abel insanity has disturbed her. I thought we'd all go as a family, but it looks as though Olivia will be leaving without me.'

'Shit. Although, I'm not surprised, bearing in mind what you just said.'

'I know. I can't pull myself together. We don't talk anymore apart from arguing.'

'Maybe she's met someone else.'

I laugh, but it's not as if I've been attentive of late. Could it be true?

Chapter 33

Olivia

The doorbell jars me from gazing into space. I open the front door and Mike is standing there with a bouquet. I think I'm dreaming, especially when he presents them to me with enthusiasm.

'For you.'

'They're lovely, Mike. Too much, in fact. What are they for?'

'Your birthday.'

'My birthday isn't for nine days.'

'I know. I'm off to a conference in California tomorrow for two weeks, so I thought I'd drop them by before I leave. I paid extra to get flowers that last. You're a great neighbour and deserve something pretty. They remind me of you.'

'That's so nice, Mike.'

And creepy. He walks past me and heads to the kitchen as though it's the most natural thing in the world. Despite the fact I haven't invited him in yet. Nevertheless, the waft of aftershave is so intoxicating, that I imagine jumping on his back. It's a cross between a Viking's armpit and summer rain.

As I close the door, I recall placing the drying rack draped with my underwear outside the front of the house to dry in the sun. It's not my date night stuff either. There are a variety of cigarette butts on the pavement, too. Most likely, Dan's. We are scumbags.

A cork pops behind me. I didn't notice a bottle on Mike's person and briefly contemplate where he had it secreted. I see the kitchen as a visitor would, and it looks like we've had an earth tremor. Despite Dan stating that dried milk and Weetabix is the hardest compound on the planet, he has, yet again, failed to clean the bowls away from breakfast. Mike has helped himself to a couple of glasses and hands me one. I'm so tired, I go with the flow.

'Cheers, Mike. It'll be like having two birthdays.'

'It's for your special day, and for your company's success.'

'My company's success?'

'Yes. I follow stocks, and I'm always reading big things concerning i-BLAM.'

We only changed our company name this week, so he's surprisingly up to date. I take a sip and can't believe how nice it tastes. The bubbles slide down my throat and I relax. I've only just got the kids to bed and wonder if Mike knew that and timed his visit accordingly.

'So, when are you going to Cali?'

This is getting disturbing now. There isn't anything in the news because it's not general knowledge yet. He notices my face fall.

'Don't you recall? You told me a while back you had the chance to go there.'

I don't remember. Another sip of my drink makes that unimportant. I decide to probe Mike, for how he enjoys living here. If I heard it from a man's angle, I might understand Dan better.

'Do you like it here, Mike?'

'Sure, you have a great house.'

'No, I mean here, in this city.'

'Of course! I love busy places.'

'Dan hates it.'

'What? It's awesome here. Not as good as Cali, but great.'

Mike opens another bottle of champagne, which makes me marvel at the speed we must be drinking it, and the capacity of his bottom if that's where he's been hiding them.

'Okay, Dan doesn't think that. Now, how should I explain it?'

'Just shoot.'

'A while before Dan met me, he and his friend travelled to Mexico for spring break. You know, where the American college students go for parties. In their minds, they'd pick up fit young chicks who'd drunk too much. When they arrived, they realised that they were fifteen years too old and with their dodgy, yellow, British teeth and beer bellies, they had more chance of farting sixpences.'

It's not often I've seen Mike stuck for words. I must admit, it made more sense when Dan told the story. Mike's a bright guy and tries to work his way through it. His blank face tells of his failure, so I explain.

'So, he didn't fit in there. That's how he feels here.'

'Ah, okay.'

He has no idea what I'm talking about. Best to get off the topic. 'I spoke to our postman today. He's unusual.'

'Him. Nuts is what he is. I keep finding him looking through my letterbox. He keeps asking me if I watch Star Wars.'

Surely my life can't be this weird. My head is heavy. It's an effort not to rest it on my arms. I decide to do just that as Dan comes through the front door. It looks like I'm sucking Mike off under the table. Dan's face is as drawn as mine. He walks into the kitchen, raises both eyebrows, pours himself a glass of champagne, gulps it in one go, smiles in appreciation, and slumps into a seat.

'What we celebrating?'

'Olivia's birthday.'

Dan's expression is priceless. I save him the torture of thinking he's forgotten. Again.

'It's for next week, Mike's away in California. He goes there regularly.'

'I know when your birthday is.'

I'm sure Mike imperceptibly shakes his head. He takes over in a brash manner.

'Yeah. I said to Olivia, I'll show you the sights. I'm often in The Golden State, we can meet up for certain.'

Sarcasm is what I expect from Dan, but he smiles and picks up a small picture of me from the shelf.

'Do you have many girls over there as stunning as that?'

He passes Mike his favourite photo of me. He took it as I posed next to a rickshaw driver on a Vietnamese street. It's in black and white and the background could be from a hundred years ago. It's the type of picture that stops you in your tracks. Dan states that when he looks at it, the buzz of the world quietens. I realise he says nice things all the time. I'm not listening because I have so much other stuff going on.

The atmosphere changes as Mike stares at it. He gently places the frame on the table.

'Not that attractive, no.'

Grace comes downstairs to break the spell.

'I'm still hungry.'

'Okay, sweetie. Dan, you get her one biscuit, that's it, and then back to bed. I'll see Mike out.'

Dan grabs a digestive and then guides our daughter up the stairs. He glances at me, his face full of accusation.

Mike changes into his charming version on the front door step and gives me a peck on the cheek. I collect my washing off the dryer, disappointed that it's still damp. That's odd. I'm sure I left five pairs of knickers on it.

Chapter 34

Dan

I stare up at the building I work in, and shudder. It's only twenty floors, but from this angle it rises forever. I will one leg at a time to enter the reception. Finally, I recognise the emotion when I come here. I'm nervous. A ball of concrete arrives in my stomach as soon as I leave the train, and then when I arrive at the office, my mouth dries, and my pulse races.

Did I always hate it here? I can't remember. In fact, this morning, I struggled to string two words together in a coherent sentence. Olivia asked me if I'd been smoking weed again. I wish I had, then by stopping I could somehow drag my head from the enormous black cloud I carry with me. My mind tells me to leave this place, walk out, never to return.

Desperate others jostle me from behind in their haste to reach their cells. They have blank faces or pinched expressions. Now I think of escaping, I'm propelled along with the tide. The lift is full. Rivulets of sweat cascade down my lower back and sides. The crush presses my cotton shirt to my skin, and I feel its dampness.

I walk on false legs towards a waving Ken and ignore disingenuous greetings from others. The room is loud with shouted telephone conversations. All I can see is anger, or is it regret? The meeting with the director and Ken is first thing. Acknowledgement of that fact makes my hands tremble.

'Come on, Dan. They're waiting.'

Ken's face smiles. What does that mean? He called me Dan? Is that important? The director shakes my hand with gusto. Words blur and flit around me. Snippets and laughs stick in my brain, but only the last sentence is stark.

'So, Dan. Are you going to be our floor manager?'

Two beaming faces grin in at me. I try to talk but my parched lips barely move. I hear my chair slide on the carpet and find myself lurching out of the room. The drinks machine shines at me as though the office is in darkness, and the crowd there slip away with worried looks at my approach. I can't remember how it works, and jab at the buttons. Turning around for help, I see a field of strangers and then another bright flash goes off in my mind.

It's quiet now. A warm ring spreads from head to toe, leaving peace in its wake. I hear voices and, apart from my legs, my body cools. In the distance, there are echoes of shocked murmurs intermingled with the whisper of my name. I'm aware my arms are outstretched and my eyes jolt open as a high female voice cuts through all others.

'He's pissing himself.'

The warmth below my belt is wet. I blink in staccato fashion and the flow continues. There's a slight release from the suppressed dam of stress that has my brain throbbing. I recall changing into my light grey suit that morning as when I hugged Charlie goodbye, he smeared jam over the shoulder of the dark one. That's unlucky. There isn't any hiding in grey. A ringing phone knocks me from my exhausted stupor and I glance at giggling work colleagues.

'Come on, Dan. This way.'

Ken drags me towards the toilet and I squelch along behind him. We stand facing each other in the disabled toilet, neither of us knowing the words for such an event.

'I have a spare suit. You'll have to go commando, but it'll get you home. I may even have gym socks. Wait here.'

After what could have been seconds or a day, he returns and hands me his clothes and a carrier bag. I think of nothing. I place my wet stuff in the bag and pull his on instead. His waist is narrower than mine, and I have to leave the top button undone.

He's waiting outside the toilets and takes me to the lifts. Past the rest of the staff. Where before every eye was on me, now everyone is busy. We go through reception and below to a basement I never knew existed. He gestures to a new Audi.

'Hop in, I'll drive.'

We depart in silence. The only sounds are the smooth gear changes and blinking indicators. I'm thankful for that. I am surprised he knows where I live, but it's not a day for those concerns.

'Is your missus home?'

I nod in reply.

'She's hot if I recall.'

Ken's still a dick, but a kind one. What would I have done without him? He steps out and walks up our drive. She comes back with him, looking worried. I try to smile but my face won't respond. They talk outside the car. I can't hear them. Time has ceased until I'm helped from my seat.

'Take whatever break you need.'

I bob my head again, and Olivia helps me towards the house. I'm unable to thank him as my only focus is holding the sobs at bay.

Chapter 35

Olivia
A month later

It's been a month since the incident. Dan hasn't set foot out of bed yet, except for the toilet. I suppose that's encouraging in light of what he did. However, for three evenings now, I've answered the door to find a takeaway guy there. The last one had two bottles of wine on him. To my shame, I carried them up on a tray.

I've been so worried I'd lose him, that I couldn't see him taking advantage of me. Beau has been great and given me the time off to look after him. My mum Dan-sat and looked after the kids for a few days to enable me to keep my hand in, but I need to return to work. If he's back to boozing, then new rules apply as he's clearly feeling better.

My mobile rings as I prepare to enter the battlefield. 'Hello?'

'Hi, Olivia. How's Piddle-i-foo?'

'I'm not sure he's ready for piss-taking, Ian.'

Dan's phone has been out of charge since he came home that day. His friend calls me for updates. I've been pondering asking Ian something delicate, so his call is good timing. Ian replies as though he hasn't heard me.

'Okay, tell him to get a grip, and meet me six weeks on Saturday at eight o'clock. At Café Bleu. He'll be fine by then. There's a load of like-minded travellers meeting for drinks.'

'Okay, Ian. Will do. Before you go, will you be honest with me?'

I expect the line to go dead, but to his credit Ian strangles a cough and replies.

'Go on.'

'Has Dan been acting oddly lately?'

'His behaviour's always been unusual.'

'I'm serious. Now I think about things, he was going to work early and coming home late for ages. I used to ring up to speak to him, but his phone would go to voicemail. Ringing the switchboard was a joke as I'd get bounced around the building. I didn't know where he was.'

'Are you asking me if he's been having an affair?'

Shit. 'Not entirely. He's not been himself that's all.'

'I'll be honest with you and say I don't know, but I'd be bloody surprised. I will admit he's not been himself, but this place isn't for him. You know yourself, he'd be happier elsewhere. We often meet for a coffee and regularly have a beer after work so I can hear him complain. I wouldn't worry if I were you. He's always moaning about how busy he is, so work is where he'll be.'

'Okay, thanks, Ian.'

I whisper, 'Twat', under my breath as I cut off the call, not worrying if my timing is out. Dan's had a breakdown and Ian's trying to arrange nights out. A few beers can be anything from six pints to an apocalyptic ending. It's annoying he's polite to me, when I know he will be tempting Dan to do something of which I disapprove.

Dan's been sleeping in the spare room. He looks up shamefaced when I push the door open. So he should. It's not even eleven in the morning and he's holding a glass of red wine. His Kindle Fire is on his lap. I see how he ordered the Chinese. Judging by the wrappers, a third bag of Cheetos has been consumed. A documentary on dinosaurs roars out of the TV.

The only sign that anyone sick stays here is the pungent smell. Even Bailey can't stand the eye-watering combination of cheese, bed socks and farts, and is nowhere to be seen. I put on my best old lady voice.

'Are we okay, dear? Still poorly?'

'A little better, thank you.'

'Get up, you malingering fool. I begged the doctor to come here as you're so delicate. Have a shower. Now. He'll be here in an hour.'

He knows he's beaten because there's no backchat, and he traipses to the bathroom.

I'm making us a cup of tea when he comes into the kitchen after Doctor Green has left. Thankfully, we have brilliant healthcare cover at i-BLAM. It's a great company to work for. Dan's lost loads of weight, but the spark is back in his eyes. He pulls up a chair at the table and sits down. I stand opposite.

'Well?'

'He said it was a classic case of stress. He wrote down all the things I've experienced: poor sleep, rubbish diet, shit job, excessive drinking, raising young children, commuting, and what sounds to him like panic attacks. You'll be surprised to hear I'm not an alcoholic.'

'That's a turn-up.'

It's a joke but falls flat.

'Are you going back to work?'

'Didn't you listen to what I said? That place is responsible for most of it, but never mind the symptoms, can you imagine showing my face after what I did there? He's signed me off for three months, and I'll get full pay. He told me to keep away if I valued my health, and him signing a further three months off later is a formality. I'd be on half pay then.'

'I would need to go full-time.'

He looks pained, but there's no alternative.

'Beau wants me in as much as possible anyway, to catch up with the backlog. Grace finishes school in two months. That's the point I need to tell him if I'm definitely going to California. The roll out begins shortly after.'

'Let's hire a camper van. Travel around Europe together. Bailey can get a passport, we'll all have fun for once. The children will learn more from that than the constant colouring they're doing at the moment.'

'Don't you listen to a word I say? This job is important to me. My career is. I can't just set this opportunity down and expect it to be there five years later. Why don't you be a house husband for a while? It's plain to everyone that your problems lie with your job and you will be fine if you leave. Enjoy spending time with our children. See how funny and interesting they are.'

He isn't going to change. It's a shame Abel burnt that rehab centre. A few months in there and I might have my old Dan back.

Charlie brings his new farm animals into the kitchen and lines them up next to Dan. It looks as though they are about to charge him.

'You'll be spending plenty of time with your dad from now on, Charlie.'

Father and son regard each other like Laurel and Hardy. What have I done?

Chapter 36

Dan
A week later

The receptionist informs me I can go through to the doctor's surgery. I sit opposite him in a comfy seat.

'How are you feeling, Dan?'

Doctor Green peers at me as though I've woken up from a twelve-hour brain operation.

'Irritated.'

'That's interesting. Go on and explain.'

'Who'd have known looking after a three-year-old full-time is such hard work.'

'Ah, I meant the other issues.'

'Oh, right. Not great to be honest.'

'Are you drinking much?'

'Nothing today, so far.'

He checks his watch, even though we both know it's noon.

'When did you last drink?'

'Sunday.'

Today is Tuesday.

'You missed your appointment yesterday.'

'Yes, I was too hungover to face the journey.'

'Drinking is often a sign of self-medicating. Why don't you try living without alcohol for a few weeks?'

That doesn't sound appealing. It can be my little secret.

'Sure. There's more to life, eh?'

The milkman is talking to Olivia's mother when I get back. Talking at, is a better description. He hands me that month's bill when I arrive. It's difficult for me not to shout out, 'How much?!', at the top of my voice when I see the amount. Olivia's mum disappears when I look up.

'Did you hear the latest news, Dan?'

'Milk is now more expensive than champagne?'

His eyes bulge. What have I said?

'Ah, a joke. Wonderful. That's a good one. They found a body in the woods, a skeleton. Old bones, but when they dug it up, there was the book *Cain and Abel*. It's our man, you understand. They've found similar unmarked graves in the past and now they think he's killed for years.'

What happened to chatting about the weather? Instead, we mention the gruesome things we are capable of doing to others. Malcolm has a furry trapper hat on his head. It has a distinctly feline air. Did he buy it off the postman? As Malcolm waffles on, I try to remember if Olivia said the postie was a cat licker or a cat killer. Both are antisocial hobbies.

'I wondered if you wanted to come over and use my gym. I've set it up in the basement. We can spot each other.'

I'd rather eat a cat than go in his dungeon. 'That's kind, Malc. I'll let you know as I currently have a badminton injury.'

'You can work on your cardio. Tomorrow night, here's the address. See you then.'

He leaves me open-mouthed.

I stagger back into the house, with the same enthusiasm as someone who has been told by a doctor that surgery's not an option. Charlie is playing quietly with his toys. He knows not to mess with Nanny. Her clipped accent slices through his boy world ambivalence in nanoseconds, whereas I could shout in his ear with a loudhailer and he'd carry on destroying whatever he was breaking.

Olivia's mother is hovering by the fridge when I get to the kitchen.

'Has he gone?' She's agitated which is unusual for her.

'Yes, for the minute.'

'I agreed to babysit on Saturday for you.'

'What? Umm, I suppose that's kind.'

'I'm sorry. He's forceful, and I wanted to escape. I didn't know you two were friends.'

'Me neither.'

She mouths 'oh' at me, and grins.

'I hope he plays nicely.'

I wait for her to make her usual quick exit. Instead, she stares at me. I begin to perspire. Her face remains impassive while she lifts an eyebrow. It's chilling and reminds me of Olivia's interrogative qualities. She reaches behind her and pulls the fridge open. It's a welcome sight but also a troubling one. Acceptable, perhaps, if I planned a party.

'Expecting visitors?'

'I tend to keep it stocked up in case I'm surprised by unexpected guests.'

'Let us hope if you are, they're thirsty.'

She slams the door and the bottles of drink rattle long after it closes.

'I think it's time we had a chat.'

Nasty. I see now where Olivia gets her barbed statements. The dog retreats to his basket and shuts his eyes.

'We've never been close, but I'm fond of you. I raised my daughter for many years, and she can be stubborn and difficult. The fact you've made it this far is encouraging.

'My husband, on the other hand, believes you to be a waste of space. He reckons you need a firm boot up your rear end. He says he'd enjoy doing it. Then again, he's liked none of Olivia's boyfriends, so don't think you're hard done by. Despite the contents of the cabinet behind me, I would say the party's over. Wouldn't you?'

She comes and stands too close. She's taller than I remember. I daren't glance down to see if she has high heels. I'm a recalcitrant soldier on parade, apart from this sergeant-major smells rose scented. She buttons up the top of my shirt and leans next to my ear. Her breath is warm and menacing.

'Don't fuck it up.'

Chapter 37

Olivia
Two days later

I power into the empty school reception and shout, 'I'm here.'

A woman pops her head out of a room.

'She's waiting in my office, Mrs Flood.'

'I'm so sorry. I have no idea why he wasn't here, and he's not answering his phone.'

'That's okay, Mrs Flood. These things happen.'

'Not on my watch.'

I didn't mean to snarl those words. The headmistress's eyes widen.

'Grace is fine.'

We both look over and confirm that's incorrect. She's a snivelling wreck on a teacher's knee. Grace sees me, runs over, and hugs me as if she didn't expect to see me again. Her wailing, high-pitched voice is at the end of the range of human hearing.

'I thought you forgot me.'

'It's okay, Grace. Mummy's here.'

I lift her and she snuggles into my neck. Her hot face stokes my rage.

'This will never happen again.'

'I don't wish to pry, Mrs Flood.'

Which means she's about to.

'Go on.'

'Is everything okay with Dan?'

'What do you mean?'

'Well, one of the teachers' partners works at the same place as your husband and mentioned he's been ill.'

Is she stopping herself laughing? Is that a small flicker at the side of her mouth? I haven't time for such thoughts. I need to go home.

'That's being resolved now, and he's feeling much better.'

'Another colleague said he arrived late for the school pick-up a few weeks back. It wasn't the first occasion. There was also a whiff of drink.'

'He was pissed when he came to collect the kids?'

'She didn't think he was drunk, or I'd have mentioned it before. He smelled strongly, that's all. You know how it is. If you haven't had any yourself, you can smell it a mile off.'

It was hardly her fault, but I don't stop myself growling at her. I need to lash out.

'My name is Miss Olivia Jones, by the way. Not Mrs Flood. In light of what you've told me, we should make that understood. Good day to you.'

I try to set Grace on the floor, but she squawks. I swap her to the other side and storm to the car.

My molten fury has chilled to cold steel by the time I arrive at home. I give Grace an ice cream in the kitchen so as not to be disturbed, and walk into the lounge. Dan sleeps on the sofa. I see three empty beer bottles, but suspect others hide elsewhere. I could kick his feet to waken him, or his chin. The alarm on his phone saves me the quandary, and he squints at me in confusion.

'Forget anyone?'

He's disorientated. He turns off the ringer, and checks his watch.

'No. Grace has gymnastics after school today.'

'Grace finished gymnastics last week. I made you write it on the planner, remember?'

He squints as he tries to recollect.

'And where is Charlie?'

'I whacked him in bed. He was doing my head in, you know, being manic. Then he fell asleep on the carpet in the middle of a tantrum. There's definitely something wrong with that boy.'

'Wrong with him? He is just a little lad. In fact, he's you! With better aim in the toilet! A smaller clone, without the beer breath.'

Dan smiles.

'Don't grin at me, you idiot. Having a few beers beforehand, were you?'

I boot the empties across the room to stop myself assaulting him.

'I only had one. Those were from yesterday.'

I at least expected him to be contrite. Instead, he's trying to blag me. I've had enough. More than enough.

'I told you to get real. But you didn't. I can handle being messed around, but if I can't trust you to walk to school and pick our daughter up on time, then we're finished. I need to know they are safe.'

The frustrations of the last few years spill from me. He doesn't respond.

'We're going to my parents, and then I'll tell Beau I will go to California. You're a disgrace. All you can think about is how you hate living here. But you have children now. They become the most important thing. You suspend your happiness to make sure they're okay.'

'Nice. You lot bugger off and leave me on my own. Thanks for trying but you aren't welcome. What am I supposed to do?'

'Your lack of effort over the last few years is nobody's fault but your own. Get a new job, stop whining, and grow up. We're through.'

I run around packing a few bits and bobs, but know my parents have most things at their house. Charlie wakes up in a good mood for once, and I lift him and Grace into the car. Dan comes to the door as I'm leaving.

'That's it? No more Daddy? Where am I supposed to go?'

Now he understands, but my sympathy is at the school gates.

'You have two months to get out. I'll stay at my parents until we leave, then rent this place out. You hated it here remember, so I'm doing you a favour.'

Chapter 38

Dan
A month later

I spent the first week thinking she'd come back. She didn't. I received a demand to take the children to the park and see them every weekend and the odd night. I offered to do the pick up from school, but she impolitely declined.

Turns out, I was right. Before I was always busy, now I have nothing to do. Without kids and a job, I am bored. I lie on the sofa and doze. My mind is filled with strange dreams. Whole days are lost to nothing. I even went around Malcolm's to his gym. To be honest, I felt I had little choice. I couldn't hide from him forever.

When I arrived the last time, Malcolm was fuming about the supermarkets. In his mind those bastards hated him and were going out of their way to ruin him. Malcolm held forty kg over my head at that point, so I agreed.

The end was nigh for Malcolm, and his wife experienced the horror of the family credit card being declined at one of those evil corporation's superstores. As he spoke, he bounced three times my poor efforts off his bulging chest. I was sweating more than he was, and I wasn't even lifting the weights.

I asked him to explain his ride in the police car a while back. He said he found the victim, and they wanted a statement. It didn't appear that way to me, but he wasn't in prison, so I suppose they must at least have had their doubts.

To my surprise, I enjoyed the exercise and was having a good time. That is until his wife arrived. He grimaced as he heard his name howled and left me down there. I listened to the mother of all rows take place. It sounded more like a bag of rats and cats fighting than humans arguing. I sneaked out before they chose frying pans, and hot-footed it home.

I have to drop more of the kids toys off at Olivia's parents. It was an order, delivered by text. That's how we communicate these days. The traffic is heavy, and I have time to think what an unpleasant experience I'm driving towards. I'll get taken into the conservatory where they'll sit in their cardigans and judge me, despite the temperature in there being around two hundred degrees.

When I arrive, her parents are leaving. That doesn't bode well as Olivia said she wanted to talk to me about a few things. Her dad is definitely losing it as he gives me the wanker sign as he walks past me. Strange behaviour from a near eighty-year-old. Olivia shuts the door after they've gone and avoids eye contact as she asks if I want a drink. I daren't ask for a beer, so coffee will have to do.

The conservatory has achieved the welcome of a foundry. I've been naked in cooler saunas. She passes me a tin of biscuits and leaves to make the drinks. The metal is hot to the touch. It's the same container they've always had in this burning hell. I've never had one before, so I'm unsure if they keep filling it up, or if it holds the original inhabitants in its fiery grip.

Hunger inspires me to take a chance. It's a terrible mistake. The sensation when I bite through the dusty, arid outer layer would be the same as if I'd sank my teeth into Tutankhamen's forehead. All moisture in my head evaporates and I wonder if this was their plan to rid their daughter of me.

Olivia returns with my coffee but fails to hand it over. Her eyes study me as she talks.

'Is that spunk on your shoulder?'

I look with a shrug. There are many stains there from when I last looked after the kids – some white, some pink. I've no idea where they came from, but Charlie springs to mind. His hands commit a multitude of crimes. I hope it's toothpaste. My mouth's too dry to respond.

'Someone strangled one of my parents' neighbours in her bed yesterday. They stole nothing. The only sign they'd been there, apart from the corpse, was a moustache drawn on a picture in the hall.'

I widen my eyes to ask if it was him.

'I don't know. The police didn't want to jump to conclusions. I asked my mum who she was, and she said she had no idea. They only lived a few doors away.'

I'm unsure where she's going with this, but can only think of the wetness in the cup she idly swings in front of me.

'Strangled! A knife, or a gun, I could almost understand. Imagine the terror. I'm glad we're leaving.'

I stand and, with caution, take the drink from her.

'You're decided then?'

'Dan, I won't continue like this. I can't wait for you to get your head into gear. This isn't a dress rehearsal. I'm sorry.'

'You're giving up on me now, are you?'

'Look in the mirror. You've given up on yourself.'

It's harsh, but true. Since she's left, I've done nothing. I've avoided speaking to work or the doctor. I certainly haven't looked for a job. In fact, it's unusual if I get dressed. The only interaction with other humans I've had has been with the postman, the milkman, and the supermarket delivery guy. My recycling bin was so full of empties and pizza boxes, I couldn't shut the lid.

I had to leave Bailey peeing on Mike's sports car and filled up his bin with the stuff that wouldn't fit in mine. That was at five o'clock in the morning. I would not enjoy an altercation with Mike right now.

'That looks like blood,' asks Olivia.

'What does?'

'The stain on your jeans.'

'I think it's from a pizza. Or ketchup, or it could be tomato soup.'

It could be anything. I don't care. Her barrage continues.

'I'll pack my stuff over the next few weeks. Beau has paid for a delivery firm to collect and store it. I'll let you know when they're coming because they have a key. You can have the car back on Thursday. Beau is lending me his vehicle as he's going to the other office for a while.'

'Could you fill the car up before you return it? I'm short on readies.'

The look on her face is the same as the one I provide her with when she asks me to bring the washing in when it's dry. She had an aversion to petrol stations even when we were together.

I stand to leave. There's little more to say. I walk through the kitchen on the way out and see two broken cups on the side. She shrugs.

'Girls do your head in, and boys do your home in.'

The door shuts behind me, and I know she's right.

Chapter 39

Abel

It's one of those nights where the gloom seeps into the buildings. The rain has stopped, but a cruel wind whips the enthusiasm from everyone. I bought the paper to keep my head dry while I select a target. The problem I have is there are too many. I can see a multitude of crimes being committed without even trying. The police have given up on this place. They say all their focus is on catching me. That's a shame, because as it turns out, I'm the cure. Let these vermin turn on each other.

The prostitutes stick together now. They approach cars with caution. Necessity forces them to be here, alongside the pimps and the junkies, but no one's enjoying it. In this one dark street, I see three different dealers. They are arrogant, but the bulge in their trousers and the odd glint of steel reveals their nervousness. Gang violence is through the roof, even at this low level.

Despite the nerves that have swept the city, business is brisk. At times, the cars are queuing for their illegal wares. It's the fat cats, snorting coke off high-end hookers' asses that I want. They are the ones who should suffer. Cocooned in their SUVs and shiny trucks, they think themselves invincible. I can't get to them, the head of the serpent, yet, so I'll start at the tail.

The article on the front page of the Evening Standard paper catches my eyes.

'Thrills, chills, and kills in the suburban hills.

'We live in a place gone mad. There's only one name on the tips of everyone's tongue. Many refuse to say it. Others dare you to chant it three times in the mirror and he'll come. It may be that he's close by, because Abel is everywhere.

'The mayor has likened it to the last days of Sodom and Gomorrah. The attitude is that a time of destruction is upon us. Whatever you want to do, do it now. There's been a fivefold increase in thrill-seekers paragliding, abseiling and just plain jumping off the tower blocks and multi-storey car parks all over the city. Suicides and accidental deaths have literally gone through the roof.

'Drug busts have hit record levels. A batch of ecstasy laced with strychnine decimated an entire year at our top private school. There is a permanent smog of cannabis and housefires over our heads. The fire department reported more cases of arson in six months than in the previous six years. New riots and marches break out on a daily basis. Huge swathes of the outer districts have become no-go zones.

'More worrying is the fact that incidents of murder and violent crime have reached epidemic levels. If people can't kill themselves, they are doing it to their neighbours. Revenge is the order of the day. Scores are being settled on a biblical level. A local priest bought an AK47 on the black market to protect himself and has reputedly run out of ammo.

'There were reports of orgies in the valley area and something described as a sex rave occurred at the manor. Our parks, recreation areas, and gardens are awash with paraphernalia of the worst kind. Bungee jumping is banned after cranes were illegally used resulting in two deaths. Freerunners pepper our skyline, and our hospitals.

'The authorities are coming under intense scrutiny. A rally challenging police brutality and inefficiency ironically coincided with a mass looting at our largest shopping centre. While our forces protected our politicians at an assembly for change, our homes, offices, and business were burgled, ransacked and destroyed.

'Amid reports of private security patrols booming in popularity and vigilantes roaming the streets, Detective Inspector Jordan reluctantly agreed to talk to us about what they are now calling The Abel Effect. Indeed, I asked her if they had lost control.

'That is simply not true. We are working around the clock to quell these disturbances and find the person who calls himself Abel. He is only one man though. Yesterday alone, we had information linking Abel to twenty crimes. He confessed to over thirty, sometimes in a female voice. He can't be responsible for everything that is happening. We urge civilians to remain calm

'It's true that crime increased by fifty per cent in three months and has since doubled. Personnel, however, have not doubled, but we are trying our best to get things back to normal. Officers from other forces are helping and overtime is being used. The days of Abel will end soon.'

'Confident words from her but sounds like rubbish to me. I can only see it getting worse. As I'm typing this, a naked jogger has run past my window. Can it be him? Well, I must say, I thought Abel would be bigger.'

I read it, and enjoy it. Fame at last.

'You looking for a good time, mister?'

I'm startled. I need to get on with the job in hand. The girl who has approached me looks young enough to be at school. In fact, she dresses as though she still is. She's someone's daughter, and that's why I'm here. I am the flame to light the fuse.

'I'm hoping for a great time, but I want a chemically induced one.'

'You sure? I could even combine the two.'

'Maybe tomorrow. Listen, I need the best stuff. Is that your pimp over there, or your dealer?'

She looks at him in disgust.

'Pimp, dealer, ring-piece, he got a lotta names.'

I pass her the list of drugs and she whistles. I give her a fifty for her trouble. She sprints across the road and he stares at me and grins. I watch him approach a rival supplier and, after a discussion and passing of objects, he jogs toward me.

Snatches of a hymn from years gone by filters through my mind. Fast falls the evening tide. The darkness deepens. I fear no foe. Abide with me. I step into the shadows, raise my scarf and hood, narrow my eyes, and become Abel. He arrives at the alley and I swing him in and shove him against a wall.

He reaches for his gun, and freezes as he stares at my cowled face. The Taser in my hand isn't needed. My legend is more powerful than any weapon. He shoves the paper bag at me.

'Take it, man. Take it.'

'I'm not after drugs. It's you I've come for.'

He was a wretched, foul-stinking disgrace before urine splattered from his trouser leg. Now he's a quivering wreck of humanity. I pull the gun from his waistband.

'Please, don't kill me.'

'You deserve to die.'

'Please...'

'Empty your pockets.'

He passes me an impressive wad of money even though he looks like he could lose consciousness any second. Abhorrent as he smells, I roar in his ear.

'Let all who come here know my name.'

He sobs as he realises he'll survive. His stench gives strength to my arms and I hurl him into a puddle in disgust.

'Tell them I will return. I am thy balm. Everyone I see will die.'

A crunching boot to his ribs delivers the message and I leave him groaning in the dark. Whoever he owes will no doubt deal with him more brutally. I stride away through the back roads thinking of a woman called Olivia.

Chapter 40

Olivia
The next day

There's no answer from the doorbell. I'm surprised Dan's late for the meeting he requested at our house. It's impressive, even by his standards. I don't miss his poor punctuality. I've spent a lot of time waiting around for him. He was often nipping out for half an hour and coming back two hours later. I regularly woke up to an empty space beside me. He would say he'd been out jogging or walking. Perhaps he had, but where to? A different bed?

Charlie woke up poorly, so I left him snuggling into my mother's bosom. I hate it when the children are ill. I despise being so helpless. Although saying that, Charlie loves it at my parents. He's clocked that Grandad's memory is not so hot, and keeps asking for sweets, pretending he hasn't had any yet. I'm not sure if Grandad falls for it or doesn't care. They are both happy.

I let myself in, and, even though it's my house, I'm a stranger. Perhaps that's because of the unusual smell. Typical man thinks a few squirts of air freshener will cover up four weeks of methane and closed windows. Grace, who insisted on coming to show daddy her school report, tugs my sleeve.

'Did something die in here?'

'Let's hope not, sweetie.'

'Maybe it's a squirrel. I watched a program on them.' Mournful eyes stare into mine. 'One bite, and you die.'

Death by squirrel. A fitting way for Dan to go. Although, the squirrel would more likely be infected by him.

'I don't think we'll find a squirrel here, honey. A massive, dirty rat is a possibility.'

Grace looks at me with worry. I pause to say hello to the goldfish. After a few moments of searching the bowl, I decide to spare Grace the sad news. There isn't much you can get past a six-year-old girl though, and she sniffles. I'm done protecting Dan for his laziness, so just give her a hug.

She repays me by sneezing in my face afterwards. Have I ever been completely healthy since Grace started at playschool? Despite the obvious malady, her cheeks bloom and her eyes sparkle. I'm not sure what happened to me. Where did my strength go? At night, I drop into bed and die of exhaustion. By the next day, I've been reanimated, but not one hundred percent. Each time there are new fault lines. Regardless, I slog on.

The kitchen announces Dan's diet over the last few days. There's a selection of beer cans and wine bottles, miscellaneous takeaway boxes, and an empty bottle of tomato ketchup. At least he is getting one of his five a day. I'm gobsmacked that he hasn't tidied up knowing I was coming. It has the look and smell of a teenager's bedroom. I daren't go in the actual bedroom. Who knows what might lurk in there.

I've been collecting various personal items over the last few weeks, and the odd bit of furniture. Strangely, a box of half used perfumes has disappeared from where I left it in the hall. I'd promised to give it to my mum as she enjoys trying new scents, yet only ever buys the same old Avon perfumes she's been getting for years. More underwear has gone walkabout, too. I hope Dan isn't selling it although I wouldn't be surprised.

I've decided to rent the house furnished. Between Charlie, Dan, and Bailey, anything of value has been devalued long ago. I grit my teeth as I notice a new stain on the hall carpet. I'm shocked to hear heavy feet plodding down the stairs. Bailey, who is not allowed upstairs, makes an appearance. How could I have forgotten him?

'I miss you, Baby Bailey,' says Grace.

He's so pleased to see us that his back end is swinging into a right angle. His brown eyes implore me to come home. With impeccable timing, Dan turns up in his badminton gear sporting a haunted expression.

'Daddy!'

He scoops her up and squeezes her, but his eyes flit.

'Nice of you to turn up. Hell, Dan. You'd be sixty minutes late for happy hour at the playboy mansion.'

'Please don't give me any grief, I've had a terrible experience.'

'Have you been doing taekwondo with the tapir?'

'Very amusing. I've been playing badminton with Felicity. She said she wanted to do me one on one, then show me the steam room.'

The twinge in my gut is unwelcome and betrays my feelings, even though I know he's joking.

'What's got your knickers in a twist then?'

'I've been doing the odd workout with Malcolm in his home gym. He's funny when he isn't scaring you. To be honest, I'm short of friends. If it wasn't for noodlehead next door, Malc, and Pete the postie, I would go days without talking to anyone.

'Anyway, I should have disappeared straight away because he was ranting and raging about his missus. He reckons her and the kid have gone missing, or left him, or something. He was all over the shop because the Dairy told him they're stopping deliveries due to the cancellations. The more he worked out, the more furious he became. That's the angriest I've seen him. Finally, he announces he will give them a piece of his mind, yanks the door knob to go back upstairs, and it comes off in his hand.'

'Oh no. Trapped in Malcolm's mausoleum. With Malcolm.'

'Yeah. You know how everyone's paranoid. I suspected he might be this Abel, killed his wife, and I was next. Scary shit. We'd had a good workout and I felt pooped. I'd have struggled to defend myself against Charlie. The expression on Malc's face was so ferocious that I backed up and smacked my head on the wall. He stared at me then like I was the crazy one.

'Two hours we were down there as neither of us had a phone. I wanted to come back and tidy before you arrived. He found an old tool kit which concerned me as he waved the screwdriver around, or the gutting implement that my mind told me it was. In the end, he did a mad war cry and drove his foot through the door as though it was made of polystyrene. I ran home.'

Maybe the time away from him has made me immune to his stories, so I haven't much compassion for him or his tale. I think I left the last crumb of that with the goldfish. I suppose I expected to come over and find him begging for me to return. Perhaps, he'd be tearful over the break-up of his family. I try to match the tanned, relaxed, handsome man I met all those years ago, to the pasty, unshaven, ill-looking wretch in front of me. It's impossible.

'Go and watch television, Grace. While Mummy and Daddy talk. What did you want to discuss, Dan?'

He appears to have forgotten asking me to come over for a chat. His laptop is open and on the side. He shuts it with a suspicious glance over his shoulder.

'Umm. Sorry, I'm still distracted.'

He looks up as though he's missing an item on his shopping list. Then a small dim light comes on in his brain.

'I wanted to know if this is it? I struggle with the fact we were a family a month ago, and not much has changed, yet now we aren't. Are you really taking my children all that way from me?'

'Why don't you Skype, text, and write? You may even find your relationship improves. We're only going for a year to start with, but we'll come back for holidays here. Maybe you can visit.'

'That's it. So, we're single? Will you be on Tinder and the rest, and hook up with whoever you fancy?' Dan grimaces as he contemplates the question.

The tears aren't far away. He's right. I hadn't thought of those implications and it doesn't sound great. However, he was always reasonable when he talked rationally. It just wasn't often.

'Yes, if that's what you want to do. I guess nothing's stopping you, Dan.'

'Isn't that typical of you? Making it out to be my fault for breaking up the family. It wasn't me who stopped having sex. You nagged me so much that I dreaded coming downstairs in the morning.'

'I tried to instigate sex with you twice recently, and you declined.'

'I was tired, and then I'd had the kids all day and wanted to sit in a dark room on my own. Surely you know what that's like.'

'Work and childcare are both easier and more enjoyable if you aren't hungover.'

'You're a stuck record looking for an excuse to split up. Ah, I get it. Now, you're free to date Beau!'

'Don't bring him into this. He's been brilliant.'

'I bet he's whispering in your ear. Saying you deserve better. I bet Beau's not his real name either. Is it Teddy, or something else geeky? These privately educated types are all the same. The prefects sodomise the younger ones, and then it's learned behaviour. When they're older, they bugger the next generation. That's where the stiff upper lip comes from. No squawking when you receive your initiation.'

'What are you ranting about? He attended a normal state school. No funding, no silver spoon.'

'Rubbish. Why then does he sound like the love child of Oliver Twist and Mary Poppins?'

I know he's looking for a reaction. He will get one.

'I stopped having sex with you because you're a drunk. I only want to make love when I'm relaxed. Stroke me, not poke and paw me. I nagged you because you're slovenly. You've no pride. Look around you. I pushed you to spend time with Grace and Charlie because they adore you. When I came back today to see you, I'd hoped you'd changed, so I'm the idiot.'

'I haven't got much going on to make an effort now. Where's my purpose?'

'Unbelievable. You still don't get it. Your children are your reasons for living. If you can't do it for me, do it for them. Become involved, take them places, draw with them, speak to them. It's easy. It might not be exciting but the reward is their company.'

He looks surprised, but I'm not finished.

'You're playing at life. This isn't a game, this is real. Our children are real. Their lives are important. I can't hang on any longer hoping that you'll wake up to that fact. I'm a fool for waiting this long. We should be happy and having a good life. Instead, you're tainting it for the children, and poisoning it for me.'

He stands there impassive. Are none of these strikes landing? Am I talking to a stranger? I should know I've already lost, yet still I shout.

'Get pissed then. Go see your friends and dig out your backpack. Try and find an existence with no responsibility or commitment. Don't you understand? That life's gone now. It's over. You're too old. Teenagers won't want to hang around with you. You'll be the butt of their jokes; 'The traveller that can't handle real life'. You'll be the one *you* used to ridicule. They will pity you. Meanwhile, your children grow up without a father.'

He looks pained and finally takes a step toward me.

'No, don't. It's too late.'

Chapter 41

Abel

The streets are empty as I look for victims. Do mothers now use my name as a threat? The day has been mild but the temperature plummets and every home hides in despair. Yet, there's a bay window on the corner with open curtains. Yellow light spills onto the street. Do they know no fear? I stand outside and stare in. At the table, bent over a book, is a tired man in a worn, woollen suit. I crack a smile. Sometimes they make it too easy.

I pull over my hood, raise my scarf, and knock. Not too hard, I'd hate to disturb the neighbours. He takes his time coming to the door, but when he arrives he swings it wide, lighting me up like a hero on stage. I must resemble a presence from the pits of his memory.

'Evening, can I help you?'

He's looking at me through rheumy eyes with no emotion. His antipathy throws me.

'I'm lost. Erm, is Turpin Street near here?'

'Turpin Street? As in Dick Turpin? Yes, it is. Now, it might be two roads along, on the left. Or is that right? You forget everything important at my age. Come in. I have an A-Z street map. Don't mind the mess, I get few visitors nowadays.'

He lets me enter as easily and enthusiastically as welcoming in the new year. Even up close his tired face shows no recognition. The house smells old. Dust frosts the surfaces. He shuffles along, and I imagine it collecting at his feet like a sorry snowplough. I place my hand on the cosh in my pocket. It feels heavy and warm.

He edges past a large table covered in books in the centre of the room. There's a war theme to them and the television has a loud black and white film playing. He opens a sideboard and roots among the drawers.

'Forgive me, I'll try to be quick. My eyesight is terrible these days, but I'm sure it was here.'

I loom behind him and notice the movie blaring out is recent, it's just the set that is ancient. My own functioning vision picks up photos of sailors and ships on the walls, many with a proud young man forefront. I spot a medal inside a small display case on a stand.

'Here you are. This is it. I recognise it from the binder around the edge. You'll have to read it. My magnifying glass helps but I've used it too much today and I've a splitting headache.'

'Thank you.' I flick through the pages, pausing to turn the television off before I get a migraine. 'Were you in the Second World War?'

His laugh is a wheeze. 'How old do you think I am? I served all over. The Middle East mostly. I loved the Navy.'

'You live here alone?'

There's a small pause and a shrug. 'Yes, I was too busy for a family. Too much fun to be had, and I wanted to see the sights. My memories are my comfort. I do have a daughter from a brief liaison many decades ago. Nice girl. She rings every year and I receive a card on my birthday most years.'

'Do you let anyone in at this time of night? I could be a burglar, or worse?'

'When you get to my age, things don't matter much. Besides, I say drink with the devil. Come on, let's have a rum.'

He moves through the door with more haste and I hear the clinking of bottles. I pick up the magnifying glass on top of a tank picture and hold it up. If the power was any greater, I could see through the brick cracks and into the neighbour's lounge.

He returns with a grumbling cough and delicately pours a whopping measure into two glasses. From behind, his bald dome surrounded by grey hair makes his head resemble an egg in a nest. Prime for cracking. What a pointless, lonely existence. I'd be doing him a favour.

Finally, his face shows emotion as his jowls quiver in anticipation while he passes me my drink with a shaking hand. The inscription on my glass reads, 'The Time Flies When You're Having Rum'.

His expression softens. 'To absent friends.'

I expect him to chink glasses, instead he downs it in a steady gulp. It feels important to do the same, and my own eyesight falters. 'I better go.'

'Sure, sure. One for the road?'

We end up chatting for a while. He led an interesting life. An existence where he didn't tend the home fire, so he's paying for it now. He has so many things he wants to discuss he hardly knows where to start. I let him talk.

Later, he walks me out despite being visibly tired. He musters a smile.

'You be careful out there. You don't want to bump into that Abel.'

I wonder for a moment if he knew all along. He chuckles but his face is open. This poor man is thankful for tonight. He's had a rare and unexpected pleasure. I consider what I came to do. I will be gracious. Maybe I'm not a lost cause and the good in me still has influence. He places a hand on my shoulder at the door.

'Please visit again. Any time you want. I'm always in, and I've always got drink.'

'You try and stop me.'

The door closes, slowly, reluctantly. I know I will never return here, and so does he.

Chapter 42

Dan
A week later

When I arrive at Café Bleu, I suppose you could call it my local, it's busy. It is so different, it's as though I'm entering inside for the first time. As I struggle to the bar, I realise I've only ever been here on midweek nights. That's why the staff were bored. Now, the place is rammed. The music pumps and even at my age, I can feel the vibe running through the place.

I'm glad I put extra effort in tonight. By that, I mean I visited a department store and bought a new pair of jeans, shoes, and a shirt. It was a daunting experience. Why the hell are there fifty choices for everything nowadays?

I remember when it used to be Levi's or the shop's own brand. Zip fly or button. I tried some skinny-fit jeans and couldn't get them past my thighs, never mind my gut. The coat prices were extortionate, so I decided to keep the one I already own. I must remove it sharpish. If it smelled any more of dog, I might as well have bought Bailey in here, draped around my shoulders.

I can't spot Ian and suspect he'll be late. My shoes pinch but luckily only when I walk. I join those queuing at the bar and, after a ten-minute wait, leave with two frothing drinks. I'm not surprised to find the beer is more expensive on a Saturday night.

My phone vibrates in my pocket and I check and see a text from Ian. 'We're in the corner'. That's not incredibly handy as I suspect there will be four of them. The crowd in here heaves as though it's breathing, so I edge and nudge my way through the massed ranks almost in a dance. I smile when I guess the right corner. I'm ecstatic to find they have seats.

'This is Charlotte, and Kathy.'

'Hi, Dan,' they sing.

Two girls, at most in their early twenties, kiss me on the cheek at the same time. They glide past on high heels. It's been many years since that sort of thing happened. Ian raises his eyebrows.

'They've gone to powder their noses.'

I'm not sure if this means they have gone to check their lipstick, or hoover up drugs. I conclude it doesn't matter either way.

'Are these the like-minded travellers?'

'Kind of. Charlotte is the receptionist at our company. Kathy is one of the PAs. They're thinking of going to South America for six months. They want to see Brazil.'

Brazil was a country we always planned to visit. The idea of the carnival and five days of drinking and dancing isn't as appealing as it used to be. Not unless they spread them out over a month.

'You know there's nothing keeping you here, now you've split up?'

'Apart from the kids.'

'I thought they were going with Olivia?'

He's right. I've been so focused on the Olivia problem that I keep forgetting that my children will be with her. They'll be gone, and I'll be homeless. I have few options. One is to go back to the home town and the house where I lived with my parents. My shoulders sag at the prospect.

'Olivia says I'm too old for travelling now.'

'What? She's messing with your head. You're never too old. You might not survive on three hours of sleep and a few paracetamols anymore, but what else is there?'

'Olivia disagrees with you.'

'People like us, we need to travel. See new things, meet other travellers. This city is one of thousands of huge treadmills around the world. Everyone should get on them every now and again, to earn money and experience it. Then you appreciate life all the more away from these soul-sucking places.'

'Well, Olivia's confirmed she is going to California with i-BLAM.'

'i-BLAM! No way.'

Ian collapses into theatrical laughter, and I fear he's already powdered his nose.

'Yeah, mad isn't it? Beau's new name for the company.'

'I reckon her boss has named it that, as that's what he'll do to Olivia when he gets her over there.'

'Hmm. You reckon. He has more pressing things on his mind. I think it stands for Banking, Loans, Asset Management. Or should I be pleased he didn't call it i-PEE, or i-JIZZ?'

'Perhaps, they're subdivisions. Anyway, here's the heads-up. Kathy has been flirting with me for weeks, but our place isn't keen on interwork relationships. Now I'm leaving soon, I don't care. She's chubbier than I'd usually go for, but her hair is so perfect, I can't concentrate on anything else. I know little of Charlotte. You'll have to see if you still have the patter.'

'I feel guilty already.'

'I wouldn't if I were you. Olivia asked me if you were having an affair. Said she didn't know where you were half the time.'

'Really? What did you say?'

'I did what mates do. I lied. Said I often meet you at the last minute. You don't want to confess to anything, do you?'

He has a strange look on his face. However, the question is forgotten as the girls return looking like they've spent five minutes plugged into the national grid. It's going to be a long night.

'So, you're Dan.'

'That's right. Nice to meet you, Charlotte.'

'I thought you'd be younger.'

'I thought you'd be older.'

'My dad's your age.'

'Excellent. You win.'

Once they come down from planet Mars, I enjoy their company. Charlotte's hair is tied back and shows off an elegant neck. She's willowy in a way I've never been. She resembles Phoebe from Friends, when I was always more of a Rachel fan. Although that's like saying if you prefer free money to free holidays, when either will do.

'What makes you want to travel?' I ask Kathy.

'We're both twenty-five and if we don't do it now, we might never. I loved living in the city and being at the centre of things, but it's changing. I'm not sure I like it here anymore. The crime statistics are off the chart. You can't even go for a jog without worrying if you're going to make it home in one piece.'

Charlotte chips in. 'I bet you two have loads of stories, being so ancient and all.'

And, of course, we do.

As the night carries on, I could be drinking in my front room because I have no idea what's occurring around me. Tonight, I'm twenty-five again. Every time Kathy speaks, Ian gets a look on his face like Tiny Tim when they wheeled in the turkey. However, the booze demands its ransom. I've resisted any drugs and I'm feeling leaden-headed. Charlotte's knee touches mine when the others disappear the way of the bathroom.

'How does it feel to be old?'

'Great. To be wise, is to be happy.'

'You're funny.'

'Thanks, I think.'

'What age does your bum go south?'

'Twenty-six. Instantly.'

She gets out of her seat and squeezes her cheeks.

'You squeeze them. Are they still firm?'

I suppose it's rude not to help a lady out. She bends over and backs into my waiting, cupped hands. I have the same look on my face as Grace did when she woke up last year and realised it was Christmas Day. I assure Charlotte everything is perfect and don't even have to lie.

'What's the worst thing about getting old?'

'Honestly?'

'Yeah. Tell me the truth.'

'For me, you feel jaded. It's summed up by films. They keep remaking classics, like Clash of the Titans and Robocop, and you wonder why. You become nostalgic without noticing. Life was better years ago. When you're young you only remember your embarrassing mistakes. Later, you recall being free in a way you'll never be again.

'You start to think you've seen it all before. That's why it's so amazing for children. Everything is new. How fucking fantastic is an elephant if you haven't seen one previously?'

'Or a hippo. Or a giraffe! So funny.'

'Exactly. Instead, as you age, there are no more first snogs or shags. Most jokes you've heard. The news feels repeated. The latest songs mean nothing, yet old ones trigger memories of special times. You don't give a shit about the drama of sports, because it doesn't surprise you. Even sunsets get boring. Finally, people you know start to die.'

'Wow. That's depressing.'

'Life can be miserable when you understand it. I can't see a meaning in it all, can you?'

'The purpose of life is to get wasted and have fun. Travel!'

I smile. I, too, felt like that. This place has changed me. Something has shifted inside and the gloom smothers me. Maybe travelling again will reawaken my interest in living.

'Why don't you come with us? You and old droopy balls Ian.'

'Talking of droopy balls, he's been gone ages.'

'They've gone home, dopey.'

That's not an unusual trick for Ian. It was nice of Charlotte to stay.

'Do you think I'm attractive?' she says.

'Of course. Young is beautiful whether you're attractive or not. Although you won't understand that until you're old. In your case, your features are in the right place and you look reasonably healthy, so I suspect most men would find you acceptable, and suitable for the rearing of their descendants.'

'Ah, smooth. Are you chatting me up?'

I concentrate on her mannerisms and deduce she's at the border of merry and steaming. It suits her. Oh, to be young and giggly again.

'I considered it, but then gave up when you told me I was older than your dad.'

'I see. Maybe that's why I'm keen. You're not trying. I find you amusing, and I feel safe with you.'

'Brillia-'

And, suddenly, we're kissing.

Chapter 43

The police
The next morning

Detective Sharpe trudges along with Detective Inspector Jordan. He hates door knocking, especially in these posh roads. At least in the flats or the slummy areas you can knock and move fast from door to door without walking up a long drive. Jordan offered to come along. She said she wanted to get a feel for the area and how people were behaving. Sharpe suspected she only wished to leave the dejected office.

Progress in finding Abel has faltered. In fact, it never got off the ground. The surge in lawbreaking was breath-taking. It was as though committing a crime and then blaming it on Abel had become a city sport. It wasn't just in this place either. The phenomenon had repeated itself up to fifty miles away. At least there had been no more religious elements to it all. They decided to keep that part of it quiet. Or there really would be a panic.

The atmosphere and general negativity had dragged everyone into the doldrums. Managers recruited civilians to answer the police phones, but the volume of cases drowned any progress. No one even knew if Abel was a real name. Their databases revealed no fresh leads. To start with, Sharpe and his colleagues loved the challenge and the overtime. Now, nobody wanted either. Sickness and stress infected them all.

He'd become run down himself, caught a virus, and spent the last ten days at home fighting sleep as he might soil himself if he lost consciousness. He was defeated in both those battles. Before he was off, it had been so manic that recording the crimes was hard enough, never mind investigating them.

'Your turn to knock next, Sharpe.'

'Great.'

They haven't spoken to anyone for ten minutes, which is odd. They can't all have left town, or perhaps they are slumped in their chairs, riddled with bullets. She recalls earlier and turns to him. 'Cheer up. Did you know something strange is happening?'

Sharpe scowls. 'I have a pretty good idea.'

Jordan is privy to the most recent crime stats and they made good reading today. She was surprised as she knows the police haven't done much different. This reminder of the positive news inserts a spring in her step. Working under such awful conditions had become unbearable. She laughs and decides she feels positive about getting the city into shape again. This is unexpected.

Sharpe gives her a strange look.

'You okay?'

'Never better. I can let you in on the latest info. Since you've been away the last week or so, reported crime has halved. This week it halved again. Across every single category, in every borough, incidents have dropped. Management can start to lay off the temporary staff. The chief fire officers have reported their quietest period for twenty years. Hospitals are dealing with low levels of violent injuries.'

'That's odd. Why does my desk have two towers of Pisa on it then?'

'That will be piles of historic stuff. We haven't even begun to process most of it. Soon a decision will be made not to bother. Resources can then move to fresh cases where the leads are hot and there's still a chance of solving them.'

'You think Abel and his friends have gone to ground?'

'I suspect Abel, alone or otherwise, is only responsible for a few incidents. There's no way he could have committed a fraction of the things he claimed, or other people blamed on him. What he created was an environment of fear. The city lost its mind.'

'That's true. Which crimes did he commit though? It was like we were living in the wild west, or even the middle ages. Revenge was the order of the day. I heard that Judge who they suspected was crooked and disappeared, wasn't on the run after all. Someone kidnapped him, and he was found tied up in a tent in a field. Minus his balls.'

'Yes, I did hear that. Many wrongs were committed over the last six months, but doesn't it make you think some were put right? Or at least they settled the score.'

'I suppose. Although you can't condone such horrific violence?'

'No, of course not. We, the police, are here for a reason. But the vigilante groups and even the general public have chased and harried criminals out of neighbourhoods. The streets where dealers worked and prostitutes touted their wares are nearly empty now. Hundreds of criminals were killed. Thousands maybe.'

'And many innocent people.'

'Yes, that too. Yet, eventually, you run out of people to target. Everyone's dead, or fled. Vengeance is taken. Scores are settled. Nobody wants to live in a permanent state of wrath, so things calm down. We may have even caught a few of the wrongdoers.'

'You're saying crime is dropping, because payback has been taken? All the bad people are gone, mostly at each other's hands? Society is cleansed, and now we can rebuild?'

'Yes. Abel was a one-man epidemic. A plague that's now burnt out.'

Sharpe looks around him, puzzled.

'Sounds far-fetched to me. People have probably just stopped reporting it as we are clueless. Besides, don't you think it's anything to do with them calling in the armed forces to maintain control?'

'That would have helped.' She smiles as he frowns at another unopened door.

'Jesus, where the hell is everyone?'

The sound of a vehicle approaching grabs their attention. A shit-coloured vehicle bumps up the drive next to them. Jordan rolls her eyes as Sharpe steps forward and opens the door to let an attractive woman in her mid-forties out of the car.

'Hi, Mam. Do you live here?'

She looks perplexed by the question which isn't promising.

'I used to. I'm going to be renting it out. Why?'

'There are numerous reports of people missing. Disappeared, if you like. The crimewave in the city has reached here as well. We're door knocking to see if anyone's seen or heard anything.'

At that moment, a creepy looking postman bounds over and gives the lady a letter. He couldn't have been any slimier unless he'd run his leathery tongue up the side of her face. She shivers, and ignores him.

'Mam, have you noticed any strange people in the vicinity?'

'It would be much quicker if I listed the normal people I know here.'

Both the officers nod in agreement. They stand next to the woman at her front door and are confused when she knocks.

'My ex still lives here.'

Jordan glances at Sharpe.

'We might as well have a word with him while we're here.'

Chapter 44

Dan

The weak morning sun peeps between the gap in the curtains. Is that a tap running, or the last drop of liquid in my body trying to escape from my poorly brain? I've never been run over before, but this would be similar. The guy who lost the chariot race in Ben Hur suffered like this as the horses galloped over him and away.

My right hip hurts so much it can only be dislocated, and someone must have removed both my knee caps. The numbness in my hands and feet worries me, but thirst dominates my mind. I hear a slight gasp next to me. My back creaks as I roll onto my side where I see Charlotte sleeping.

A guilty feeling washes over me as her young skin reminds me of Grace. My memory gently arranges last night's jigsaws. Charlotte was slaughtered, and I had to hold her up on the way home. Her singing could have woken the dead, never mind the sleeping. I recall seeing Mike the neighbour in his dressing gown, standing in his doorway, smiling a victorious smile as we passed by.

Then, a kaleidoscope of advanced sexual positions flickers through my subconscious. I'm lucky to be alive after all that! So, I guess it's expected that I can barely move. As I admire her lean body and pert breasts, I must say it's a shame. My memory is so fuzzy, it feels as though it happened to someone else. I do remember thinking this is how I used to have sex. When it was new and exciting. It was fast and frantic with Olivia at the beginning, I recall.

I slide out of bed and stream treacle into the toilet. My squinting eyes only able to move in slow painful jerks. I'm disorientated but make it back between the sheets. Charlotte wakes and smiles at me. She whispers.

'Have you got a toothbrush?'

'Of course.'

'Go and use it.'

I assume that's a slight on my breath which could split atoms at this moment in time, but I grasp she has other ideas. She will need a defibrillator if she thinks she can get me going again. I stagger off, she follows and stands behind me. As I brush, she fiddles. She takes the toothbrush off me and then cleans her own with it. I think her doing that is what perks up the old boy.

Eight minutes later, my ruined body straddles the bed. It was weird, but exciting, as she manhandled me into each position and more-or-less rode me like a pony. Maybe sleepy seaside donkey is more accurate. The number of times I had to think of Ian or Bailey to stop myself peaking early is too many to remember. Life is weird. I had sex with a stunning young woman and spent the majority of it thinking of my best friend and a dog. Her youthful confidence is shocking.

'That was brilliant.'

'You didn't do too bad yourself, old man.'

'Please, that's too much. Lay off those heavy compliments.'

'What you lack in stamina and agility, you more than make up for with enthusiasm. Anyway, I'm off home. We're all meeting next Saturday at The Blue Brick Bar. I'll see you there. We can plan Brazil.'

She doesn't notice the look of horror on my face as she glides into her jeans. My body will need to be kept in an oxygen chamber for a month to recover from the previous twenty-four hours. Did we agree to go to Brazil last night?

'Where's the Blue Brick Bar?'

'I'll send you a link. It's banging. You'll love it.'

I hope banging means it's cheap, quiet, and has many comfy seats. I know from experience now is not the time to think about anything new. Mind numbing television and the hair of the dog are what I need. A movie I've seen a hundred times would be perfect. She rubs her head searching for her bra. I have a flashback of seeing it downstairs.

She shrugs and pulls her top on without it. 'No worries. Bring it Saturday.'

She looks in the mirror next to me. Last night the difference was twenty years. This morning we are two species separated by generations of evolution. I'm the one which sank back into the mud. There are scratches on my chest too, like I've been in a bar brawl. I can't recall if Charlotte did them or I received them elsewhere.

'Come and wave me off, point me towards public transport, and I'll get out of your way.'

I find my boxers, but nothing else. So, grabbing a T-shirt from the pile on the landing, I pull it on and follow her down the stairs.

Next to the door she creases up. My T-shirt fits like a second skin. It's bright pink and says, 'Tonight's forecast, 100% prosecco'. She kisses me on the lips, squeezes my cheeks, and, as she places her fingers on the handle, the doorbell rings.

I pray to a God that's never loved me. Please, let it be anyone but the police or Olivia.

Of course, it's both of them. I expect to hear a booming laugh from the heavens. The first face I see is Olivia's. Perfect. The yawning door reveals a pair of serious faces above suits. It's the female one of these who talks. She frowns at my T-shirt as she does so.

'I'm DI Jordan. We're doing door-to-door enquiries. Have you seen anything unusual around these parts? Suspicious people, that sort of thing.'

My pickled brain is unable to perform. I can only grin like a fool. I glance at Olivia as I talk.

'Nope. I love it here.'

'How about your daughter?'

Charlotte bursts out laughing, and winks at me.

'No, sorry, nothing. See you, Dad.'

She bounces out of sight. Olivia scowls.

'She came over to get a travel book.'

I've never learnt that it's sometimes best to keep your mouth shut. They aren't detectives for nothing, and immediately pick up on the tension.

DI Jordan smirks at me and shakes her head. The male suit repeats my words. 'She came over to get a travel book?'

'That's correct.'

Bailey chooses that moment to join us with a red bra in his mouth.

Chapter 45

Olivia

The sound of the police laughing stops as they knock on the next house's door. I'm sad and angry, but do I have any right to be? Dan and I stare at each other as if we've never met.

'Are you going to invite me in?'

I think he'd rather work in an old people's home for a year, but he steps back to let me through. God knows what that girl's done to him, but he looks drained. I follow him into the kitchen and watch him hastily shove discarded clothes into a cupboard. How lovely. We can talk where it looks like he's been doing the dirty deed. In my house!

'I came here to give you move dates. Beau is relaxed about specifics, he just wants me there as soon as possible. You need to be out of here in a month. Painters are coming and the removal men will take the things I'm not leaving.'

'Okay. You didn't have to come here to tell me that.'

'I know. I wanted to make sure you had somewhere to go. Whatever happens, I still care about you.'

'I haven't seen you for two weeks. I have a relationship with your mother and the children now. You've moved on fast with your new exciting life.'

After what I saw leaving my house, I snap. I'm so furious, I'm only able to deliver bullet-points through gritted teeth.

'I've moved on? That tart seemed nice. Pretty. Uni student, is she? Did you give her what she wanted?'

'You know nothing about her.'

'I bet you don't either. She's young enough to be your daughter.'

'Is that what's upsetting you? Her age? Not that she wants to do things you can't be bothered with.'

'You bastard. Did I mean so little to you that you leapt into bed with the first whore you met?'

'Did I mean so little to you that you gave up on us so easily? I knew we weren't happy, but I never thought you'd throw me out. We have kids. It's about hunkering down.'

'How dare you say that? You can hunker off.'

I pick up my handbag and want to shove it down his useless throat. A small voice tells me this isn't solving anything. If he can't be civil, then I need to be the bigger person.

'Why didn't you say you were thinking of leaving?' he asks.

'I did.'

'Well, I didn't hear.'

'That's because you don't listen.'

'I thought you believed in meditation?'

'If by that you mean mediation, then I distinctly remember you telling me in a drunken stupor that all counsellors are cocksuckers.'

'They are!'

'Nothing gets through to you. Don't you dare blame any of this on me. I came because I still care for you. It's me that's an idiot! But I need you to be okay, so our children can spend time with you. I need to know they are safe and with responsible adults. What are you going to do with them? Hang out with teenagers? You need to find somewhere to live.'

His eyes narrow, but not in a harsh way. In true Dan style, he's not thought further away than his next meal, or beer.

'I'm off to see my mother in a few days. I'll take Chucky. Sorry, Charlie. She's not seen him for over a year. I suppose I could stay there for two or three months. Get my head together.'

I've only met his mother on a few occasions. They have the kind of relationship you'd expect if he had been sent to boarding school at eleven. Only he wasn't.

'Isn't that out of the frying pan and into the volcano? Didn't you say the only ones that return to that town are people on day release from prison?'

'God, you're right. Admittedly, it's not ideal but it will be free. There's nothing keeping me here if you go. You know I've not been happy. I've lost who I am. There are too many people and towering buildings. Too much traffic and constant noise. I can't find a niche, because I don't understand why anyone wants to live here. From the moment I wake up, I feel I'm forcing myself to breathe.'

He's being a little dramatic, but I know these things. Although, it's the first time I've heard them in a list. Should I have known he was this unhappy, or is he making excuses for his lack of effort?

'You refused to embrace it here, Dan. You've never given it your all. You constantly resisted this city. You hid behind sarcasm and alcohol and refused to let this place in. I was here, your children were here. Do simple things. Sober. Visit the theatre, or cinema. Cycle around a park, re-join life. There are galleries and shows open every day and night.'

'Theatre, art galleries, opera? That's not me.'

'Is it anyone? Maybe not to start with, but you try, and then you talk about it. Even if it's to slag it off. That way, eventually, you'll find something you love. There are stadiums, water sports, rock-climbing, and architecture. Join a chess club. Discover museums and exhibitions. You made me go to countless war stuff in Vietnam and Cambodia.'

'I do enjoy a good museum.'

'Yes. See. Have you been to one here? I'd have gone with you if you'd only asked. As long as they have a cake and coffee shop.'

I smile and he does the same. His fades away.

'It's so expensive and busy here. It stresses me out.'

'You've got an excuse for everything, haven't you? Yes, it's hard. It's easy to sit on the sofa, watch movies, and get pissed. Is booze free? If you spent the beer money on experiences, we'd all be happier. Which do you think is the healthier and more rewarding?'

A car horn outside sounds three times.

'Who's that?'

'It's Rachel. I told her I was coming here. We're going out for a bite to eat in town at that new tapas place.'

His scowl is back.

'It's still a city full of wankers.'

I give up. 'Yes, that's true. It's a shock you didn't fit right in.'

Chapter 46

Olivia

Rachel is talking to Mike outside when I stamp past. I ignore them both, walk up to what I hope is her car at the kerb, and climb in. To my annoyance, it takes Rachel a further minute to join me.

'He's so dishy.'

'Please can we get out of here? I have numerous appointments in town, all of them with wine.'

'Went well with Dan then?'

'He's so frustrating.'

'Am I allowed to say I told you so?'

'Only if you want to go for tapas on your own.'

Rachel drives off in a smooth manner. She's one of the few people on the planet who calm down behind a wheel. She becomes a sensible, rational person. My blood cools. She brakes sensibly as lunatic cyclists hurtle past. These spandex warriors drive me crazy. I've lost count of how many times I've almost been knocked over by them. There's a bunch who go out near our house and terrorize the roads. I often feel like throwing things at them.

By the time we've nipped into our favourite bar for a pre-lunch relaxant, I'm ready to talk.

'You were right. He hasn't changed. He picked up his single life as if the last eight years never happened.'

'Has he put any effort in at all?'

'Not a huge amount. He's argued, not begged, the fooker.'

Fooker is what Rachel likes to call useless men.

'They're all fookers, don't be surprised.'

'I know. But it doesn't feel right. I imagined if we ever split up it would be because he'd cheated on me and shagged someone. I never imagined I'd give him the boot for not trying hard enough, and basically tell him to shag other people. Now he's gone and done it, I'm devastated.'

'What!'

I finally understand the reason why Rachel doesn't get as drunk as I do is because she is always spraying me with her drink. Half of each glass gets to go down her throat, the other part is blown in my direction.

'Yep. I turned up, and he was letting a hot young thing out the front door. Skin like a baby's bum, and, well, I should think a bottom like one too. The bitch.'

'Not the girl with the vein-tight jeans and no bra I saw at the bottom of your street?'

'Ponytail and red high heels?'

'That's the one.'

'I don't suppose you ran her over, did you?'

'No, but we can turn around and find her if you want. I'll do it really quick?'

'Don't joke about that. Dan found a dint on our car. He reckons it was me that scratched our neighbour's car. Besides, I know it's not her fault. Shall we just give her a glancing blow.'

'Come on, Olivia. You're better off without him. You have an amazing opportunity coming up — which is the chance to get drunk with me in California. Then the new job's okay, too. Happy days.'

'I asked his friend if he thought Dan was having an affair. He said he'd know and he wasn't.'

'Come on, Olivia. Would he really tell you the truth? 'I guess not.'

We settle in and talk rubbish. My problems always dissolve for the time I'm with Rachel. I must say it will be good to have her close by. We pop to our second favourite bar and she buys me another vat of prosecco. She's driving, so I feel a bit guilty, but not too bad. I plonk the empty glass onto the table with a sloppy grin and notice her distraction.

My eyes narrow. 'What's got into you?'

'Nothing.'

'You look guilty of something.'

'Me? Is it a crime to be enjoying your company?'

'If I didn't know better, I'd say you've had sex today.'

'I have not. How dare you? It was yesterday.'

'Surely not…'

'Yes. Herman the German. He's proved to be an efficient lover.'

'A big German fooker!'

This time I'm covered in mineral water. I suppose that's an improvement.

'In many ways. I'd never have thought effective, resourceful, attentive and persistent would be my bag. But my knees are still quivering.'

'Wow. That was unexpected. What's the story?'

'I got him drunk that night and dragged him to his place. I thought he'd fit the 'ein zwei, ein zwei, vielen dank, und gute nacht' tag. So, in the morning, I left without a backward glance. I didn't bother to give him my number as I'm going back soon and expected not to see him again.'

'And?'

'Next day, I get lilies at my desk, and he's keen as mustard. I've seen loads of him. All of him, many times, in fact.'

'That's brilliant. Here, that's Mike, isn't it?'

She turns around and sure enough, coming through the door is Mike. There's a hint of the man from Del Monte about his attire, but he wears it with confidence. He swaggers over.

'Heh, ladies. Fancy seeing you girls here. What'll you have?'

'Prosecco for her. I'm driving,' says Rachel.

He strides to the bar and Rachel is shamefaced.

'What a surprise.'

'Rachel!'

'He was coming to town for a business lunch, so I said to pop in and see us for a drink. He's got the hots for you.'

Mike comes back with two glasses and a bottle. I get the feeling I'm not in control.

We have a brilliant hour. Suddenly, I'm a free spirit. The laughs and jokes come easy as does the fizz. Rachel excuses herself for the toilet. Mike looks at his watch and stands up.

'I need to shoot. I'll take you for a drink and a steak one night. There's a great Argentinian place not far from here. How's Saturday?'

'I don't know, Mike. I'm leaving London soon.'

'Come on. You're single now. Have fun. What time shall I collect you?'

Alcohol has robbed me of a reason.

'Seven-thirty?'

'It's a date.'

He kisses me on the hand, and leaves before I can change my mind.

I catch Rachel poking her head out of the toilet to see if the coast is clear. Sneaky cow. She attempts to look innocent as she sits.

'Got any plans for the weekend?'

'Nothing will happen. It's just dinner.'

'I suppose you won't be taking him back to your place. Talking of which, where is Dan going to go when you leave?'

'He's thinking of moving in with his mum.'

'Ah, I always knew he was a motherfooker.'

Chapter 47

Dan
Two days later

The children have only seen their grandmother on my side twice. She refuses to visit the big city, as she calls it, because it's so dangerous. Now this Abel thing has started, there's no chance she'll come. I'd take the kids more often, but she lives over two hours away, and isn't interested in them. She talked about moving back to where she grew up, over four hours away, which would have meant we'd never see her.

Grandma, as she insists on being called, likes to pretend she's a sweet old lady. In fact, Grandma makes me think of the sweet lady in Little Red Riding Hood. I wouldn't fancy the wolf's chances. He'd end up mopping the floor and doing odd jobs around the house while she waved a shotgun in his general vicinity.

One of her many flaws is failing to answer the phone, then berating me for not having rung. I've kept a log of missed calls for when she mentions it this time. Grace is at school today but Charlie doesn't have playschool, poor thing, so he's with me.

Looking after kids isn't as hard as you think. Well, as long as your expectations are low. Car journeys for example are minefields. However, if you get organised it can be easy. All you have to do is knacker the little darling out beforehand, give him a bag of crisps at the start of the journey, and then a trip to McDonald's as soon as he wakes. It must be my lucky day because he hasn't pooped his pants either. That's despite him insisting on having my Big Mac, leaving me four suspicious nuggets.

The bungalow looks as it always does from the outside — unlived in. Not that the garden is overgrown or untidy, it's unloved. More someone's buy-to-let than a home. A place where they've done the bare minimum to keep it acceptable for when the tenants move in.

'Who lives here, Daddy?'

'Grandma.'

'Grandma?'

'Yes, you know, like the one in Little Red Riding Hood.'

I can see him thinking about the wolf, too. He's a boy though and easily distracted.

'You have two Grandma's. Your other one is Nanny. You've been staying at her house.'

That works as now he looks disorientated. He was nearly two when he last met her. I note the doorbell doesn't work. I wouldn't be surprised if she'd unscrewed the battery herself. I peek through the front window and she's watching a *Carry On* film on a massive LCD TV. She rocks in her seat with laughter. She reaches across and takes an industrial swig of a dark, red liquid in a small glass. Sherry, I expect.

I go back to the entrance and give it a resounding knock. The door opens an inch and a cautious eye looks me over.

'Hello,' she says in a frail voice.

I can see it's going to be one of those visits.

'Open the door, Grandma. Charlie has come to see you.'

She widens the door and continues the charade.

'Sorry, Daniel. My eyesight's not what it used to be.'

She examines Charlie in the same way Robocop judges villains. Analysing the threat and assessing his danger levels. I imagine her saying, "Come quietly or there will be... trouble." I smile.

'Charlie. Kiss your Granny hello.'

'Grandma,' she corrects.

He looks like I've asked him to check a ferocious lion's mouth for cavities. He approaches her with appropriate caution. I notice too late that he has most of the baked beans he had for breakfast all over his top. The only way he could have got in that mess was to have rolled in them. Grandma's noticed. It's lucky she doesn't have a gun on her hip, or Charlie's head would be a smoking mess. They both settle for an air kiss a foot apart.

'Saying that, Granny has a nice ring to it. You can call me that from now on. Can you remember Granny? Like Granny Smith, the apple.'

'He's a three-year-old boy, not a greengrocer.'

I watch her wondering where to take the little dirt-ball to minimise the mess. She limps to the next doorway and directs him into the kitchen. She has aged and is favouring one side. The years catch up with everyone. I see the pictures of the family we send are on her wall. She can be supportive and interested as long as there's a safety zone of one hundred miles between us.

'What a nice surprise. Although I'm going out soon.'

'What do you mean, you're going out? I told you I was coming a week ago.'

'Did you? It's my memory. Everything's fading. It's unlucky because I'm so rarely out nowadays. Sometimes I get lonely. You should ring once in a while.'

'Here's the list of times and dates when I've rung. You don't answer.'

She scowls at the piece of paper. Unhappy that she's been exposed.

'Folk from the church take me shopping. Maybe I was doing that.'

'Is that where you're going now? I'll drive you to the shops, or church if you want.'

'It's okay. Arthur is picking me up.'

'Who's Arthur?'

'A companion.'

Ugh. Why does that sound so nasty? I think I'd have preferred her to say fuck buddy.

'Perfect. I've driven all this way, and can't even have a cup of tea.'

'Stop being silly, Daniel. We have time for that. How about you? Would you like a juice, Christopher?'

I don't bother to correct her. She reaches up to the cups. I assume the grimace on her face, which resembles a soldier being shot in the back, is to let me know her crippling arthritis still plagues her. Charlie and I watch her wipe dust off the top of the orange squash bottle. His expression says, 'Do not leave me here'.

'How are things then? You're getting out a little, at least.'

'Seldom, seldom.'

A phone beeps, indicating a message has been received. Her head shoots around at the sound like a hawk hearing a mouse squeak. She has the same cruel expression. The sneaky cow. I wasn't aware she had a mobile. She carries on and pours the tea, clearly thinking me a fool. It beeps again to let her know the game's up.

'Did I say I had a new phone? I must give you the number.'

She hands me a cup with a trembling hand and lifts slices of cake out of a plastic tub. It's the quietest I've ever seen Charlie. She considers herself a good cook. As his hand reaches towards them, I consider warning him. I don't. There will be an important life lesson occurring in this room shortly. He picks up a piece, and his fingers meet in the middle of it. I wisely pass.

'How's your girlfriend, Olive?'

I check to see if Charlie is listening, but he's distracted by the foul damp thing he foolishly stuck in his mouth.

'That's kind of why I'm here. We've split up.'

The bird of prey expression returns. 'Oh, really?'

'Yes, I need to get out of the house in a month, and they signed me off sick. I don't think I'll be going back to work.'

'Good, good. Things will pan out.'

'I need to leave that city. Have you seen the madness on the news?'

'You know I don't watch television. Where will you live? You wouldn't want to come here.'

'That's why I'm visiting. I was thinking just that. Could I?'

'You'd hate it here. I couldn't cope with children tearing around either. Not at my age.'

'The kids are going with Olivia. It'd be only me.'

'If you had nowhere else to go, you could stay for a few days. A week at most. If you're desperate.'

This time, her phone rings. She picks it out of her handbag and walks out of the room.

'Alice, darling. I'm glad you rang. Are you still on for tomorrow?'

There's a calendar on the wall covered in writing. I imagine the Queen has less engagements. 'Come on, Charlie. Let's go.' I finish my tea and guide a now green-looking boy to the hall.

She comes back having finished her call. 'Are you off?'

At that moment, Charlie nudges a tall thin table in the hall and a vase on it drunkenly wobbles. I've seen professional goalkeepers move slower than the speed she saves it.

She opens the door for me as an open-topped classic car screeches to a halt outside. A silver-haired lothario waves from the driving seat. I hope he doesn't get out and do stretches. I get a perfunctory kiss on the cheek from Granny and sit the boy in the booster seat of my car. We're half way up the road when I recall she still hasn't given me her phone number.

I think of pulling over but there's no point. I wouldn't be surprised if my own mother wrong-numbered me. Staying there is out of the equation. I curse under my breath as one of my few options disappears in the rear mirror. Charlie pipes up from the backseat of the car.

'Daddy. Did you say cluck?'

Chapter 48

Thomas, the neighbour of Judith the birdwatcher

Thomas walks down the street feeling sicker than he has ever felt in his life. Last night he'd gone to meet his boyfriend, Larry, at the cinema as arranged. He stood in their usual spot and waited. His dignity went home after an hour and yet still he stayed. Larry's phone was turned off, and Thomas received no messages in reply to his many.

When Thomas eventually got home, he chain-smoked, and finally fell asleep at four. What did it mean? There was no chance Larry would blank him. They were in love. Thomas had never fallen so deeply, not even close. He sometimes felt like he should inhale him, or climb inside his body. That way, they could become one.

The past few months were a blur. He had walked around in a daze, seeing shows he couldn't remember and places he instantly forgot. The world and time had ceased to exist. He'd been in heaven, and he was positive Larry had, too. So, where was he? There could be a nasty explanation, and that was the man they all feared. What had Abel done with him?

He knows he isn't thinking rationally. It's unlikely to be anything so dramatic as a serial killer, but his gut is telling him something bad has happened. He checks his phone again, wanting to shake it to get some answers out. The thought of going to the advertising office today is unappealing, yet he has no choice. He's missed many days with a reluctance to vacate Larry's bed.

He needs this job though and invests the money he saves. The dream is a flat of his own, even though he understands they won't let his mother live with him. Not now she has deteriorated so badly, but it would be a tranquil place for them to have. Sudden guilt makes him flinch as his conscience reminds him of his lack of recent visits. Thomas knows he's been neglecting everyone and everything. He'll go this afternoon. As soon as Larry is safe.

The traffic is heavy outside the railway station and he stops to text their only mutual friend. It was she who introduced them that memorable night. Thomas's face lights up as a snapshot of Larry and him slow-dancing to Bryan Ferry's *Slave to Love* burns in his memory. The pair of them whispering the exact words to each other. Both changing the 'her' to 'him' and 'woman' to 'man' in perfect harmony. Choking exhaust smoke straightens him up and he hurries inside.

He has five minutes to wait, so he strolls to the platform and takes a position at the far end hoping to get a seat. His mind now conjures up images of Larry bound and blindfolded in a chair, blood pouring from his ear. Abel smirking in the background. Thomas remembers watching Reservoir Dogs the previous weekend and grins at his stupidity.

He misses the *text received* sound as they announce his train but feels the phone vibrate. He pulls it from his pocket with awkward fingers. The message is terrible.

'Hi, Thomas. I didn't know you and Larry split?'

His bowels shrink in horror. A numb thumb stabs out a reply.

'When did you see him?'

He can hear the train's rapid approach. She responds in seconds.

'At the club yesterday. He was all over his ex and they left together early.'

My God, he's been a fool.

The push in his back is almost gentle. Perhaps he wouldn't have lost his balance if he'd not been so utterly distracted. Thomas has time to turn his head and see the look of surprise on the driver's face before the edge of the train hits him under the chin.

The massed ranks of commuters support the decapitated figure upright. Blood sprays in the air like a shaken-up can of Coke being released. Three more die in the stampede while the perpetrator slips away unnoticed.

Chapter 49

Olivia
Saturday

I've had a frustrating day. Someone let all of my tyres down overnight. My dad said he'd pump them back up before I rang the breakdown people as it was probably kids who did it. They seemed fine afterwards, so he was probably right, but it made me late for a big list of things. It wasn't the first time something odd had happened to my car either. I keep finding my wing mirrors and windscreen wipers in strange positions, too. I've spent the day in a foul mood, and I can't wait to have a few drinks.

My mother follows me around the house when she wants to impose her will. It's comical. I lock myself in the bathroom trying to escape the inevitable questioning. She is there when I come out. Skilled interrogators need to see their victims' faces. The taxi won't be here for another five minutes, so I might as well get it over with.

'Olivia, are you going anywhere nice?'

'No, Mother. Nothing special. Just a steak.'

'Ooh, lovely. Is it with anyone I know?'

'Rachel.'

My voice is reedy and less than convincing. My mum has a history of seeing through even my quality lies.

'You're going to a lot of effort for her, dear.'

'I don't need a lecture, thank you.'

'Please, Olivia. Stop for a minute and listen to what I have to say. Once I've said my piece, that will be finish of it, and I won't bring it up ever again.'

It's amazing she can keep a straight face when she says that.

'Okay, okay. I'm meeting a man. It's nothing but a meal. He knows I leave soon. I want to feel like a woman for an evening, as opposed to a mother. I need to talk about art, or music. Anything but potty training and how expensive school uniforms are. One night as me isn't too much to ask for.'

'I understand relationships aren't easy. Look who I'm married to. I really know what I'm talking about. This stage with young children is the hardest. You think it will go on forever, but things change. You get your life back. If you've quit already, you lose out on the best part.'

'Which bit is that?'

'The looking back on shared experiences. Knowing it was tough, and you stuck at it. He'll always be their father, you can't replace him.'

'I'm not trying to. It's him that's given up. Dan won't change.'

'The most important thing for the children is to be with their parents. In the same house. Even if you argue all the time. It's important for them to see you having a row and resolving it afterwards. You're the benchmark for their future relationships. Do you want them to think it's okay to quit at the first sign of trouble?'

'No. Although I'd hardly say eight years is the first sign of bother.'

'Pish. Eight years is a speed bump on life's journey. What have you told the children?'

'I said Daddy wasn't feeling well and needed time on his own to get better. They're fine with it.'

'Is that right? Then why did Grace ask me if you'd ever be a family again? Charlie piped up, and said, "Family. That's Mummy, Daddy, Gracie-May, baby Charlie and baby Bailey". They miss him.'

'Nothing's changed for years. I want to be happy.'

'Well, you shouldn't have had children.'

I think Mum's joking, even though she looks fervent. Incredibly, she believes what she's saying. She's not finished either.

'Men are strange beings. They take a long time to grow up. Your dad was only twenty-five when we got together. Imagine what bollocks I've had to endure over the years. He used to be a scrapper, you know. Age mellows everybody.'

She laughs but I can tell tears aren't far away. My phone beeps, telling me the taxi is outside.

'It's too late.'

'Don't be silly, sweetie. It's never too late. Until the male of the species realises what they have, and they might lose, they're only boys. Most of these boys grow into men. Be there when yours does.'

'I'll think about it, okay?'

'And remember, Olivia. I know you. You will have your head in the clouds by now and believe it's all his fault. Is there anything different that you could have done? Have you been perfect? Is some of the blame to be laid at your feet?'

She hugs me and closes the door.

Brilliant. What a depressing start to the night.

Chapter 50

Olivia

The restaurant is called 'El Hornero'. I wonder if that's Spanish for the horny one and is a portent of things to come. I Google it in the cab, and I'm disappointed to find it means 'The Baker'. The driver is talking but there's too much going on in my head for any of it to register. I smile and nod at him in the mirror, and hope he isn't asking me if I wanted to go back to his place to see his sex swing.

I have butterflies. It's been a long while. For me at least. I often have them when I watch the children in a show or at sports day. I like how it feels, then and now. Despite my mum's efforts, I will keep Dan out of my mind and have a good time. Tonight, I've got no kids, Dan included, to hog my energy. My parents sleep as though they've been tranquilised, so I don't need to worry what time I get back.

Mike is waiting outside the restaurant. He looks suitably keen. Almost eager. He scores points for that immediately. Whenever I meet Dan somewhere, he's either late and leaves me hanging around, or he goes in and gets stuck into the beers. I've always had a thing for shoes as well. I think they represent a man's attitude to personal grooming and cleanliness. Mike's are shiny and immaculate. Most encouraging.

He smells as good as he looks. Of course, he opens the door for me, and pulls my seat back when we reach our table. He rattles off rapid-fire Spanish at the waitress. She gives him a funny look and disappears.

'Very impressive, unless she has no idea what you said.'

'If she returns with next door's dog, I won't try again.'

She returns with the sommelier.

'Here you go, darlin'. I'm new and don't speak Spanish.'

She has the thickest Texan drawl I ever heard, and we burst into laughter.

Mike asks if he may order for me. He visits here at least once a week and wants me to taste the best dishes. There is something arousing when a man flits between languages. He checks I eat certain food and drinks in English and then converses with the staff member in Spanish. The wine arrives, and it's superb. I take a big glug and empty my mind of my responsibilities.

'How long have you lived here for then, Mike?'

'Three years now. I opened a dentist surgery. That's what I do. I have a few dotted around. I get them started, and then when they're established, search for another place to put one. It's time to move on to the next, but this city feels like home. I love it so much that I've stayed longer than expected.'

'What do you enjoy doing here?'

'There's loads to do. I'm never bored. I can wander around, seeing the sights, or get dressed up for the opera or theatre. I feel as though I'm at the centre of the world. To top everything off, I have a great neighbour, too.'

He holds my gaze for longer than usual. My stomach gurgles in anticipation. For the food, or maybe for something else. Unless, I have wind, of course.

'Same question to you. What are your passions?'

I think for a moment and remember the lady about town I used to be.

'I loved seeing concerts.'

'What stopped you going?'

'Well, the kids for one. They're too young to leave on their own and so everything needs to be planned months in advance around work and babysitting. After a while you get lazy and don't bother. Dan hates that sort of thing. He feels claustrophobic with the crowds.'

'There are always great shows here. We can use my friend's box for free. We should go. You needn't concern yourself with Dan's lack of enthusiasm anymore. I've seen him have the kids, so do it then. That's one of the benefits of splitting up. While your ex has the children, you finally get time to yourself.'

I dislike him dismissing Dan. In fact, I hate thinking about Dan in the past tense, but he's right. Dan wouldn't do anything like that. He'd never bring me to this kind of place. Or if he did, he'd moan about how expensive it was.

We share smoked ham and mozzarella for starters, followed by wondrous ceviche. When my steak arrives, I expect the table to whimper under the burden. It's cooked to perfection. It almost wilts when my knife approaches.

'I love it when the blood oozes out.'

'It's not really blood, per se, by the way. It's a red liquid made from water and myoglobin which is an iron and oxygen binding protein contained in muscle tissue.'

He's so clever and interesting. And cultured. And handsome. I'm so drunk. We've had a different wine with each course so far. They've matched the food so well, I might as well have been drinking pop. We chat effortlessly over our mains, and I smile as I realise I have no idea what the time is.

'Everything okay?'

'Perfect, thank you. I'm just nipping to the ladies'.'

'No problem. I'll order dessert if you still have room.'

'There's always space for ice cream.'

'You're in luck. They do great sorbet.'

The toilets are immaculate. It's a shame ours were never this clean. I sit on the seat and take deep breaths. Now is the time to decide, before I'm steaming, how far I should go with Mike. I'm not naïve. He's a man, and will go all the way. I shouldn't. What kind of yoyo-knickered slut-bag gives out on the first date? Mind you, he is extremely charming. I bet he'd be an attentive lover.

This is how I imagined life to be. Trying new restaurants and immersing myself in the culture. Instead, I'm submerged in the washing-up. Or worse, in Charlie's underwear. Tonight, I am brave and modern. I should be able to enjoy nights like these. What to do about later though? I decide I want kissing with passion again. It feels good to be desired.

My treacherous mind brings up the image of that young girl leaving our house. The look she gave Dan told of dirty times. With that vision forefront, my choice becomes simple.

Chapter 51

Dan

Now I don't see Olivia all the time, many things remind me of her. Earlier, I glanced up from a newspaper to share some madness, only to remember I was alone. The rooms in the house suggest I've just missed her when I step into them. Sleep eludes me because my senses are alert. Smells and sounds, real or imagined, open my eyes.

I miss seeing the kids every day. Which is weird because they often did my head in when they were a permanent feature. I am a different person now I don't work at that awful place. There is an undercurrent of anger that Olivia has given up on us, but I'm becoming normal again. Well, as normal as I ever was. Still, it will be nice to see hot Charlotte again.

I arrive at Ian's flat and ring the buzzer. He only lives around the corner from the bar where we're meeting. He has the top floor penthouse which his boss owns and lets him have for nothing. How rich can they be to make gestures like that? Would I be happier here if I could look down on everything and everyone? It's a chilly night, and the git takes his time to answer. A squall of rain blasts me through the door when I hear it click.

I never see anyone else here, yet there are fifty flats. How strange. Ian says investors buy them and don't rent them out, keeping them immaculate when sold again. They're so rich, they ignore rental income to save themselves the hassle. It's as though he lives in a few rooms in an empty castle.

'Come in, mate. Ready for a big one?'

'Not particularly. Why the hell are we meeting at ten? That's the time I suggest a whisky for the road.'

'The nightclubs don't shut at two like they did in our day. These kids will still be going at six. As will we!'

'Nightclubs, yuk. Six o'clock in the morning. No chance.'

My interest wanes somewhat. Ian smiles. He thinks I'm joking. I can do without the drugs, too. The payback would be awful in my vulnerable state.

'Is it the four of us again?'

'There's two others going. Blokes unfortunately. They'll no doubt be trying to cut our lunch.'

That's one of Ian's favourite sayings. He used to find it amusing when we travelled that blokes attempted to move in on other men's women. If you were chatting up a girl and left to get her a drink, by the time you returned another fella would be giving her full patter. It might well have been Ian.

'Did you bring that Kathy back to this place?'

'Yeah. She's dead keen. I hear you had a little visitor.'

I try not to think of Olivia's face as Charlotte left. Charlotte's bra burns a hole in my pocket. I wondered whether I should wrap it up or something. I've been out of the game too long to remember the etiquette for such things.

'It's all right for you. I'll have to rent a room in a shared house after I move out. At my age. You know what that entails.'

'Yeah, that'll be revolting. Eight other bedrooms and only one bathroom. Someone sneaking a slice of your ham and a drop of your milk. Then many others doing it until you have none left. Everyone denies it and looks at you as though you ate them yourself and forgot. Margarine becomes a valued commodity. People steal it with gay abandon. You walk past bastards with so much on their toast it drips on the carpet.'

'Cleaning it will come out of my deposit. The atmosphere is dark. People form cliques. Except me, I'm too old and become ostracised. The weirdo in the basement plays Nick Cave songs dead loud and at strange hours. Oh no, wait, I'll be that weirdo.'

'Someone's been in your room, even though you're sure you locked it. Nasty. I don't envy you that at all!'

'Funny, isn't it? I wanted to live like a youngster, and I shall. I will have come full circle. Indeed, it was me who used to steal the others' food.'

'Life bites you in the arse once more.'

'It's not fair. House prices have rocketed in the last few years. If they hadn't, I wouldn't be living at Olivia's, we'd have bought a home together. That way, my name would be on the deeds, and now we're splitting I'd get half the equity. I wouldn't be rich, but I'd be a damn sight more comfortable than my current situation.'

'Life's not reasonable. You know that. Let it go. Think of it as security for your children.'

I wanted him to agree with me, not blow my argument out of the water. It's better if I change the subject.

'I've never heard of this bar? Is it new?'

'No, not especially. It's next to El Hornero. You remember, that Argentinian place you considered going to until you found out the price of the steaks.'

'Yes, I remember. We joked it was called the horny one. They were outrageously expensive. I could get a week's shopping for the same amount as their porterhouse.'

'You always miss the point with that kind of thing. It's not just the food, it's the experience. Soft lighting and excellent service are included in the bill. I wouldn't pay that much for a steak if they threw it at me in a polystyrene box.'

'I understand that, but travelling has ruined me. We used to pay ten baht for Pad Thai in Thailand, fifteen if you wanted egg in it. Here you pay twenty times that price and it isn't as good. Talking of money, I haven't got much. You still thinking of going with these young'uns to Brazil?'

'Yeah, definitely. I said something would turn up, and it did. We'll have fun, and it's cheap there. You won't believe the size of the bonus I get in a few weeks. I'll pay your way if necessary. It'll be my pleasure. I want to live life again.'

His enthusiasm is catching. Although, I'm not sure going on a booze cruise around South America counts as living life.

'I have a bit of cash in a bond that matures next month, and those shares you made me buy have done brilliantly. I was keeping them for something that escapes me. Now I have kids it doesn't seem right to be spending my savings on happy pizzas and skydives. Saying that, I've already cashed in some of them.'

I should have taken Olivia for that steak. When was the last posh meal we had? One we could remember and look back on. I suspect we wouldn't have had sex afterwards as we'd both have been too full, but that's a benefit of being in a secure relationship. You don't need to as there will always be another time.

I was saving the money for the future. I know that much. Was that to make our lives more comfortable? To enable us to pay for experiences together. There's great pleasure watching kids' horizons broaden. I want to be there when they see their first real pig. Or deep down did I think we'd split up and I'd need a buffer?

'I'm ageing by the day here, Dan. Let's drop this country and get sun tans. Think of the carnival and the beaches.'

'Don't you consider yourself an impostor? Do you remember being underage and sneaking in pubs and fretting over getting served? That's how I feel now, except this time I'm too old. That someone will come over and shout, "Good try, mate. But you need to leave".'

'No. I don't think like that. They're lucky to have me. To have us. We're older but we've got spending power. In the end, it's all about money.'

'Easy for you to say, seeing as you have a load. I can't drink the way I used to, and nor can you. Admit it. You take days to recover from a big one, and I'm sleepy by nine-thirty.'

'We don't have to get up the next day. There's no nine-to-five. What's really bothering you?'

The answer is immediate.

'I'd miss the kids.'

Ian locks the door and gives me a hard look.

'They aren't going to be here though, are they? There's nothing in this place for you now. In this country even. You said to start with she was leaving for a year. That's a long time. You might as well face facts. If you wanted family life, you'd have tried harder.'

Chapter 52

Dan

Ian's words stay with me on the walk to the restaurant. I stifle a yawn, and he follows suit. We cross the road and sure enough, there is the bar next to El Hornero. The Blue Brick Bar looks like a goldfish bowl full of Christmas lights. There's a queue outside which we join. I roll my eyes at Ian, who shrugs. We aren't the oldest in the line, and, even though it's one in, one out, it is moving at a good pace. That makes me feel better.

We line up along the windowed frontage of El Hornero. I point out the astronomical prices and raise my eyebrows in mock shocked surprise. Most of the menu is in Spanish. I learnt a fair bit of that language on our travels. I could have impressed Olivia with my linguistic skills. Although it would be rusty as I was never fantastic.

I often got words mixed up. I remember ordering two chamomile teas in one place (Manzenilla) after a mad all-nighter. We'd found it the most soothing thing for hangovers. The waiter gave me an unusual frown but thought it best not to question the wild-eyed gringo.

He came back less than a minute later with a grin and two pats of butter (Mantequilla). Ian said at the time the only way we could save face was to rub it on our faces. Good times. Man, I used to laugh so much. Why are there only things to moan about nowadays? I need to change my method of thinking. Be more optimistic. Expect little and celebrate the smallest wins. I should take onboard Olivia's advice and look to people's strengths as opposed to highlighting their weaknesses.

I peer between the menus on the window and can make out that weasel neighbour of ours, Mike.

He is grinning and laughing as though he's on drugs. His expensive dentistry glows in the subdued lighting that Ian mentioned earlier. I can't see his date but I hope she's ugly, or better still a blatant escort. I suppose it would be too much to wish for it to be no one, and his mind has gone.

Ian is peering through, too. I grin as we resemble a pair of peeping children.

'Here, isn't that your neighbour? The git with the flash car?'

'Yes. Mike, el rich bastardo. I can't see who he's with, can you?'

At that moment, the queue moves. We shuffle forwards like old men collecting their pensions. And there, highlighted under a spotlight, is Olivia.

She has her hair up and wears the purple dress I bought her before she got pregnant with Charlie. It was for her Christmas party. She looked stunning with it on, but by the time the party arrived it no longer fitted. She always joked she'd never be thin enough again to wear it.

It's one of the great truths about break-ups. The emotional trauma women go through causes them to stop eating and they lose weight. While the men can't cook and therefore eat takeaways. They search for oblivion in belly-enhancing beer. Hence, they look awful and their exes look fantastic.

Something looks amazing on Olivia, and judging by the direction his gaze keeps dropping to, I have a good idea.

She often moaned I didn't pay her attention, yet I always told her I loved it when she wore her hair up. Especially if she wore glasses. I must have a secretary fantasy. I saw her in both on rare occasions. I told her I liked her in high heels, and she only ever wore them when she partied with the girls. She has a dangerous looking pair on tonight.

I expressed a desire to have sex when she had full make-up on, like before she left for the office. She snapped she was too busy. Get up fifteen minutes earlier then, I said. Or five minutes if you put your glasses on. I'm not in the mood at that time of the day, she said. Would once have killed her? How about when you return? No, too tired.

Modern life is a barrier, children a cage. Work can take everything and leave nothing for home. She'd come back exhausted, scrub off her lipstick and foundation, and try to cuddle when I slept.

All the time and effort invested in our relationship will be wasted with our impulsive decisions. We discard our pasts because making something new is easier. Maybe we shouldn't ask why people split up, instead only exclaim surprise when they stay together. She and Mike have recreated the special bond we had with no bother. Their dinner has no baggage or regrets.

I'm glad I had little to eat myself as it would be everywhere. Instead, my mouth fills with bile. When did she last laugh in that manner with me? He offers her a morsel of food on a fork. She nibbles it off but it drops on the table. He leans forward, and whispers. She throws her head back and I recognise the signs. I loved her most when she was drunk. I saw the girl she left behind. That scene was us before responsibility held the reins.

I watch him top-up her wine when she's talking to the waitress. Ian elbows me and beams.

'Look at that weasel. Very low. Filling her drink up when she's not looking.'

Everyone knows wine oils the wheels of romance. The line moves again and we move out of sight. Ian places his arm around my shoulders.

'You can't complain too much. Think what you're queuing up to do.'

He's right. Yet, why do I yearn to lie on the pavement? I want to turn back the clock. There's a ruckus up front and they eject six men from the club. One goes to throw the bottle he's still holding, but sees the size of the bouncer and thinks twice. We smile as that's enough bodies leaving for us to enter the premises.

It's three deep at the bar which is discouraging. Ian can't see the others so we stand together and after ten minutes of being jostled and bumped, we get our drinks and move to the side. We scan the horizon like meerkats for hyenas. I see them first. The four of them appear how you'd expect two attractive young couples to look.

I glance at Ian who doesn't look his best. He's moist and harassed. The man who's chatting to Charlotte is focusing on trying to cut my lunch. And my dinner. She grins and giggles at his vigorous face. I sense defeat. I note Kathy's bloke is more forward. He could have stepped out of a rowing boat and has a meaty arm draped over her shoulder. Ian will be pleased.

I watch them in their innocence and know we're interfering. Ian spots them, and his eyes narrow. He sees the danger.

'They're over there. No way, those toads are all over our chicks. Game on.'

He's a snake in long grass as he cuts through the crowd and beats me there by a good half minute. Ian knows the rules. I watch a master in action. He introduces everyone, manoeuvring people into space to shake hands. When the dance is over, he has Kathy in the corner with him blocking her in. Charlotte finds herself jammed against the wall by me, and the two goons stand together with jumbled expressions.

Ian delivers the coup de grâce by handing his victim a credit card.

'There's a tab behind the bar. Get the drinks in and you can have what you want. Shots, you name it. The night is on me.'

Rowing must not pay well as he's pleased with the trade. I suspect, looking like he does, free drinks are rarer than keen women. My foe is not so easily vanquished. A song I've never heard before starts to play. He takes her hand and cheers.

'Come on, let's boogie.'

She doesn't even pretend she's not interested. I watch in horror as they sashay to the edge of the revellers who have succumbed to the beat. No hiding behind others for this guy. Brilliant. My enemy dances. It's the ultimate trump card. The sound of a guillotine sliding into a thud echoes in my mind.

Ian gives me a shrug and shouts over the din.

'You'll have to ask if you can have the next dance. Hopefully it will be something from Dirty Dancing and not YMCA. Failing that, use my gloves and slap him around the face a couple of times and demand satisfaction.'

'I'm going for a piss.'

I take as wide a route from them as I can, suspecting Ian is laughing. No one wants to see that. I walk through the crowded bar and don't see a single person who looks as lovely as Olivia did tonight. I doubt I would, even if I stayed in here for a whole year.

As always, the toilets are the first place to show the effects of a busy establishment. They're on the edge of disaster. The floor will be tiptoe only within the hour. The urinal overflows as I pee into it. I have to stand back and can see how the problem started. Another bloke is urinating into a cubicle from a metre away.

The soap has run out, but I rinse my hands. The towels are long gone. The face in the smudged mirror that returns my stare is worn-out. What am I doing here? I must have been dreaming. I'm not up to the challenge of Ricky Martin out there.

My heart isn't robust enough for this lifestyle. It's hard to recall after so many years how merciless the dating game is. People are ruthless with your heart, and you with theirs. You forget how difficult it is to discover someone similar. How rare to meet a person who can tolerate you and your idiosyncrasies. To find a person who loves you more than your weird behaviour irritates them.

I used to think Olivia and I were the same kind of crazy. Maybe she altered, and I didn't notice, and she hoped I'd change, and I never did.

Both Ian and Olivia were accurate concerning travelling, and they were both wrong. Ian is right, I'm not too old for long term travel. Sure, I can't do three nights in a row or live off local beer and noodles anymore, but that's about knowing your limitations. On the other hand, Olivia is correct too, because a traveller is not who I am now. I'm past it because of my commitments. If I go to Brazil, every experience I have will be blackened by the knowledge I didn't do the right thing by my children. Or at the least, attempt to.

Why haven't I tried harder? What am I doing here? She will leave without me, and I'll be on my own. My children countries away, and even Ian is leaving. The old adage is true; you appreciate nothing until it's missing. I must talk to her, and I need to sort myself out.

I exit the toilets and stare at the sea of animated faces. I don't belong here. Not anymore. Ian catches my eye as he scans the room. We've been together in a thousand bars in a hundred cities. Our eyes meet and that's enough. He will know I'm leaving. I surge toward the exit. It's as though I've fallen into dark water and only now, just before I drown, can I see the light and how to escape.

The clear air makes me gasp in relief as I step out the doors. The bouncer looks at me and shakes his head.

'Too much for you in there, is it?'

He turns his back and laughs to his mate. He's loud and cocky, and pleased with his local accent. A knee to the balls would wipe off his smile. A girl in the company uniform walks by and he slaps her arse.

She shrinks away from him. I slip Charlotte's bra in his coat pocket as I leave and hope it costs him dear. The rain is torrential as I walk into the open, but I'm unaware.

Should I approach Olivia now while he's there? I can't imagine accosting them when they're both loaded would end well. One's thing for sure, I'll never be eating at El Hornero. A terrible thought rips through my mind. What if they fell in love? Perhaps she wouldn't leave the city. Mike moves into my house and becomes a father to my children. I'd have to knock on their door and wait for him to open it.

A surge of panic makes me turn towards the restaurant. I must talk to her now, even if I don't yet know what to say. It needs to be immediately while my mind is focused. The restaurant's neon sign flashes outside and I see an employee leave. He doesn't lock the door so I stride over to the entrance. A suited man pulls a bolt across his side of the glass as I approach. I rap my knuckles hard enough to bruise. He mouths 'We're closed,' and disappears into the gloom.

I strain my eyes to penetrate the streaked windows. I can't make out if anyone is still there. A flash of lightning reveals the place is shadowy and empty. I'm too late.

Chapter 53

Olivia

Mike and I stumble through the expensive hotel entrance. The doorman tips his hat to Mike. They know each other. I wonder if that's because he brings all his dates here. Am I the most recent of many? The carpet is thicker than our duvet at home. That and the wood panelling make the atmosphere subdued and I feel cloth-eared. My heel snags but Mike catches me before I fall and links his arm with mine.

We wander through a confusing array of corridors and find ourselves at a secluded bar. There's a handsome guy behind it, and one other patron — an elderly gentleman snoozing in a high-backed armchair. Mike slurs a bit as we sit although I'm not convinced. I've noticed him top my drink up more often than his. Let him think he's in control. The decision has been made, and it doesn't matter.

'What'll you have?'

'Not what that guy had.'

On cue, the old man starts to snore like an elephant seal.

'Wine?'

'Oh, no. No more of that. Let's have an Irish coffee. Perk us up a little.'

The last sentence gives Mike the green light he's been waiting for. I see him relax. I expect him to go to the bar. Instead, he nods at the barman who comes straight over with a smile.

'Two coffees, with Jameson's, please.'

He seals the deal next time we laugh by putting his hand on my leg. I don't remove it. The coffees arrive with a hushed voice.

'Thank you, Mr Armitage.'

I find them knowing his name unsettling. In fact, it's like I'm underground somehow. The old man has gone. I have a vision of Mike pressing a button and a section of the wall opening and the man and his chair revolving into the space before it closes.

Mike picks up on my discomfort.

'I'm associates with the owner. I play golf with him and a few other similar-minded professionals. One of those is the man who owns the stadium I mentioned earlier where our tickets will be free. We look out for each other and assist as best we can. I'm brilliant at what I do, and they know. I help them, and in return, they me. I stay here for free whenever I fancy. It's a privileged club.'

I find extreme wealth an aphrodisiac. Yet, these powerful men have always hurt me. I gave them everything and was left with pieces. Dan only had his confidence. Where he lived his life, it was all he needed. I brought him to a place where money rules, and without it you're no one. I didn't ask him, and I didn't explain. He came knowing nothing. I'd forgotten that.

The Irish coffee slides down, and it's a good one. A mellow pick-me-up was what I needed. Now, I'm in control.

'Shall we check that room out?'

He can't help but grin. He is the unappreciated author who finally sealed a book contract. Taking my hand, he helps me out of my seat. He's certainly been here before as there's no mention of any bill. We glide along the corridors and then take a lift seemingly to heaven. I might have known it would be the penthouse. The view is incredible.

'Not bad.'

'This room is often free as few can afford it.'

'It was presumptuous of you to get the key beforehand.'

'I wasn't presuming, only hopeful.'

I wander over to the tall windows and watch sheet lightning flash above the skyscrapers. The city looks moody and threatening, but exciting and powerful. I sense him next to me and he passes me water in a heavy glass. It's like he knows my mind. I look over his shoulder and hope I can't see a grand piano. If he sat and played on one of those, the cheese factor would be off the scale.

'I've liked you for a long time, Olivia. You deserve happiness.'

He chinks my drink with his and then, while holding my hand, escorts me to a pair of mirrored doors. He pushes them open to reveal a huge bed with shiny black sheets. They wouldn't last five minutes in my house. Thoughts of my family crowd in on my happy state. I still have a house, but I don't have a home.

My glass feels heavy, and I clunk it onto the bedside cabinet. I drop my handbag beside it, noting the whisky is winning the fight. There's a pair of surgical gloves atop a dresser on the other side of the bed which is weird. I suppose he is a dentist. He follows my gaze.

'I find these things everywhere. I must go through twenty pairs a day.'

He joins me, and kisses my lips. Gently at first. The room spins and I have to re-open my eyes. It's strange to be touched by someone who worships you. His hand traces my face, my neck, and guides the zip of my dress down my back. It feels wonderful. I can finally relax my stomach before it escapes through the stitching.

His breathing quickens as he releases my breasts and fondles them in a manner they're unused to. At this point, Dan would have squeezed them and shouted 'yeah baby'. I reach down with enthusiasm, but Mike stops my hand, and pushes me onto the bed.

'You first.'

I sprawl in what I hope is a sexy way and watch him undress. He doesn't spend every moment of his time at work. His shaven chest is far removed from Dan's hairy belly.

Moving to my side, he eases my pants off in a swift practised manoeuvre. He kisses shoulder to hip and then further below. He teases me. My tiredness departs as my hips raise towards him. A few moments later, my concerns have vanished. He turns me onto my front and pulls me into the doggy style position. I can't help a smile. Men, eh? So predictable.

Only, I'm wrong. He continues with his lips, tongue, and breath. I'm ecstatic, vulnerable and dirty. A lady, a lover, and a whore.

So much for being in control. Dentistry is not the only thing he's brilliant at.

Chapter 54

Dan

I catch the night bus home as the last train has gone. It's a mistake. The only people who get on these are the young and fun, and the sad and lonely. You can imagine where I fit in. I avoid the energy and sit amongst the other jaded folk in their forties.

The buses are too slow during the day because of the traffic, but at this time of the night I arrive at my stop in fifteen minutes. It's a long quarter of an hour though, full of wondering, imagining and blaming.

The lights are out at Mike's house. Does that mean they're already in bed? At separate houses or together? I can't imagine they would come back here. Olivia isn't that punishing. Maybe I'm fooling myself and Olivia's lack of enthusiasm for our relationship is due to long suppressed feelings for Mike. That's why she was so tired. Perhaps when he came over to borrow stuff, he was coming for a different type of sugar.

I let myself in the front door and the dog's waiting for me. Bailey's such a good boy. He's even done a shit on the kitchen tiles instead of the hall carpet so it's easier for me to clean. How considerate. I forgot to take him out, so I'm at fault. I open the fridge and remember the four pack I bought in case Charlotte wanted to come back here and needed more booze. Buying them, and the thought processes surrounding that, is from a different life, in a faraway galaxy.

In the lounge, I find Olivia is right, and it is nice to return to a clean house when you've been out. However, I hope she never discovers my reasons for tidying. I slump in the chair, not bothering to turn the light on, and open the can with a tsk. I should go to bed, but I often do this. Why not retire as opposed to guaranteeing a painful head in the morning? I hear Bailey bark. I wonder what he wants as it can't be a poo.

There's somebody at the door. A brief surge of optimism is quelled as the opaque glass doesn't hide the fact the person has grey hair. I can only think of Olivia's mother, and I'm correct.

'How was the nightclub, Vivienne?'

'Shut up, you cheeky boy. Let me in out of this rain.'

'Tea, something stronger?'

'It's not a social call. We were passing, and I saw your lights on. We attended the theatre for a fabulous show. Do you go?'

'Not for a few weeks now.'

'Right. I thought I'd pop in to see if you'd misheard me last time we spoke?'

There is a vague recollection of speaking to her recently. I don't remember the conversation as such. Something about Harold not liking me. That wasn't a surprise as he called me a penis once at the dinner table.

'I said to not fuck it up. Does that ring any bells?'

She oughtn't to use the f-bomb as from her mouth it sounds strange and unsettling. Ah, I see her purpose, and I also recall those words now.

'That sounds familiar.'

'Well, you appear to be doing exactly that.'

'You're right. I have, haven't I?'

A tear trickles from my eye and my shoulders heave. I don't think I've ever so much as touched her before tonight, yet she still envelops me in her arms. It's difficult, but I manage to stop howling and she guides me towards the kitchen.

'Come on. Let's get you a cup of tea.'

The light pings on and she comes to a halt. I try to peer beyond to see what's stopped her and then remember Bailey's present on the floor. Before I can warn her, she nudges it with an expensive shoe. The crust comes away, releasing brown liquid, a piece of carrot, and a terrible aroma. She looks at me in horror.

'Oh dear. I thought it was fake.'

'Freshly laid, I'm afraid.'

'I'd take him to the vet if I were you.'

When she's made the tea, I decide on action. I tip the rest of my can of lager into the sink and fetch the others from the fridge. She pours one away with me.

'My husband used to drink. He stopped, give-or-take, and we've had a great life. Relationships are a journey. A rollercoaster really. There are big dips but the highs come soon enough. Only the crazy ones jump off and leave their kids behind.'

'I think I'm too late. I've lost her.'

'Rubbish. You know nothing about women. Especially one who has your children. It's gestures she wants. Effort and commitment. Show her you're trying and you want to make things work. Even if she leaves, she'll remember. She can't replace you like-for-like. Deep down she knows that.'

'What do I do? Flowers? Sing to her from the driveway?'

She fires me an intolerant look.

'Harold would shoot you if you started singing near the house. Where's the rest of the drink? We'll get rid of everything.'

'That's it. I drank the rest. Alcohol is only a temporary guest here.'

'Pull your finger out, young man. I should go, or he'll think I've forgotten him.'

At the door, she stops for one last question.

'Do you know where you'll go? I asked my husband if you could stay at ours in the short term. He said over his dead body. Or better still, he'd let you move in and kill you while you slept. He's such a joker.'

'That's a shame as my possibilities are limited. Thanks for stopping. I will give it my best efforts and we'll see what happens. Any inside tips on what makes your daughter work?'

'Stop drinking so much. Although in your case, it might be wise to not drink anything at all. Invest your time. That's it. It's the most valuable thing we own. Then talk to her about your hopes. She says she doesn't know what you're thinking. Let her be aware of your feelings.'

'You make it sound so easy.'

'It is. You'll have to marry her, too. No half measures. Not many blokes want to get hitched, so don't think you're unique. Pretend if you can't show enthusiasm. Happy wife, happy life.'

Bailey looks up and whines when she leaves. His sadness reflects mine. How do I begin to correct things? I need to convince Olivia she also has to try. It's not totally my fault, although I accept I am mostly to blame.

I take a quick picture of Bailey and trudge up the stairs. It seems I will use any technique or method, however low, to further my cause. I'm tired now and know I'll have more enthusiasm and ideas in the morning. Nevertheless, I attach the photo to a WhatsApp message with the words, 'I want the family back. And I want you back.' I press send and my phone beeps to confirm it's gone.

Bailey takes that as go-go-go for upstairs, and he shoots past me and leaps on the bed. I climb in clothed and he snuggles up behind me. Is Olivia doing the same?

Chapter 55

Olivia

My mouth is open to utter the words, 'Please, just do me,' when my phone informs me that I have a WhatsApp message. Whenever I receive a text at night and I'm not with my children, I always think it concerns them. Even though it feels like I'm unwinding myself off a corkscrew, I still have to see what it says. Mike's tongue must be a metre long with the tensile strength of a cable from a suspension bridge.

'Hang on a minute.'

I grab my phone and enter my PIN.

'I want the family back. And I want you back.'

Great timing from Dan as always. Then the words sink into my addled state.

'What's wrong?' asks Mike.

All of a sudden, everything is. My brain is way past subterfuge. Dan's text and my mother's advice fight for dominance over my lust.

'Sorry, I need to read this.'

I stagger out of the room and sit on the toilet, reading it again as though I'd imagined it. I'm not sure what it means, or even if what he's saying matters. Searching my feelings, I know that's not true or I wouldn't have experienced the jolt. Splashing water on my face doesn't help. Explaining to Mike that I'm going isn't a nice proposition. But, I need to get my head together. I must speak to Dan.

Taking a quick look at my smudged lipstick and with a deep breath, I walk out the room and dress.

'What is it?'

'Something's come up.'

It's a poor choice of words as his impressive boner wilts with disappointment.

'Is it the kids?'

'Kind of.'

He collects my clothing for me and passes me my handbag, apparently oblivious to his naked state. I find it hard to look at him when I reach the door. I glance at the magnificent panorama. I don't want this. Whether I stay with Dan is a different question. I shake my head as I realise I'm not ready to move on. That's the wrong thing to do as it confirms Mike's fears.

'It's him, isn't it? Dan.'

He spits his name out. His raw anger is shocking.

'It's family.'

'When will you wake up? He's a loser. I can make you happy. Give me a chance, Olivia. I've waited for years.'

He lets out a wail. Maybe Dan was right, and he is insane.

'Goodbye, Mike.'

The twisted grimace is pure rage. I don't think I've ever seen an angrier, redder face, and both my babies had constipation.

I pull the door shut and hear the smash of a glass on the wall. There's another anguished cry and this time it's the door that's hit. I've been here before. I could be twenty, or twenty-six, or thirty-five again. Why am I attracted to mad people? Dangerous, violent men have been a feature in my life.

The reception staff ignore me. They're well trained. The doorman is still outside and holds the door for me. He waves for a taxi to come over. I dive in and bellow my parents' address at the driver.

'See you again, Ma'am,' says the doorman as he shuts me in.

'I bloody hope not.'

Chapter 56

Abel

My mission to ruin this city draws to an end. Everyone knows my name. Newspapers are the records of the damned as they list the crimes I've inspired. Decision time approaches, but that is out of my hands. Fates hang heavy upon her decision, because no one rejects me. Forget the good book, I'm out of control. I wasn't religious anyway. I relaxed in the peaceful surroundings of the churches we attended, and only zoned in for the vengeance and wrath.

The lessons are over now, and the city has been cleansed. Now it's personal. I've felt little through these months, despite the excitement for others. The only satisfaction I experienced was for a job well done. That gold tooth was real, almost like I'd treated myself. When I hold it, I relive the moment. I deserve another bonus, so tonight is a treat. I bought a boiler suit, just for the occasion.

The mechanic's garage is at the bottom of a dead end, so traffic is light. They close at six, so it's unlikely anyone would arrive at that time. There's an easy escape path between two houses nearby, so if I'm quick, no one will even know I was here. Not until their families wonder why they haven't come home.

The last customer pays her bill in the office. I watch from the shadows. Thieving Terry, the manager, grins when she turns to leave. He conveniently lowers the blinds. She departs with a grim look on her face. I wore that same expression when the cost exceeded my expectations. The mechanic waves her off with a smile. The lady gives him the finger. Another satisfied client. Their final one.

The mechanic is a man of routine. He sits on the tyre, facing the office, and rolls his smoke. I dread to think of the oil and filth on the papers. Isn't it unhealthy enough already? Our houses are full of weapons, and today's is a screwdriver. Sharpened, of course. These victims are special. I want them to know it was me before they draw their final breaths.

I approach through the ramps from behind him in silence. My boots have anti-slip soles on them. The advert said prison officers wear them. The mechanic is a big, fat man. Hair sprouts from his greasy T-shirt. I raise my hand and drive the sharp edge straight into his spine. His back arches. The second screwdriver I deliver underhand and it spears the area where his right lung should be.

I'm surprised. I expected more drama *and* more blood. He rolls off the side of the tyre and lies staring at the ceiling with a stunned expression. Crouching next to him, I pinch his ear and lift his face to mine.

'Remember me?'

He nods, and I shove another screwdriver into his solar plexus and towards his heart. I haven't got time to dawdle, so cover him with a sheet from my backpack. The strides to the office take seconds. They've ripped me off in here loads of times, so the manager, Thieving Terry, smiles and offers me his hand. I shake it with my gloved one. His grip is strong considering his sprightly pensioner persona.

We sit opposite sides of his cheap desk and I book in my car for a full service. While he taps away at his computer as though it might bite him, I squirt baby lotion over the floor underneath and around his seat. The last squeeze covers his leather brogues.

He glances below with a puzzled expression and when he looks up, I lean over the table and plunge the final screwdriver in and out of his stomach. I sit again. His eyes are wide, the question obvious.

'You are a dishonest man, Terry. Because of that, today, you die.'

He curls up in pain and then lifts and throws the desk at me with a howl. I wasn't expecting that, but I'm ready. His frantic gaze looks for an escape that doesn't exist. He opens his mouth to shout, but instead bends over in agony. The word "Son" comes out as a gasp. The mechanic, I guess.

'He won't be much help. He has a few holes in his radiator.'

Terry's preservation skills, to my surprise, are admirable. He tries to run past but slips to the floor. A stab in the shoulder is his reward. He shouts out in pain and rolls onto his back and away, splashing around like a dying fish.

'Are you sorry, Terry?'

'No.'

'I release you from the burden of life.'

His gaze follows the approaching bloody screwdriver. His chin raises, and he spits straight into my eyes.

The next moment I'm aware of is when my hand slips from the weapon, leaving it embedded in the top of his head. Have seconds past, or minutes? Judging by the pulpy body at my feet, it's the latter.

I've had my revenge, but searching my thoughts, I feel no different. The zip sticks as it slides down my splattered boiler suit, but frees with force. After taking out my hoodie and putting it on, I fold the incriminating garments into my backpack. Spotting a panel full of switches, I sink the garage into darkness. With a quiet whistle, I leave without a backward thought.

Chapter 57

Dan
Two days later

It's two days since I sent that text asking for her back. Olivia and I have had a few chats on the phone. She's coming to the house this morning with the kids to have a further talk and take a walk. She says it's up to me to decide where we go and what we do. In the past, I've directed us towards somewhere with a play area for them and a bar for me. Even if it was only eleven a.m. Do they have big plastic slides, giant Jenga, and a climbing frame in the last chance saloon?

I leap from the bed sheets when a car stops nearby and look out the bedroom window to see if she's arrived early. I don't need to pull the curtains as I didn't close them. It's like those weird functionless cushions she leaves on the bed after making it. They're both pointless and time consuming.

The street is empty and looks peaceful. Summer is coming, and the sky is bright. Pete the postman has his shorts on and hops from door-to-door. He appears to have grown a ponytail overnight unless he had it hidden. Ian always said never trust a man with a ponytail. I think it was to do with people like that having no shame. It could be a clip-on one, or a pet ferret. I hope not. Either would make him weirder than I thought.

There is something of the sixties about Pete. The decade rather than his age. He's light and jolly, the same as how you see the Beatles singing on old newsreels. Maybe that's what makes him good at martial arts. I feel like Scrooge throwing back his window on Christmas day.

Instead of singing for a large turkey, I could drop a stinky sock onto him. He looks straight up at me.

'Morning, Dan. Great weather.'

Hmm. He doesn't miss much. He's right though. When Olivia arrives with the kids, I will recommend we take a walk in the park. They have a new sand and water feature. Best to enjoy it quick before the cats ruin one and the rats get to the other. There's also no alcohol allowed, so that removes any temptations to break my two-day hiatus.

Worryingly, it's been a struggle to stay clean. It doesn't help not having a job. There's plenty at stake here though. If I'm unable to quit for this, then I have a real problem.

I've had a lot of time to think about what to say. I practised in the mirror like I was rehearsing a speech. Now I'm stone-cold sober, I understand I gave up on us. I don't remember when, so can only assume it was a long while ago.

That said, I'm not the only one with blame. I hope Olivia will accept her share. She needs to make changes as well. I can't sell myself short, or we'll go to California with a suitcase full of trouble. We could take it as hand luggage and get it out on the plane.

The city appears to be recovering from its malaise. Is it returning to normal, or might it be a lull before the real storm? There are people pruning their hedges and mowing their lawns. Has the promise of summer pulled them from their fortresses? Of Abel, we hear little. The media have new targets. Foreign wars, corrupt politicians, and bronzed bodies dominate the headlines once again. Of Malcolm the milkman, there has been no sign either.

The dog and I scamper down the stairs with an enthusiasm neither of us have shown in the last year. I flick my eyesight to woman-mode and analyse the cleanliness and general condition of the interior.

Ten minutes later, I'm showered, shaved and dressed.

Bailey and I have cereal and toast. I can't ever remember to buy dog food. I've reached the stage in my life where lists are necessary. However, to my credit, I prepared the picnic last night in case the weather held. I leave the house with it and stand there waiting for her to arrive. It would be for the best if she doesn't go inside.

I tie Bailey to the gate and take a few deep breaths of the air. A shadow flicks past one of Mike's downstairs windows. I want her back, but I can't deny seeing his face when she turns up will be the icing. A plastic water bottle rolls down the street, blown by the breeze, so I catch it and place it in the recycling bin. Despite my recent abstinence, there are still many signs of an affection for alcohol.

I tried to sneak a few into Mike's bin but when I opened his, I found it full to the brim with empty wine bottles. He must have had some party. God knows when as I heard nothing. Perhaps he misplaced my invitation.

The windows in Mike's house are open. The whole street is doing the same to blow away the stale winter. One of his curtains isn't billowing like the rest. I edge closer and stand on a pile of bricks I promised to move in 2014. There is little movement because the curtains are secured to the wall and stitched together in the middle. There is a thickness to them that tells of letting in no light.

The brown beast containing my family turns up at that moment. Olivia gets out and stands before me. She looks great. She blushes. I know when she's apprehensive, nervous even.

'Hi, Olivia.'

I give her a slow kiss on the cheek. I bet Mike's watching. Whilst holding both her arms, I declare my intentions.

'Let's go to the park with the new kiddies' play area. I've done a picnic.'

Olivia is suspicious.

'They have new swings and a weird horse thing the kids can knock their teeth out on. They'll love it.'

She always was a sucker for enthusiasm.

'Are we walking?'

'No, let's drive and save our energy for the fun stuff. I've change here ready.'

She's confused. Usually, there's no way I'd pay their shameful parking prices. My teeth clamp at the prospect, but I would prefer her not to be near the house and the desolation within. That, as the joke goes, is the lesser of two weevils.

She also knows getting a three-year-old boy to go for a walk without ruining the experience is tough. She smiles and returns to the car.

Before she gets in, I touch her shoulder and murmur in her ear.

'Look at the window on the right at the top of Mike's house. Notice how the curtains don't move.'

'Oh, yeah. That's weird.'

'They're secured by tape.'

I wait for her eyes to widen in shock. They don't. I explain.

'He wants no one seeing in there. It's where he takes his victims.'

'What victims?'

'The joggers he's been accosting. He'll have a dentist's chair in there, with straps. That's where he performs his experiments.'

'Do shut up.' She gives it a second glance.

'It is odd though, isn't it?' I reply.

'If you say so. I reckon Abel was the milkman,' she adds. 'You said you haven't seen him or his wife for ages.'

'No. I even popped over to see if he was okay but nobody was home. The milk just stopped. Way before the date it was supposed to finish. The dairy tried to charge me for it too, the serpents.'

Olivia gives me a spooky look. Her voice is a whisper. 'My guess is they've arrested Malcolm. We haven't see him because he's in prison being questioned. They found his wife. He divided her into three-hundred different yoghurt pots.'

'Gross.'

'I'm in a playful mood.'

'Now you say that, I bought a pack of cheap bacon off him before he disappeared. The kids loved it.'

Olivia slaps my arm. It feels like old times.

Chapter 58

Olivia

I watch him place the so-called picnic in the back of the car. He's either bought particularly heavy vol-au-vents, or there are bottles in there. He has a backpack, too. Does he plan to sleep there? Still, it's nice to see him. He looks fresher-faced. Or maybe fuller-faced. When he was ill he somehow managed to look gaunt and chubby.

I'm pleased he's made an effort with his appearance. Being clean shaven is a big deal for me. If he has one day's stubble and I kiss him, my skin will erupt the next morning.

'Daddy!' the kids say as he opens the door.

He gets in the driver's seat. I like that. I always prefer him to drive when the children are in the car. Otherwise, I find it hard not to look around at them. I'm forever finishing a journey and finding Charlie has undone his seatbelt.

I untie Bailey from the gate. That must mean Dan rates the picnic as a higher priority than the dog. The children are trying to tell him everything from the last few days all at once, at the same time. We find a space and Dan grudgingly pays for a ticket. The grimace on his face as he examines the tariff is worth the entrance fee alone.

The park is a different place to the one of a few months back when Abel was everywhere. The kids see the new council-built wooden castle and run on ahead. Dan takes my hand. We say nothing. I hope he is thinking the same as me. There will be much that needs to remain unsaid if we're going to reach the other side of where we are.

I can tell it'll be a good day because when we get to the picnic section which overlooks the kid's play park, someone vacates a nice bench and seats. Dan sets the huge cooler on the top with relief.

'Drink?' he says.

'What have you got?'

He gets two litre bottles of mineral water out and hands me one. That's why it was so heavy. Dan is over the first hurdle.

'I don't suppose you brought any cups?'

'No, Dan. Pass it here.'

I take a sip. At least it's cold. The kids return full of enthusiasm.

'There's a sand and water bit,' Grace says. 'Can we take our shoes off and paddle? We should have bought our buckets and spades.'

'Sorry, honey. I didn't bring anything like that.'

Dan clears his throat next to me. He opens the backpack as though he's a confident magician and pulls out their sandcastle making equipment. He also retrieves two pairs of socks and a couple of towels. To my amazement, he reveals their beach shoes.

'Who are you, and what have you done with my boyfriend?'

He smiles, then bellows out after the running children.

'Watch out for needles.'

We have one of those days which people without youngsters might not appreciate. Usually, even if you visit an expensive theme park, it's a trying experience. You are hectored. It can be for a wide range of things; an ice cream, more ice cream, sunglasses on, sunglasses off, more money, it's my turn, he hit me, she pushed me, I need a wee, I've had a wee, play with me, carry me, I want to go home five minutes after arriving.

Today, we have none of that. They come back on a regular basis, even though we can see them. We hear their laughter from our table. They eat the food placed in front of them, even though most looked like it came out of a vending machine. They have one ice cream and no tears. Bailey lies in the shade.

The woman's face next to us is a picture when Dan presents the cheesecake (still frozen) and flourishes a foot-long carving knife. There are no beers. The water, two tins of corned beef and an entire watermelon (mouldy) made his load hefty.

We are a family, even if it is just for one day. That said, we are here to talk, so before the afternoon wanes, I begin.

'Your text. What does it mean?'

The kids choose that moment to return to type.

'Mum, I'm hungry.'

'Eat more picnic.'

'No, I want a hotdog.'

It was too good to last, but we had a decent run. The stall is next to the toilet which is worrying, but at least close by. Grace seizes the note I give her, and they run off shrieking.

Chapter 59

Dan

Olivia has asked me to explain my text. She's querying my behaviour over the previous five years. Where do I begin?

'I'm not sure what happened to me, not really. This city stole my identity. I forgot to appreciate you and the kids. In a way, I self-medicated. I should have left that job, but I had no confidence for another. It felt as though I was punch-drunk and couldn't see a route out. I suppose I didn't want to let you down, either.'

'How many times did I say leave that place, and you wouldn't listen?'

'You were always shouting at me.'

'You need shouting at. You all do. That's how I prevent us living in chaos. What about the drinking?'

'I've stopped. I'm not daft enough to state I won't have more, but since I left my job, I don't need it in the way I did. I want to be present. We've both been missing days like today. Sitting here, chatting, watching the kids. It's what I gave up for. That, and you.'

'We're leaving soon, Dan.'

I feel pathetic. I know begging isn't the answer, but I say it regardless.

'Can't I come?'

'Have you ever thought it was me that made you unsettled?'

'I think you could have put in more effort.'

The scrunch of her nose indicates her displeasure.

'In what way, exactly?'

I take a deep breath.

'I had a poorly-paid job I hated, in a city I disliked, with an indifferent woman, in her house, where I didn't have sex. Could you see why I might have been unhappy?'

'It might be the same there. It's still a big place.'

'I won't have that job. I've woken up, or even grown up. The time and space to get my thoughts together was what I needed. Besides, our children will be the main ones who suffer if we separate. They won't understand why we don't want to live as a family. Were we that miserable?'

'I was for a while. I understand what you're saying. If we're going okay, and it's up and down, but not too low, perhaps it is sensible to have another try. Should I ask Beau if I can stay for a while to see if we can make it work?'

Shit. I'd hate to remain in this dung hole any longer than necessary. After my fantastic picnic, I hoped to have smashed through her barriers. Particularly with that delicious cheesecake. I've done a great job today. There wasn't much in the cupboard but I cunningly bought a few bits from the petrol station. 'I thought we were having fun.'

'We are. This isn't real life though, is it? The hard work starts with the mundane and the routine. That's where you struggle. You want to enjoy everything whereas sometimes you have to crack on. You need to be a robot to get things done.'

'I disagree. If that's okay? Can't you choose to be happy? That's why I struggle with you sometimes. You've been funny, dry, sarcastic, relaxed and witty today. Great company. You look pretty and you've made an effort, but I only see that side of you on the odd occasion. I can't remember when I saw the loving, affectionate, vulnerable Olivia. When you're in full automaton mode in the morning, getting the kids ready, the house has a terrible atmosphere. Can't you be nice *and* efficient?'

'I haven't time to pander to your ego. I work, raise the children and do all the jobs for the family which not only do you not do, you aren't aware of.'

'That works both ways. I don't see you changing lightbulbs, or sorting out the insurance.'

'Mike changed the last bulbs that blew. We'd have been showering in the dark if I'd waited for you. Have you ever cleaned the bathroom? Or the dishwasher, fridge or washing machine? Do you think the elves provide the children's clothes and shoes? Does Amazon kindly deliver presents for the other boys and girls as and when needed? I don't recall you wiping the skirting boards either.'

Damn. What's happening here? We're way off target, I'm losing the argument and her mouth is set.

'That's true. The old Dan didn't do those things.'

She laughs. 'Nice recovery.'

'You must admit, to a certain degree, you placed the house's cleanliness above my happiness.'

She considers. 'I suppose so. I do want to have sex too, you know, but it always feels as if I have one more task to do. When everything is done, only then can I relax. You're often unconscious by that point.'

'If you weren't such a jellyfish giving in to their multiple story requests in the evening, we'd have more naughty time.'

'I agree, but they won't be young forever. I don't want to miss a thing. Looking after small children shouldn't put you in the mood to have sex, anyway.'

Now, it's me who chuckles. She continues.

'Sorry but I need to get my skates on, Dan. I'm out with Rachel tonight because she's going back soon. I'll come to the house after work tomorrow. If you drop me off, you can keep the car and I'll catch the train. Banish the kids to bed and we'll have a proper chat. I'd kind of made my choice. It's hard to know what to do.'

It appears I was a little over-optimistic and misjudged her state of mind. We round up the happy children and wander to the car.

'Hey, man.'

I look up to see who's blocked our path. It's the homeless guy of the junkie couple. He looks like he's had a rough time of it.

'Not seen you for a while?'

'Slim pickings here when it's cold. It can be decent when the families are back with the better weather.'

'Where do you go in the winter?'

'We have squats all over the city. Some warmer than others.'

'I see.'

'Got any spare change for food?'

'I have the next best thing.'

I slip Olivia the keys behind my back and she swiftly shuffles the kids away. There's only one item left in the cooler, and it's his. Lucky guy.

'What do I do with it?'

'You smoke it.'

I leave him scratching his head and holding a large pork pie.

Grace and Charlie are strapped in when I return. I pull into the light traffic. The children cheer when they hear they are sleeping at mine. I worried they might not be keen. Olivia kisses me when she gets out of the car. Half lip and half cheek. That's progress. She gives me a 'look after my children' glare when she arrives at her front door. Half serious and half joking. I suppose that's progress, too.

I have to sing in a loud voice to stop Charlie falling asleep on the way home. When we pull up, I give them a serious talking to, army style.

'Now, Grace and Charlie. Listen up. You are not to tell your mummy that our house is in a state. Okay?'

We step inside together.

'It's really messy!' says Grace.

'Yes, that's true. It's a secret.'

'Secrets cost money,' says Charlie.

I'm not sure where he learnt that. However, he is correct.

'Pizza anyone?'

Chapter 60

Olivia
The next day

Weather-wise, it would be hard not to have a more different day. Whereas yesterday was balmy, today is barmy. The dusk is oppressive despite being early evening. The low, heavy, black clouds brim with rain, and a harsh wind beats people off the streets. As always, public transport struggles on days like these. I was about to ring for a cab, but Dan told me that the main road out of the city had flooded.

The weather must be why we resemble miserable third world cattle as the carriages limp through the outskirts. When I get off at my stop, queue for the barriers, and step outside, the taxi line is frightening. Dan said it could be bad on wet nights. I stick up my umbrella and plunge into the night. I understand Dan's complaints now. It's been a torrid, exhausting experience, just getting home. Imagine doing that journey to work, then doing a full day, knowing you have to repeat it on the way back.

The Dan conundrum distracted me in the office. Beau could see I wasn't present, squeezed me on the shoulder, and left a cake at my desk when I nipped out for a walk to get my thoughts straight. I haven't spoken to anyone about it as *I* need to decide. The facts are out there. He's making an effort. There's no doubt of that. Yesterday, I knew him again. He made me feel normal and special. Fortunate, even.

There was also a glimpse of the woman I want to be. Who aspires to be a sour-faced moaner who is always on the look-out for problems? I want to be carefree and good company. I need to be able to relax and enjoy life. When was the last time I had a few drinks with Dan? When did I become so uptight? That said, one of us has to remain capable of driving if something happened to Grace or Charlie.

There are many reasons why I shouldn't take him with me, but the main concern is his drinking. Stress can do that to someone I suppose, and I've had a snapshot of his miserable routines myself tonight. I could still go to California for a year, or even six months, and let him completely find himself. Although, that's a risk. He could find someone else.

I've never been away from my children for more than an odd night. This morning, I missed their funny games and unbridled optimism. By leaving alone, I'd be denying him that for a long time. Grace and Charlie would lose their father. The drinking and messiness aside, they are learning important things off him as well. I would be responsible for the loss of that.

No doubt something will occur which will cement my choice. I hope that leads to taking him. It's strange to be so analytical about such a serious and heartfelt subject. I suppose that's what having children does to you.

Dan sent me a jokey email containing ten things a man wants in bed, but I know him. He agrees with it and is making me aware he isn't the only one who should change. He forgets he needs to be pleasant to get me in that frame of mind.

After I leave the bright lights of the station, I sense the dark's embrace. A gust sprays dirty, freezing road water over my legs. Due to the things on my mind this morning, I forgot to pack my trainers for the walk home. My skirt is too short for the wind. Something else I didn't consider first thing.

I get a sense of being followed immediately. Yet, when I turn, there's nobody there. I consider going back to the taxi rank but it's exposed to the ruthless elements. Was it my imagination? It's the type of night when terrible things happen. I try to walk faster, but I can't without fear of injury.

I lower my head and focus on the paving slabs. One foot in front of another. There are many ridges and crevices with malevolent needs. Another flurry twists me around and almost tears the umbrella from my grip. The part that matters is ripped and useless. Except, perhaps, as a weapon.

I turn back once more. The streetlights only reach their immediate vicinity. There's nobody near me. There's one other person on the street and they are so far away I can't tell if it's a man or a woman. A seemingly driverless solitary car sluices past me and delivers a wave over my high heels.

An icy chill has me by the throat, but I can only continue. I'm ten minutes from my house in one of the busiest cities in the world, but I am alone. I pick up the pace once more and cross the road, checking behind me.

There is still another on the street with me. They are closer now but only a dark mass. It's the same person as their silhouette is identical. Did they run to close the gap? Fear moves my legs and I stumble but keep my feet. I turn a corner and march onwards.

It's unlikely they mean me harm but my rational part has disappeared with my calm. My breath shortens, and I regret the bag of crisps I ate on the train. Be strong, I won't be a victim. I force myself to stop. Whoever it is will walk past me. It's my imagination. I'll still be in control.

My heart pounds with the same intensity as the now torrential rain. The gloom draws ever closer. I imagine a man. He'll be around that bend any moment. My fingers tighten on the handle of my useless umbrella.

Then, nothing. No one appears. I will myself to loosen my grasp, and my breathing slows. I slow to a trot. At the next bend, my pulse is nearly back to normal. I don't want to glance over my shoulder but I must. I regret it.

It is a man. I can tell by his gait. The visibility is so poor, I can't see exactly what he's wearing, but I know his clothes are black. A gust stretches his scarf out. His hood looks like a cowl. Realisation drains the strength from my legs. It's him.

The wind blasts me across the road and onto a doorstep. I look up and Abel stands at the corner I've left. I turn and search for a bell. There isn't one, so I bang my hand on the door. Next to the heavy rain it sounds like a slap. A curtain twitches and a kindly-faced lady peers out, haloed in warm light.

I stand with my back to her entrance and wait for safety to come. He's still at the corner, waiting, watching.

Incredibly, the rain intensifies further and leaps off the asphalt as though it's landing on a molten surface. A bus speeds along the avenue and briefly lights up Abel. There are no features to him. No eyes.

I turn to hammer the door once more, and this time it's a weak smack. She knows I'm out here. The truth dawns on me. She isn't coming.

I step off the pavement and stand in the road, shrieking at him.

'Who are you? What do you want?'

He walks toward me and my head spins. Panic engulfs me. I trip up the street with my brain incapable of coherent thought. I gasp as I remember Dan. His face is a beacon in my mind. Cowering in poor cover provided by a tree, I pluck my phone from my coat pocket, and hit dial.

I beg the heavens for him to answer. I stare through the torrent and can't see Abel. I twist around the tree, and he's there – barely thirty yards away on the other side of the road. Rivulets run down my face, making my vision blurred. Yet, his clothes are baggy and tattered. Water pours off him like evil. He is the embodiment of the darkness inside of me.

I hear a muffled voice answer through the earpiece.

'Hello?'

'Dan, please...'

Chapter 61

Dan

I'm getting the hang of this child raising lark. The key is to get them outside as early as possible and knacker them. Before they demolish the house. We visited the park again as we had such a good time yesterday. I found my pie uneaten on the ground and told the homeless guy off. He regretted leaving it, but said he lacked the dentistry to tackle something so dense. The day deteriorated fast, and we were home by lunchtime.

I drove them to an activity barn in the afternoon. Bastards charged me to enter, too. Was I going to be playing in the ball pit? I think Charlie pissed in there, anyway. Serves them right.

Then you feed stodgy food into them, so we had a pasta bake. I messed it up somehow, but covered it in cheese and they ate it. Next, into the bath, splash around, tidy up downstairs while they're doing that. Cartoon and ice cream and up the stairs for a story and bed. To my surprise, I enjoyed the reading part.

Usually, I can't stand the monotony. This time I focused on the children and their enjoyment. Olivia was right. I felt involved and even glowed a little.

I debated getting a bottle of wine for Olivia's arrival, but I might have drunk it by now. I'm supposed to be impressing her, not seducing her. I'll see if she wants a takeaway.

I hear my phone ring from the other room and debate whether I can be arsed to answer it. It might be Olivia, so I better had.

'Dan, please. Help me!'

'Olivia? What's wrong?'

'It's Abel.'

'Where?'

'He's staring at me from across the road.'

'Where the hell are you?'

'Turpin Street. I was walking home, and Abel followed me.'

'You walked home in this weather? Why?'

'Dan, I'm scared.'

I can hear her teeth chattering.

'What's he doing? Has he attacked you?'

'He's waiting for me. Glaring at me. Should I ring the police?'

'I'll come and get you. You're only two streets away.'

'No, don't leave the children.'

'Shit. Look, they're in bed. I'll wait in the middle of the road. You're around the corner. Just fucking run. I'll see you in thirty seconds.'

'I've got high heels.'

'What?! Take them off. Leave them.'

'They're my favourites.'

I can hear her sobbing. I bellow.

'Olivia, we'll buy new shoes. Remove them, drop them, leave everything. And run. This is what you've been training for. All those nights of hard work. All those calories counted. Run, run, run. Run to me. Run for your children.'

There's a clatter and the phone goes dead. I assume she dropped it.

Jesus, women. Worrying about her shoes.

I pull my trainers on and barge through the door. The rain is absolutely pouring. I'm drenched in seconds. It's so hard it stings my bald head. I charge up the drive.

The glare from a car's lights blinds me for a second and then the road is empty. I stand in the middle and peer through the rods.

She appears as if from nowhere. She drives hard up the white lines, arms and legs pumping, with a determined mad desperation on her face.

'Quick,' I roar. I dash towards Olivia and she almost knocks me to the floor as we meet. Her body shudders.

'Come on. It's okay now, I'm here, and you're safe. Let's get you inside.'

We stare back down the street. No one's there.

Chapter 62

Dan

As I steer her towards the house, Mike comes out of his.

'Hey, is she okay?'

We both ignore him and leave him drenched and open-mouthed. He looks forlorn until his face hardens into a snarl that tells of revenge.

I trip over Bailey who made it as far as the front door in his quest to help. He never liked the rain.

I grab a dry towel from the radiator which I forgot to move to the airing cupboard. God knows how long it sat there as it's crispy. It is nice and warm though. I dry her off as best as I can, but she's water-logged. Gently, with her shoulders still heaving, I remove her clothes. I leave her in the now-soaked towel and run up the stairs to get another.

She follows me up with giant leaps. Confused, I look at her as she walks straight past me and into Charlie's room. She then reappears and enters Grace's room. Olivia comes back and I encircle her with the biggest towel we have. I pull her trembling body into mine and rock her from side-to-side.

She's a tough broad and recovers fast. That's just as well because I'm drenched too. I run a bath and she slides into it with a sob. I'm unsure why as it's not something I've done before, but I light candles and place them in there. After she gets in, I leave the door open and play quiet music in the background.

She surprises me in the kitchen an hour later. I didn't hear her come down the stairs. No harm seems to be done. I pass her a hot chocolate and she giggles.

'Very dramatic.'

It's typical of her to laugh. She's so robust and resilient. Only now do I respect such admirable qualities. Such necessary assets in order to be a good mother. I remember the health worker asking her if she felt low or depressed after the birth of Charlie. She replied she didn't have time for any of that. Yet, on odd occasions, I would catch her drying her face. The real troubles can be the ones we fail to acknowledge.

We sip our drinks together in silence. She has a duvet around her shoulders from upstairs. I wear her dressing gown, so look my best. She finally talks.

'Should I dial 999?'

'I wasn't there. Did he hurt you, or say anything to you?'

'No. Nothing. He wasn't even close enough for me to describe him. Maybe it was all in my head?'

'No. You said he was staring and waiting. Do you think it was him? It could have been another weirdo on the Abel bandwagon. I wouldn't tell the police though. You don't want the authorities thinking you've been imagining things.'

Her eyes note the items on the kitchen table. Her rising smile is a welcome sight.

'You found them.'

'Yeah. I jogged back and fetched them. The phone might not work again, and the umbrella isn't up to much, but you have your shoes.'

'Come here, you.'

As we kiss, hands find their way into her dressing gown. She pulls me up the stairs.

Chapter 63

The prostitute

Carly stares at the people carrier, willing it to stop. She is frozen. The air hangs solid around her, permeating into flimsy clothing. She's used to it now. In fact, Carly struggles to remember a time when she wasn't cold. Even when her landlord lets them have the heating on, she shivers. It's as though her veins flow with coolant as opposed to warm blood.

The gnawing of addiction refocuses her mind, and she undoes her jacket to display her wares. She feels loose teeth as the chill clamps her jaw shut. Her pimp will be along soon, demanding the money. Her cut is heroin and a damp bedsit. She knows not to hide it, or she'll have to blend her food.

Carly can't quite believe she has only been here eighteen months. That naïve runaway is long gone. A hand comes around and covers her mouth, she leans back unsteady on her heels. She doesn't struggle as Damon laughs. He's been doing that from when they were girlfriend and boyfriend. He was a big, strong, beautiful man when he found her. She'd never met anyone like him before. He was a rainbow, mixed from the best of men. His crumbling frame shows that to be a lie. Hard drugs have no mercy.

'Hand it over then?'

She does, and he glares at the notes. He should be happy as she's tired from the roaring trade. Abel has scared off all but the most desperate street workers, but the demand is ever-present. Nevertheless, if Damon didn't control her every moment, she'd be elsewhere. Perhaps even home.

She remembers the clumps she received from her alcoholic mother. Carly couldn't wait to escape. Ironic that she ended up in a similar place.

The strange men don't bother her anymore. She endures their antics until she can return to the oblivion she yearns for. She has to give credit to Damon. The transition from lover to master was so smooth she barely noticed. Now, she makes good money, but still can't satiate their burgeoning habits.

Anger rises on Damon's face as he pockets the cash. However, the vehicle she saw earlier pulls alongside and distracts him. His cruel grin greets the customer as the window glides down. There will be time for violence later.

'You looking for fun?'

'I need to party. Back at mine. You know, a bit of music, some drugs, just don't want to do it on my own.'

Carly examines his face for clues. She's become expert at identifying those who blur the line between pleasure and pain. He thumbs behind him and she notices three other hookers in the gloom. Their emaciated frames look comical, like children dwarfed by their seats on the way to school. She knows them all, knows them well. They are the only friends she has. They grin back.

It's not unusual for a normal man to want to pick up a few prostitutes and have a wild night before returning to his family. Most of them end up too caned to even trouble the women for sex. They pay, guilty men always do.

'Fifty now, and fifty when you leave. The drugs are included.'

The see-through plastic bag of narcotics he waves in the air seals the deal. She would have gone anyway. Hell, the warmth from the car was so enticing, she'd have sucked him off for nothing if he let her sit in it for half an hour afterwards.

'Hey. You want to party with my girl, it will cost more than that.'

Trust Damon to be greedy. It's past eleven now and there'd be little more trade. His face is interested though.

He's clocked the others in the rear seats. He is jealous. The man notices.

'You can come too, buddy.'

'You not some kinda faggot, are you?'

'All are welcome in the House of the Lord.'

Carly misses the strange statement as she smirks at Damon's bravado. He is already climbing in the front seat. She climbs in the back and they pull away. The driver has a baseball cap on, so it's hard to see his face. He isn't nervous which means he's done this before. That's good news as he'll know the score. She smiles as he tries to give her the money. Damon takes that and holds the zip-loc bag of drugs up to the windscreen. All eyes are on the large stash. The journey is ten silent minutes, their minds full of anticipation.

They pull up in a quiet street. Carly remembers a young teenager and her best friend going to a house party. Her dad getting out and opening the door for them like a chauffeur. They ran off giggling. She wished now she had gone back. Told him she loved him. Maybe he had the blood clot floating around his body then, biding its time before it killed him. She will never recover from that shock. Her mother certainly hadn't.

The house is sweltering. She feels as though she's walking into a baker's oven. It's heavenly. He guides them into a room with two sofas facing a large flat screen television. She fails to consider the doyleys and Toby Jugs. They ignore the family pictures which don't include their host. Their focus is on the prize, and they get stuck in.

***

The first thing she notices as her eyes struggle to open is the sour taste. A slow breath pulls fetid air into her lungs. Her heavy head sways to regard her co-workers. They all snooze, lined up on the sofa. For a few seconds, it's a Christmas scene from years ago.

Damon could be her father, gently snoring in the armchair. Tears slide off her chin. It wasn't supposed to be like this. She didn't deserve this.

Carly can't summon the energy to rise out of her seat, but instinct tells her she must. Rolling off, she crawls out of the room. The hall is quiet save for the tick of an unseen clock, the floor hard to her bony knees. It's as if she's fainted, but remains conscious. There's a mewling sound coming through a closed door. It swings open at a gentle push. A smashed window and ripped curtain allows the moonlight to display an old lady, duct taped to a recliner. She sobs in silence.

A wave of overwhelming drug euphoria causes Carly to rest her head on the parquet flooring. Blasts of icy air grab her attention but can't prize her eyelids apart. Despite her confusion, everything that is wrong with the scene registers. This isn't the home of a forty-year-old man. It shouldn't smell of petrol here. She doesn't need sight to know Abel has opened the front door.

The click of a zippo lighter opening becomes her world. She prays for oblivion, before she burns.

Chapter 64

Olivia
A week later

The traffic to the airport is light, and with extra time I park in the short stay and enter the terminal building. Rachel checks in and I buy coffee from Starbucks. Even I smart at the cost. Dan would have had a heart attack. We sit and have a last chat.

'How's Herman?'

Rachel beams. 'Excellent. Coming out in a month to see me. I almost daren't say it, but he's proving lovable.'

'That's good to hear. I'm pleased for you. I hope he's the special one.'

'So, have you decided to take Dan with you? You said you've half moved back in. I can see you're happier. God only knows what you see in that eejit, but you love him. Your pizazz has returned.'

'My pizazz?'

'Yeah, you know. Your kaboom!'

'I will miss you, you know.'

'Well, it won't be too long now. It'll be great, even if you bring Dan Dan the domestic man. Although I still can't rate him as a househusband.'

'He is trying, but he's by no means a natural. We call it man cleaning. He does the hoovering and tidies the kitchen. Then I go behind him and do it properly. It's not a perfect system but I get it done much quicker. I blame his mother. How did he not learn how to iron?'

'Ironing is for people with too much free time. You know that.'

'He's always been brilliant with the washing machine though. He rarely wears anything more than once before he cleans it. Although God knows where him and Bailey get to, because they're often covered in mud.'

'Enough about domestic chores. Are you looking forward to getting stuck into your new job?'

'It's a great opportunity. And great money.'

'I'd say you are delighted for yourself.'

'I am that.'

'Perhaps you could get Beau to give Dan a job. They'll need someone to clean the bogs at the new office.'

'Stop it. You're terrible. Now you mention it, that's not a terrible idea.'

'I'm joking.'

'I know, but Dan has skills. Beau might be keen as it would make me happier.'

'That fooker better not end up sitting next to me. I can do without being surrounded by his beer farts all day long.'

'He's getting fit as it goes. Running, weights at home. I even saw my Davina McCall DVD out on the side.'

'I suspect he's been doing a different pump to that.'

'Ha ha. He told me that Charlie spilt a yoghurt on the TV.'

'You always take it too far.'

'To be fair, Dan's a changed man. He's stopped drinking, and the weight is sliding off him. Dan actually wants to do things. We're having fun, even when it's boring, if that makes any sense. We're going somewhere tomorrow morning as a secret treat.'

'You don't say? Are strip joints open in the morning?'

'Give him a chance, Rachel. He's not all bad.'

'I still need convincing. I was beginning to think he was Abel with all his weird behaviour.'

'Can you imagine? Him and Ian. A deadly duo wreaking death and destruction.'

'Perhaps the criminal genius will take you to a football match.'

'Dan's smarter than that. I think. I suspect he's taking me to a...wait for it. Car boot sale!'

'The sneaky little gombeen. He is pulling out the stops.'

There was a flyer next to the computer and with minimal cyberstalking, I found the website on his browsing history. I love car boot sales, and it's a huge one tomorrow. I experience a strange thrill when I arrive. There are bargains to be had there. You can get strange quirky items you wouldn't even think of buying. I've found fantastic ornaments in them.

'It's exciting. I can't wait.'

'I'm glad I don't live with you anymore. Every time you found one of those markets, we'd end up with a flat full of shite.'

'Oi, cheeky. We had loads of good stuff.'

The tannoy announcements always rattle Rachel in airports. She's paranoid she'll develop narcolepsy, thereby missing her plane. She likes to reach the boarding gate first and sit right at the front, her thinking being that if she drops off, they will see and wake her. And there's me thinking airport seats are designed specifically so you couldn't fall asleep on them. We all have our foibles.

'I better get going.'

I check my watch and smile. She has two hours.

'Give me a hug. Keep in touch.'

She holds my arms and squeezes them hard. 'Be careful. It feels a bit like I'm escaping from this place.'

I watch her walk away with her little pull-along suitcase. That Herman has tightened up her arse. She worries too much, maybe things are coming together. Can life be simple after all?

Chapter 65

Dan

I chuck Bailey a handful of gravy bones and walk towards our waiting shit-mobile. Olivia is in good spirits and waves like a crazy person. I climb in next to her and kiss her on the cheek even though she only left to drop the kids off half an hour ago. She has her denim dungarees on as I told her to dress casually. It's weird that I find them her sexiest item. Possibly hotter than the purple dress. It's confirmation I'm straight, as Super Mario never did much for me.

'I'll drive if you want?'

'That's okay. You always drive. Now, where to my little munchkin?'

I nibble my lip. She's a wonderful driver, in some respects. Way better than me, apart from one aspect. She is the clutch-killer extraordinaire. I must remain calm.

'To the stadium near where you used to live?'

'Eh?'

'You know. Near the monument.'

'Oh.'

I'm not sure why she looks annoyed. She pulls away and rides the clutch as though she wants to punish the car. I swear I hear a strand on the cable pinging. I can't help myself.

'Remember what we discussed?'

'Can it, Dan. Do I tell you how to drive?'

'No, but I haven't gone through two clutches in three years.'

'Don't start. We're having a nice day together. Focus on that. No bitching. Where are we going?'

'There's a big car boot sale on the stadium car park. Thousands of stalls. Full of lurking treasures.'

'Brilliant. I thought for a minute I'd be forced to watch sport.'

'Well, I know how you enjoy bargain hunting.'

She reaches over and squeezes my hand and gives me a cute look, hair up in a bun.

We pull up at the far end of the stadium where there are still spaces for parking. If Olivia was any more excited, she'd have her legs crossed. Tables fan out as far as I can see, but it doesn't appear too busy. We're reasonably early as she always reckons the best stuff goes first. Not too early though. I know it's going to be a wearing experience.

Olivia kind of floats through the stalls. I've seen her do it on other occasions. It's ethereal. She glides along with all the time in the world, a half-smile lighting up her face. As an accompanying man, it is terrible. You should go with a plan, get what you want, and come out. She's looking for something she doesn't need. Madness.

After an hour, we agree to hunt alone. She said I was ruining the experience by hanging around like a bodyguard. I find a sports memorabilia stall that's interesting. It uses up a bit of time but I buy nothing.

We meet back at the car. She struggles with bags and carries an enormous fluffy rabbit.

'Haven't our kids grown out of big furry toys?'

'What? No. You never grow out of them when they're this big. I couldn't resist him. He's so cute, isn't he? He's for you. He likes you. A lot.'

She pushes me over the bonnet and simulates the rabbit giving me a rough ride. Olivia's giggling so much she's dribbling.

'You want it, Dan. Don't ya, don't ya.'

It's proof we live in a big city as no one says a word, despite many walking within a metre of us.

'Very amusing. You fancy a burger?'

'Aren't you taking me and the rabbit for lunch?'

'I suppose so. That was the best sex I've had in years. We can go for a meal next, but I'm starving now. Come on, we'll share one. You love dirty burgers from filthy vans.'

She thinks for a minute and bursts into song.

'I want a burger all of my own.

I ask my boyfriend, what will it be

Will it be bow wow?

Will it be roadkill, or maybe a rat?

You'll have to wait and see.'

I leave Doris Day and Que Sera behind and join the queue. One minute later, I'm back and getting into the car. Without any burgers.

'Where's the food?'

'He wanted ten for two burgers.'

'That's steep.'

'Yes! That's what I said. I asked him why it was so expensive.'

'Was it wagyu?'

'My comment exactly. He replied, "No mate. It's beef, and that's the going rate". He then said something about having to cover the costs of getting his van here and the customer pays for the convenience. I told him it was a boot sale in the car park of a city stadium, not Everest base camp.'

'Ah, no way. I want a burger now. Can we still have one?'

'No, I can't go back.'

'Why not?'

'I insulted him. If he's close to his mum, he'll be upset.'

'I see. Some things don't change.'

'Shall we get a pizza?'

'Yes, let's get out of here. It was closing up anyway. I reckon I have all the best stuff. Thanks for bringing me. I had a great time. It was perfect to wander without worrying about the kids.'

Chapter 66

Dan

We stop at a local pizza place. I have a Groupon voucher in preparation and swagger through the door. Groupons always make me think I've got one up on the restaurant. We skirt around the California paradox until the desserts arrive. Then, Olivia tells me the news I hoped not to hear.

'I'm sorry to say this, Dan. We're going without you. I know you've been trying, but it's early days. This job needs all my attention, and I want to start the job with no aggravation. I need to give it my best shot while I'm calm and settled.'

My tiramisu spoils in my mouth. I force it down with a frown.

'Is there anything I can do to change your mind?'

'Come and visit. After a month or so. It'll give us both chance to breathe. We can see how we get on and take it from there.'

It's a reasonable gesture. A sensible one. I try not to think of missing the children for that long. Getting cross wouldn't help either. Should I blame her? They always say absence makes the heart grow fonder. What choice do I have? Or am I giving up too soon? She hasn't gone yet.

'Are you going to continue living at your parents' house?'

'Yes, if that's fine with you. I think it's good for both of us.'

I give her a smile I don't feel. She gives me a sad look in reply, then remembers something.

'Guess who I saw with a stall?'

'Mad Mike, our neighbour, selling souvenirs from his murders? I can see him running a pickled finger stall.'

'No, but close. Joseph Wickmeyer.'

'Who is that?'

'You know him as Pete the postman, or The Taekwondo Tapir.'

'That numpty. What was he doing?'

'He had a stall. Bric-à-brac mostly. He was selling Star Wars toys. I haven't seen yours for a while. Did you let him have them?'

'I gave him a couple. I thought you'd moved them?'

'No, I didn't. He was also selling second hand perfume. You know, half used stuff. Quite a few of them looked like the ones I had. Did you give him them as they've disappeared as well?'

'No, I didn't. The little stoat must have nicked them. Did you challenge him?'

'I wasn't sure to be honest. I said hello, but he wasn't fazed. At least I couldn't see him selling any of my underwear that disappeared.'

'I should think he was wearing that, or he had them for breakfast with Nutella. How brazen though. I'm going to have a word with him. I'll drop around on the way back to yours.'

'It's not worth it, Dan. It was a load of old rubbish. Let's not ruin today.'

'That vermin has been in our house. That's bang out of order. Besides, you've already ruined today.'

Chapter 67

Olivia

To my surprise, the postman lives in a reasonable neighbourhood. I don't ask Dan how he knows this. By the strain in his jaw, his toes are over the edge. I suspect it's nothing to do with this guy stealing our stuff, and more to do with my decision.

I tried long and hard to choose for us all to go together. Yet, a part of my being willed me to leave with just the kids. Almost as if my molecules were telling me it's time to be on my own. Is my instinct begging me to get my head together so I can give it another shot, or is it imploring me to start again? Without him.

'It's nice around here.'

Dan ignores the high terraces and swept paths. He grunts as a cyclist nearly commits suicide on our bonnet, and stops outside a shabbier place than the others. He pops the compartment near my legs, reaches in, and pulls an orange hammer out. My eyes follow as he slips it into the inside of his jacket so smoothly, it's like he's pocketing someone's business card.

'Expecting trouble? Don't be daft and put it back. In fact, why is there a bloody hammer in our car?'

'It's an emergency glass breaker. I'm not turning up swinging a mace.'

'Why take it at all then?'

'He's The Taekwondo Tapir remember. What if he's also Abel?'

'The newspapers reckon that Abel is dead. They think he got caught up in that shootout in Chinatown. It was like something from the movies. The Chinese said a man had been terrorising them. He killed scores of dealers until they cornered him in a busy supermarket of all places. Thirty people died. One of them had a beard, a hoody, and a scarf.'

'When was that?'

'This morning's news.'

'Shit. Abel probably bumped into Malcolm ranting over them undercutting him on milk. Malcolm snapped and slayed everyone there, Abel included. So, it's over?'

'Let's hope so. It could have been a copycat they killed.'

Dan returns the hammer to the glove box.

'I'll still give this guy a talking to. Although I agree, I doubt I'll need to beat him to death with that useless thing.'

He gets out and walks to the front door. He doesn't appear nervous whereas I'm jittery and jumpy. Like an exciting movie is starting. I also feel a tiny bit aroused. It's a side of Dan I don't see. He has passion and, in a way, he's protecting us. That weight training is paying off, too. I noticed while we ate pizza that his biceps bulged as he placed each piece in his mouth.

From where we're parked, I can look into the house when the door opens. A frail lady with crazy white hair is not who I expected. She's so small that when she steps forward, Dan has to look vertically down at her.

She points a crooked finger up at him, and even from here, I know she's told him to piss off. Dan turns with an incredulous expression. The postman arrives in the doorway. I'm still not sure what to call him. He takes the woman's hand and guides her back into the house. When he returns, he wears a big smile.

He talks animatedly for a minute, oblivious of Dan's angry visage. The lack of response from Dan ensures it sinks in and his face becomes expressionless. It's the same impassive look he wears when delivering the post. Dan slips into full ranting mode. He points across at me, and I see the postman's hand rise. Dan grabs it and leans in toward him. I'm holding my breath.

The gesticulating carries on for a further minute and, gradually, Dan's shoulders drop. An odd grin sneaks on both faces. They shake hands and the door closes.

Dan enters the car and releases a whoosh of air.

'Is everything okay?'

'I guess. He apologised for taking the things. He reckoned I said he could have them. I'd tidied the perfume bottles up and left them downstairs. He assumed they were out for him to take.'

'Did he try and hit you?'

'I don't think so. I think he thought I was going to whack him. Must be his training. He's such a finely coiled specimen, his body responds automatically.'

I feel terrible laughing. 'I bet Pete watched *The Karate Kid* when he was younger and wanted to take lessons. Instead, he was frog-marched to cubs. Then, too many episodes of the *A-Team* warped him. He has become a deadly weapon.'

'His mother had venom. She weirded me out. After he guided her back to the lounge, he said it's her property, and she has dementia, so he moved back in to take care of her. She lives on the downstairs floor as the stairs are too much for her. She did say to thank you for the underwear although next time she'd prefer something more modern.'

'How rude! He's still been in our house though. What did he say about that?'

'He said the door was open, so he helped himself. To the toys and perfume that is. He denied the theft of your sturdy undergarments. I felt bad for him, looking after his mum must be hard. He did ask me if I wanted to go up to the first floor to look at his collection.'

'Oo-er. What does that mean?'

'God only knows. Maybe he has a selection of the city's ladies suspended on meat hooks up there. Like a human abattoir.'

'Yeah, I can see it. Or he takes his honeys there for love of a tapir kind.'

'That's not something I'd recover from seeing. Come on, let's get going. I feel deflated about everything. We might as well drop you off at your parents' house.'

'Let's leave the kids there for a while.'

'What do you want to do? I could eat ice cream.'

I have to leer at him, lick my lips in a comely manner and squeeze my boobs before he gets the message. Men really are simple beings. Slow learning, too. Even Bailey would have learnt to read the signs by now. I know I'm giving him mixed messages, but I don't care. For me, there's a sense it may be our last time.

The drive home is uneventful. I can't help staring up at Mike's window when I get back.

'What would you use curtains like that for, Dan?'

'You mean apart from sinister reasons? I should think it's a dark room.'

'For developing pictures?'

'Yes, all psychopaths are the same. He'll want mementos of his sick acts to prolong the fantasy. Mike takes photos of his victims and the foul things he's done to them. You can't upload them to Snapfish for obvious reasons.'

'I've never heard him mention an interest in photography, have you?'

'No, nothing. Although they've said Abel's gone, I'd still love to have a snoop in there.'

'Promise you won't, Dan. Please.'

He leans out of the car before I can read his face.

Chapter 68

The cyclists

Cyclists. Demons in spandex. I hate them all. The silver-haired six will be my victims. They'll need new shorts after today. Saying that, it was hard getting my hands on a gun. I stuck knives into two scumbags until that drug dealer let me borrow his, and ammunition is scarce. Blanks were easier to find, and they should suffice. Fear is more effective than murder. The living spread the word faster than the dead, and it's less dangerous for me.

You could set your watch by these guys. Seven o'clock they will glide through this underpass. Like a flock of angry geese. They go straight to the pub and stand around in their outfits thinking they own the place. I overhear them discussing the merits of the house red and want to ruin their comfort.

There's an escape route through the allotments if necessary, but I hope at least one of them will need CPR after the firework display. I should be able to wander away at my leisure. They come into view and I note there are more than six this evening. Excellent.

I light the Catherine wheel I pinned to the wall, and retreat to the far end. The six rockets nestle at my feet. Four seconds fuses, so I touch them with my lit cigarette. The sparks in the dark from the first firework are shocking, and the leader falls off his bike. As the rest come through the smoke, I step into view, raise my pistol and fire five blanks at them. I imagine false teeth falling out of their horrified faces. The rockets take off and scream into the gang like scorpion missiles from a helicopter gunship and my victims clatter to the floor.

Out of the wreckage climbs a man. Big, strong, and raging. I bolt up the bank and enter the allotments. It's darker than I remember and the ground is treacherous. I curse my choice of footwear as my work shoes slip and slide. Incredibly, the old fart is still after me. His cycling trainers find purchase where my steps fail. I plunge into a freshly tilled patch and fall to my knees. He stops at the edge and clenches both fists.

Close up, he's younger than I thought. Perhaps he was one of their sons. The enormous muscles in his legs bulge as he stamps towards me. Revenge is his business, but so is it mine. And I have a gun. The final round was in it when stolen. I pray it works. With a blast that surprises me and shocks him, I despatch the bullet to his heart.

Chapter 69

Dan
A week later

There's been something nasty floating around the house, and, for once, Bailey isn't responsible. It's my mood. Olivia has been over on numerous occasions but it isn't the same. It feels like the end of a holiday romance when you know you're going separate ways.

I've been on my best behaviour, but, I'm a man. A slovenly one at that, and I couldn't maintain the high standards. Therefore, the bickering has begun. I believe a certain amount of arguments are inevitable when you look after young children. They wear you out. They grind you down. They are relentless.

My mum was right when she said you can't have anything nice when you have kids. The LCD TV has what looks like nine mallet marks on the screen. Any night time scene is completely black. The sound levels have a mind of their own. Yet, still the children pray to their cartoon gods.

The fridge has been yanked back on its hinges so many times, it will only stay closed if I tape it that way. I've lost so much stuff by our sticky-fingered magpie son I forget what's missing. I found him wearing female sunglasses and stroking his hair with a strange brush. He said he found them in the garden. On top of that, we've found poops in beds, wardrobes and even our shoes.

But, there's no malice to him. He's being a boy. However, it's unreasonable to expect your fuse to be anything but non-existent after a day with him. In comparison, Grace is the golden child. Although she does wind him up when she thinks no one's watching and is becoming prone to manic outbreaks of divadom. They go to bed and what's left of you hunts for oblivion on the sofa. Romance is gazed at on the television, or read about in a magazine.

Olivia asked to see that picture of her in black and white. I had to tell her its location was a mystery. She was upset. I hope she wanted me to have it to remind me of her. When she does things like that, it makes me confident for our future. I expect her to change her mind and take me with her. Explain that she can't live without me. She hasn't.

It's too late now, anyway. The removal vans are booked, an apartment rented, school places reserved, and flights paid for. Olivia came over and involved me in where the children would be educated. As for the rest, I'm not even a fly on the wall.

The doorbell startles me, and then Beau surprises me.

'Hi, Beau. She's not here at the moment.'

'That's fine. It's you I want to have a chat with.'

'Oh, step inside then. Would you like a cup of tea?'

'Yes, please.'

'If you're happy to cover your work clothes with hair, Bailey's waiting in the lounge for a playmate.'

'Cool.'

I wonder what Beau wants. It's unlikely to be good news. Perhaps, both my children are his. He's here to tell me he'd like to adopt them. The reason Olivia has gone off sex is because she has so much fantastic stuff with him. He feels sorry for a wretched soul such as me and has come to end it. When I return with the drinks, he'll be lurking behind the door, and bludgeon me to death with that rock-hard *Thomas the Tank Engine* toy I'm forever stepping on.

The kettle boils and brings me back to planet Earth. I hear him wrestling with Bailey in the lounge. Two docile creatures together. I hand him his drink.

'There you go. What's up?'

'I've been playing golf nearby and thought I'd pop by with a proposal. This is informal and, of course, far from being set in stone, but I might have some good news for you.'

'Okay. What did you have in mind?'

Olivia had told me Rachel's joke about me scrubbing shite and vomit off the floor of i-BLAM's new office toilets. Not so amusing for me although Olivia was close to a breakdown when she repeated it.

'What do you know of FinTech?'

'About the same as I know about skiing.'

'I didn't know you skied?'

'I don't.'

'Ah, I see. I'll explain. Fintech is the great leveller in the banking field. It's nimble and has minimal overheads and commitments compared to traditional finance companies. There is expansion at an incredible rate all over the world. The Office of the Mayor of London for example, claims 40% of the London workforce comprises financial and technology services alone.'

He keeps talking, and it is English, but every third word isn't in my vocabulary. It sounds dodgy to me. He mentions 'On-boarding' and 'Payment gateway'. Is that porn? Underbanking sounds painful, too. I bet the dentist next door does it already. "Right madam. I'll underbank you while you're unconscious, I'll probe your payment gateway and participate in some thoroughly fast on-boarding".

Just as I stop listening completely, and wonder if I could measure his top lip, he offers me a job.

'When we're up and running, we'll start a call centre there, and I'll need someone to manage it.'

My eyebrows hit the ceiling. I'd be sceptical, but this is Beau. I try to run the reasons and implications of what he's said through my mind.

'Doesn't it matter if I understand little about Fintech?'

'You have experience of managing people. It's a service. The guys on the phones will know the tech stuff. You only need to oversee them. Ensure we hit our KPIs, service levels, that kind of thing. The technical side will get picked up in time.'

'Sounds great. I don't know what to say.'

'Say you'll consider it.'

'I will. I will.'

'Well, that's fab. I better run.'

He and Bailey climb off the sofa. They are both sad. Bailey because Beau's leaving, and Beau because his trousers have a million hairs on them.

'Were you aware my fiancée was mugged?'

'Felicity? Was she jogging?'

'No, it wasn't Abel, if you're thinking that. I suppose they could have been mimics. A bunch of lads did it outside the office, late at night. The police keep saying that crime levels are now at record lows, but it doesn't feel like it when you're the victim of what's remaining.'

'No, I guess not. Congratulations on your engagement by the way. I always thought you fancied Olivia.'

I regret saying the words as they slip out. He's offered me a job, and like an imbecile a few seconds later I'm stirring up trouble. Beau doesn't seem to notice.

'She's a great girl. You're a lucky man. I'd never jeopardise our working relationship. Besides, Felicity and me aren't into sex at the moment.'

'You're not?'

'No, Felicity and me are celibate. We think sex complicates things. I need to focus on my business right now. It's not forever. How much time is wasted on relationships when you get too involved on strategising, analysing, and agonising over love.'

He's lost me again as I fondly remember the perspiring Spandex-clad Felicity picking up a stray shuttlecock. Jesus, what a tragedy. He looks cross as he continues.

'Everyone's sex-mad. If you took drugs, sex and prostitutes out of the equation, the world would be a better place. I'd wipe them all from the planet.'

Bailey and I wave him and his sports car off as it hurtles up the road. I want to thank him for confirming it isn't just me. It may be that I've a few loose marbles, but in this city, everyone's mad.

Chapter 70

Dan

After Beau is out of sight, I stand and stare back at our house. It's strange to think we won't be living here. We'll be leaving many memories behind. Although it might be for the best, we had great times, too.

I allow myself to reminisce on our lives here. I expect long Christmas scenes or complete birthday parties to flood into my mind. Yet, like fireworks on a dark night, flashes of the past light up in my head. Two children giggling in the bath, Grace asking for the fifth time how long dinner is, a little boy's face around the door in the morning, a lounge resembling a bombsite, tears and jokes, fun and laughter.

There is no way I can stay in London after Olivia's gone. I've decided that I'll go travelling for a few months. I want to see India. In this day and age, internet cafés will be everywhere, so I can easily stay in touch. I applied for the visa online and it arrived in a few days. I'm deserting the dog, but Olivia's parents have agreed to take Bailey in the short term.

The rat-race beat me. I lost sense of who I was. I became everything I swore I'd never be. A victim. I joined the haunted ranks of lifeless victims circulating this strange place. I could feel no pleasure. My breaths were shallow. I wasn't living. I'd sacrificed my soul for the daily commute.

The old Dan is more or less back now. I see the world. There is beauty and pleasure in everything around us. We need to stop to enjoy it. Before, I was in such a rush to go nowhere, I couldn't taste my food or smell the air. Not that you'd want to do too much of that in the centre here, but you know what I mean. I can't wait to find open spaces. We all deserve solitude and peace. Dare I wish to live a life without the accompanying sounds of the modern motor car twenty-four hours a day?

I received an email from Ian. He's still going to Brazil but not with the girls. He partied with them for a weekend and by the Sunday he couldn't take any more. He has since heard that the local ladies in the seaside resorts in the north of Brazil want to snare rich foreigners and have few morals. He said he will be in hog heaven. I try not to think what that means.

I didn't hear from Charlotte again until yesterday when I got a Facebook message. It simply stated, 'Remember me'. I certainly won't forget what being with her taught me — I'm not twenty-five any more.

My phone rings as I walk back down the drive. It's Olivia.

'Hi, honey.'

'Hi. Sorry to be abrupt but I'm at work and I need to collect the last few bits from the house. I'll be there in fifteen minutes. I haven't got my key, so you'll have to let me in when I get there.'

'No problem. I'm packing my stuff today, so knock when you arrive. The kids are playing nicely upstairs.'

It's the school holidays, so the children are staying overnight. By nicely, what I mean is I can't hear them. They could have beaten each other into submission but I've found it best not to disturb them unless absolutely necessary.

'Just a quick question, Olivia. Did you ask Beau if he could find me a job?'

There's an infinitesimal pause. How depressing. Olivia has resorted to begging for jobs for me. On the plus side that means she is thinking of our future. In fact, that's good news. It's confirmation we'll only be separated for a few months, before we begin the next phase as a family.

'No, why has he offered you work?'

'Kind of. A possibility of one anyway.'

As we talk, I notice Mike has left one of the downstairs window open.

'Interesting. Mike has a window ajar. I'm sure he's out as I saw his car leave. I might have a little peek and see what's in that room.'

'Don't you dare. That's burglary.'

'I think it's only burglary if you take something. I'll be trespassing.'

'Dan, give me a break. I need to talk to you about Mike. He's been sending me weird messages. I've had a few missed calls from him at strange hours as well.'

'Weird in what way?'

'I'll show you when I get there.'

'Okay, no problem.'

'Do not go in his house. Besides, who'll be looking after our children?'

'Yeah, yeah. See you soon.'

I walk back inside and upstairs to check on the kids. Charlie has fallen asleep on his bed, and Grace is reading on hers. The urge to look is overwhelming. I'll be quick. I grab my rucksack, just in case he has too many bottles of wine in that cellar he keeps banging on about, and sneak out the door.

The window lock has come loose and I can pull it wide open. The problem is it's higher than I imagined. I'm debating pulling a bin over to stand on to make things easier when I get a tap on the shoulder.

It is a close call on the underwear front. Pete the postie grins.

'Did anyone tell you not to sneak up on people?'

He's oblivious, and gawps.

'Mike's left his window open, so I'm going to have a quick check inside his house. You know, make sure he hasn't been burgled by a junkie. Give me a lift, and then I'll help you in. Safety in numbers and all that.'

'I don't want to go in there.'

'What! You can't be scared of an emaciated, thieving, heroin addict? You're a vigilante. The Taekwondo Tapir no less.'

He looks bewildered and frightened at the same time. It's not flattering.

'Mike would be angry if he found us in his house.'

'We're doing him a service.'

'I don't care. He's been mean to me. He said if I couldn't be quieter sticking his mail through the letterbox in the morning, he'd kill me.'

I'm not surprised. Mike's behaviour over the last few weeks has been most unusual. I've heard smashed glasses, raised voices and heavy thumps through his walls. Maybe it's not such a great idea to enter his lair.

No, I have a purpose. I am also dying to see what's in that room with the taped curtains. He'll never know I nosed around.

'Okay, you be lookout. Make sure my kids don't come out of my house either. Now, give me a bunk up. By the way, I'm disappointed in you.'

Pete fails to mention the rucksack. I clamber in and tiptoe through what looks like a dining room. I put my dog walking gloves on before I touch anything. There's a lot of high-end furniture covered in a thin layer of dust. Mike doesn't appear to have had any dinner parties of late. I nip into all the rooms downstairs, but the house feels empty.

I creep up the stairs, find the evil room, depress the handle and push the door. The sound of Velcro coming apart causes the hairs on my neck to stand on end. It is pitch-black. I flick the light switch and a dim red bulb lights up above a desk. I've seen enough horror movies to know a dark room when I see one. The paraphernalia is there, and it looks well used.

There are photographs in frames covering a wall. They're of animals — foxes mostly — and taken at night by the looks of things. There's one of a cat rooting in an overflowing bin. The next picture is the same animal disturbed, with a violent look on its face. I knew Mike was weird.

Then, there's Olivia. The shot is of her leaning over and buckling Charlie up in the car. Her skirt has risen and there is a glimpse of underwear. Pete would love that photo. There's also a close-up of her outside the local bakery. She's smiling at something in the distance. It's a good shot of her; natural. Even in the poor lighting I notice the glass is smudged. Kiss marks maybe? Mike has a problem.

I back out of the room. I definitely don't want him catching me in there. Nerves send adrenalin flowing into my body as I recall Mike's face that rainy night when we ignored him. Tell-tale cramps rumble through my bowels. I might have to use his facilities. Imagine if he came home and found me on his throne, flicking through his latest copy of *Outdoor Photographer*.

Just before the door shuts, I notice the black and white photo of Olivia from our house siting proudly on his desk.

Thieving bastard. What's wrong with this city? In the place I grew up, I never used to lock my door. If you do that here, it's carte blanche for every Tom, Dick, and Harry to take what he fancies. I'm glad I bought the rucksack now as I pop the stolen picture in it. I'll leave him a few presents in exchange. Maybe I won't flush afterwards. That will help his mental state.

I steal into what must be the master bedroom. It's shambolic. There's smashed wine glasses on the floor and strange stains on the walls. Even I would consider the duvet cover is in need of a wash. I have a quick glimpse in the wardrobes and under the bed, but see nothing of interest.

I step back onto the landing and notice a security camera with a flashing green light in the far corner. I spy another one on the stairs which I only notice on the way down them. There's even one in the room where I entered. I should have pulled my hood up.

Pete, frozen with terror, is still waiting outside the window, but it's now shut. He flinches when I knock to attract his attention. He almost pulls my arm out of its socket getting me through.

'Bloody hell. What the heck have you been doing in there? Why were you so long?'

'I had to check every room. It's okay. The place is empty.'

'Good. Pull the window to and let's get out of here. It can be our secret.'

'Nice. All on me now, is it? You were the look-out, remember. I have disappointing news. I didn't think he'd have security cameras.'

Pete takes an instinctive step back. 'Oh my God. He'll know. You'll be in trouble.'

Someone with that much security inside must have more outside. I stare up to the eaves of the house. Pete follows my gaze.

'Oh, shit,' he says.

'Oh, shit, indeed.'

Knowing Mike, he would have the cameras linked to his phone. We hear a slight screech of wheels in the distance. Our eyes narrow as we regard each other. We both jump as an enraged Mike pulls up in front of us.

Chapter 71

Dan

Your natural instincts take over at times such as these. We flee. I don't think I've ever seen anyone as furious as Mike when he saw us outside his house. And I have annoyed many people over the years. I sprint through my front door, thankful this time it isn't locked. Pete flies in after me, and I slam it behind him. I fumble for what feels like a long minute but can only be seconds before I slip the key in and flick it shut. We both exhale together.

I remember what Malcolm did to that internal door at his house. However, this is a bulky, wooden, external one with a good lock. I rest my hand on its solidness. A hard thump causes it to vibrate. We back away along the hallway as another heavier thud arrives. I hear a small ripping sound. Surely there's no way even Mike can kick through that. The final boot coincides with a tearing sound, and the frame splinters and snaps. Mike pushes the door open and steps through. His face is determined and wide-eyed.

We back up to the kitchen, the oven stopping us from melting into the walls. My hands are numb and I force myself to take deep breaths. Mike comes through the doorway sideways. He's so pumped up maybe his shoulders won't fit straight on.

'I want a word with you.'

The words are growled as his temper flares.

Pete whimpers next to me. I can smell the rancid stench of diarrhoea. Fleetingly, I consider telling him that Charlie does that, too. I've managed to calm myself. This isn't a movie. Although, for a minute, I am convinced I'm about to be terminated.

Nevertheless, it's real life. He might be mad, but I'm sure he's not a killer.

'Morning, Mike. That's some knock you have.'

Mike's movements are slow and jerky. He is on the edge of insanity. A smart man wouldn't provoke him.

'You. I hate.'

He can barely get the words out of his clenched jaw. What do you say to that? He's not getting a cup of tea.

'Mike, I'm going to have to ask you to leave.'

'I'm going nowhere. You, are a waste of space. Every day I see you with everything and you're too stupid to realise it. You have two wonderful children and the most fantastic partner and you don't give a shit. Olivia deserves better than you.'

'Someone like you, perhaps?'

'I suggest you stop talking if you want to survive this experience.'

Hmm. Too many *Die Hard* repeats for this guy. He's unlikely to kill me in front of an admittedly ill-looking Pete.

'I'm rich, I'm clever, I work hard, I've done everything right, and a bum like you has what I deserve. It's handed to you on a plate.'

My hackles rise.

'Is that right, Mike? Did you know I lost my job? You're rich, I'm not. I've got to move back in with my mother for a week. No longer than that, mind, as she doesn't want me there. Olivia and the kids are going to California without me for at least six months. Possibly forever. And my neighbour is a grade-A psychopath. What I have, my friend, is fuck all.'

My rant releases a little of his steam. Although the psycho comment was unnecessary. Stupidly, I'm not finished.

'She doesn't want you. Family is important to her and you're not it. Not only that, you are weird. All this Cali this, Cali that. It's bullshit. I bet you've never even been there. I checked it out online, and anyone who knows California calls it just that. Cali is for tourists and tosspots.'

I question my intelligence as I watch Mike reflate. The silence stretches on, perpetuated only by Pete's sobs.

'You broke into my house,' he snarls.

'You left a window open. I checked for burglars.'

'Rubbish. You are a thief along with every other flaw in your pointless body.'

Mike edges further into the kitchen. The big table sits between us. For that, I'm extremely grateful. I can't believe this is happening. For a start, he's a hypocrite.

'You can talk. You've been in here stealing things. I saw your dodgy dark room, you sick cretin. Photos of my Olivia everywhere and you stole my favourite picture from here, too. She'll love it when I tell her about that. Come on, Mike. When does the stalker ever get the girl? You've lost. Now leave, I'm ringing the police.'

His left eye squints when I say Olivia's name. He bares his teeth in what could be a smile or a sneer. This time, he shouts.

'You don't win. In fact, you deserve to die.'

With that, he launches himself over the table. Pete is immobile with fear and in my lunge to escape we become entangled and fall. Mike pulls me up by the back of my collar and bangs me against the wall. He turns me to face him, and slams me again. My head rings with both impacts.

Pete snivels on the floor. I shout, 'Use your martial arts,' but he's a lost cause. Against Mike's rage, he would be as effective as attacking a giant tortoise with drumsticks. However, I'm not so easily defeated. A murderous urge comes over me as his fingers grab at my throat.

I jerk my knee up hard into Mike's groin. He releases me and clutches himself. I look for a weapon to finish him off but remember the children are upstairs. I figure if I can get them out into the street, they'll be safe. I dart to the hall, and glimpse back. Mike seems to be in a lot of pain. What about Pete? I can't leave him. I tiptoe past the now-leaning-over Mike and help Pete to his feet. He staggers in the same way as a newborn fawn.

We scuttle past Mike with my hand guiding Pete's shoulder. As I edge out of the kitchen, a strong hand grabs my ankle. Mike powers up and takes my foot with him. I manage to stop my head hitting the floor and spin out of his grasp. We circle. Pete stands open-mouthed in the doorway. I get my phone out and Mike's on me. It spins away and we bang against the fridge.

I'm thankful for my recent weight training as Mike is strong and solid. We struggle in a clumsy waltz, neither of us gaining the advantage. He grunts with focus and my tank empties. Mike's innate strength and years of conditioning will overcome mine. He realises that at the same time.

I spit in his face and push him away. My eyes notice the knife block and I feign right and stretch left to grab one. Mike's too quick and the knives scatter along with the glass of water I'd left on the side. I slip on the now wet floor and he's on top of me. His meaty hands circle my neck.

I have no purchase in the position I find myself. My breath catches but I wedge my thumbs under his palms. I strain and release an ounce of pressure, but he's too powerful, focused and angry. My eyes implore Pete to do something. He staggers backwards and runs out the house.

The perimeter of my vision becomes black. Mike blinks sweat from his face in slow motion. His eyes burn into mine. My grip weakens. All that remains is a shrinking circle of light with a grimacing Mike at its centre. As even that dims, a salient fact becomes evident. Mike is capable of murder.

Chapter 72

Olivia

I wince as I hurtle past a police van. I'm miles over the limit but I have an awful feeling. Knowing Dan, there's no way he won't have gone in Mike's house. The policeman has sunglasses on and doesn't turn his head. I pray he sleeps. I remind myself to be rational and cut my speed.

My hands slip on the wheel as I career into our street. A car brakes in front of me on the wrong side of the road and I steer away with millimetres to spare. Mike's car is haphazardly parked over both drives — the driver side door swings in the wind. I screech to a stop behind it. My stomach lurches as Pete tears out of the house, and tries to sprint past me. Petrified doesn't come close to describing him. I grab his jacket.

'What is it, Pete? What's wrong.'

'It's Mike. He's gone mad. He's killing Dan.'

'What? Where?'

He slips out of my grip and sprints away. I think I hear him shout kitchen. I holler at him to ring the police. The door looks like a mule kicked it in. My thoughts are for my children, but I can't lose Dan. I charge in and race towards the kitchen. Mike is red and bulging with effort, crouching over Dan, who is purple and dying. Both men's eyes are glassy and veins bulge in their heads.

I struggle to pull Mike off him. It's as though he's set like concrete. Dan's eyes close. Panic and hysteria empty my brain. There's a carving knife on the floor. Instinctively, I pick it up and ram it through Mike's neck. His face turns in shock. Mine has the same expression. I step back, leaving the weapon in place.

Yet, still, he squeezes Dan's throat. I jump forward with a howl and yank the blade out. A spurt of hot blood blasts me in the face. Mike looks dazed now, sleepy. A second spurt covers my T-shirt. Mike slides forward and goes limp.

I drag him off Dan by pulling on his belt. Dan's spluttering, and the purple becomes less vivid.

'Where are the children?'

He rubs his throat, eyes wide and searching.

'Where are the fucking children?'

He points upstairs. I take the steps two at a time. Frantic.

'Grace, Charlie.'

I cry their names again and again. They aren't in either of their bedrooms. I push our room's door open, sobbing with worry. There they are.

Never have I cried with joy to see they've pulled the cushions and covers off our bed. They peek out from their den, oblivious to the insanity downstairs.

'Momma's home!'

I gather them up, covering them in gore. I don't care. They're safe.

Chapter 73

Olivia
Two weeks later

The last two weeks have been surreal. I left the kids playing upstairs and returned to see if Dan was okay. Mike was far from fine. His blood covered the entire kitchen floor. That bastard postman hadn't rung the police, so I did it. Dan sat in the pool and hauled in deep breaths.

To our great relief, they believed us straight away. You could make out the red finger marks on Dan's neck. The swelling dissipated after a week, and the bruise is still visible now. Dan was taken to the hospital, the kids went to my mum's, and they drove me to the police station. They caught Pete hiding at home. They brought him in for questioning, too.

I was exhausted and traumatised when they let me go. Dan had to give a statement on a gurney and they released him shortly after. He came to stay at my parents' and we've all been there ever since. We're a family again.

I found myself having hallucinations. I can't remember hearing the flesh being sliced when the knife entered, but the sound is in my dreams. Last night was the first that I slept for more than a few hours. They told me two out of three people don't develop PTSD. I hope I am one of them. I'm still on edge, but that's fading now.

Dan's been brilliant. I watch him with the children and he's so natural. They love his rough play and foolishness. His control of Charlie is impressive. He knows exactly how to distract him when he begins the slide into a tantrum. Charlie and Grace yearn to be chased, hauled in the air, and rolled around. They need their father. I was wrong to consider taking him from them.

More so, because I'm no innocent myself. Too soon we forget our own crimes. Who listened when I prayed for my own children? Did I make a trade? I understood what I was doing when I stopped taking those pills in Asia. I knew I had met someone I could raise a family with and it was my last chance. Perhaps my only chance.

Dan was oblivious, and two weeks later, I was pregnant. Dan accepted it with good grace and enthusiasm. He never once told me he regrets what happened. Yet, at the first real rocky patch in our relationship, I cast him aside. I wanted to get married and then incredibly I fell at that first hurdle. I need to remember we are partners first, because without that, the rest doesn't work. We can be lovers and friends further down the line.

I don't regret not telling Dan as him saying no was a risk I wasn't prepared to take. I have the children I dreamed of. That's not to say there's no shame at how I did it. But I'm selfish. I think most of us are.

Even my dad is happy with the current living arrangements. He gets to spend as much time as he likes with the children without being ultimately responsible. On the plus side, he and Dan seem to have made a truce from their bickering. I suspect they won't be going for a beer together, but it's better than I hoped.

As always, Beau has been brilliant. He told me to take as long as I needed. I'm hoping for closure from today. Then, we'll go to California as a family. That decision is final. If it doesn't work out, so what? We'll have done it together and given it our best efforts.

I find myself staring at my hands. The questions won't go away. Did I need to kill Mike? I know it was self-defence, but sometimes it feels like I executed him. Should

I have just stabbed him in the stomach, or slashed his face. Who made me God?

Dan has been more attentive of late. He holds me close and doesn't judge me. He loves me for who I am. I need to return those feelings, because we are lucky to have him.

Chapter 74

Olivia

The doorbell rings. The police said they would be at our house around midday, and they are punctual. My parents have taken Grace and Charlie to the park, so Dan and I wait alone. He gets up, and drones, 'duh-duh-durrr'. He pulls the curtains to one side and sneaks a peek out the window.

'There's a prison van parked outside. Do you think it's a coincidence?'

'Shut up, idiot.'

Detective Constable Sharpe and Detective Inspector Jordan walk into the room. They politely decline Dan's offer of a drink. They're both smiling, so it's good news. DI Jordan talks first.

'I'll get to the point. This was clearly a case of self-defence, so there'll be no trial. There will be an inquiry, of course, which you must attend. The powers that be are happy for you to continue your life as normal with no restrictions. I know you're moving, so you are clear to proceed.'

'Phew.'

It's still a release, even though I'm expecting it. But what other outcome could there have been?

'Everything that happened to you has been kept out of the press for the moment, but it is unrealistic to expect it to stay that way. We'll release a statement tonight. We believe Mike was Abel. At the moment, we can't know for sure as there have been so many copycat crimes. Put simply, we're overrun.'

'Why do you think Mike was Abel? Couldn't he have just been deranged? Those texts were weird.'

'The messages are part of it. The photos in his house were concerning, as was stealing the picture of Olivia from here. You confirmed that it was your underwear he had. The texts show he was plunging down the slippery slope. Unless that is, you were going to elope with him. Perhaps he lived in a fantasy world. However, it was the other things we located that gave the game away.'

He pauses and gets out a notebook.

'There was a fake beard in his kitchen cupboard, along with a pair of mirrored sunglasses. In his wash basket, we found a black scarf and a hooded sweatshirt. He owned black jeans and a big black coat. There was a Taser in his bedside cabinet, and a large lock-knife under the bed. A locket with an old lady's photo and a used hair brush were there too. His DNA was over everything. In one of the kitchen drawers there was a gold tooth which we believe came from some gruesome crimes not far from here.'

'We've yet to match the DNA to any of the crimes attributed to Abel, but there are so many, we don't know which is which. He couldn't have done all of them. Saying that, he was clever. There's so little evidence. We might never have caught him if he hadn't been obsessed with you. It won't feel like it, but you've done the city a service.'

DI Jordan stands, walks over and sits next to me.

'Try not to be too hard on yourself. You did what any normal person would have done. You should get a reward, but I'm not sure we do that for taking a life. Maybe he isn't Abel, but we found bondage magazines, too. Not complete filth, but kinky stuff. I assume that might leak first. We think he was a deviant, but we'll never know for sure what he did and didn't do. I don't think the world will miss him.'

'I thought Abel died in that supermarket massacre.'

'Mike will be the third Abel to die although he is the most likely candidate. It turns out Mike beat a sexual assault rap five years ago on his wife. We'll re-open the case. We're trying to trace her, but by all accounts, she disappeared with his son soon after the trial.

'The press will be outside his property when this gets out. There's nothing they like more than this. You must be prepared for that. It's good you are staying with relatives until this blows over. I wouldn't talk to the newspapers. Nothing good can come of that.'

My resolve is firm. 'We won't be living back here again. Not after this. All I see is that river of blood. I covered my children in it. I had to tell them it was ketchup.'

'Well, let's hope he was Abel. It looks that way as the incidents where he 'confesses' have dropped to almost nothing. That said, the lull in crime we experienced is over now. It's business as usual.'

I show them out. Dan stands next to me, and I put my arm around his waist. A fresh start with my family is what I need.

Chapter 75

Dan
A month later

'Passengers, please fasten your seat belts for take-off.'

Mine is already secured. I redo Charlie's, for the sixth time. He looks at me displaying a satanic grin, then kicks the seat in front of him. I've lost count of the number of times he's done that, despite me telling him if he does it again he'll have to go in the cargo hold with Bailey.

The bloke whose chair is being booted turns around and gives me a death stare. I say sorry to him, but hey, what can you do? He has a turbulent journey ahead. Grace has her colouring pencils out but is staring wide-eyed at the air stewardess. She must look glamorous to a seven-year-old.

Grace flew on a plane before when she was three but can't remember anything, so everything is new. I think back to my conversation about seeing hippos and giraffes for the first time. Imagine flying for the first time. Her exhilaration, anticipation, and joy make me happy, and that, in a nutshell, is the pleasure of parenthood.

Olivia is across the aisle sitting next to her parents. She gives me a smile that says a thousand words. We're bonded now, in life, but also in death. She's recovered from our ordeal like the trooper she is. Yet, I detect a shadow where there wasn't one before. I'm sure she'll be fine.

There's been a marginal decrease in nagging levels, and I've made friends with the hoover. Neither will last.

Her parents are sitting beside her. I get a thumbs up from her mother. She's wise and feisty, and scary. I'll need to watch out for her. Olivia's dad catches my eye, too. He mouths 'dickhead' at me. How lovely.

My passport is still in my jeans pocket after going through the departure gate. I flick it open and smile at my convict picture. My finger traces across the details. Imagine if I'd used my real name. Abel Daniel Smith.

I have no explanation for what I did. It seems when I'm stressed, a dark and dangerous part of me comes to the fore. My mother called it the sickness. I don't recognise the person I became. I don't recall my actions. Even now, it's hard to comprehend that it was me that instigated this torrid spell.

Yet, deep down, in the part of us all that knows the truth, I knew it was me.

I have no pity for Mike. That's what's wrong with me. Who else have I damaged beyond repair? Innocent people, for sure. Mike, however, was broken. Many others are. He'd also have killed me, given the chance.

What is it about our society that makes us become animals as soon as order breaks down? It's the herd mentality. Like when seemingly normal people join in with looting. Have their lives before this been a disguise, and is the creature climbing through the broken glass who they really are? We stampede over the cliff-edge together.

I'm glad I planted those things in Mike's house though, because I've escaped scot free. It was genius to rub everything over his dirty laundry to get his DNA on it. They found me sneaking about the place on Mike's CCTV, but Pete backed up my burglary story.

It's hard to believe I'm capable of such horror. I believed there's enough murder, violence, and slaughter without me adding to it. Yet, from a young age there was something missing inside of me. What I do remember is owning up to those black acts and then sewing them together into a dark cloud that hung above the city. Indeed, it was poison rain.

I became soulless. My time was spent walking the streets when everyone slept, or trawling the web for dark doings to confess to. I'd find myself posting letters I had no memory of writing, finishing calls I didn't remember starting. Then, it was as if Abel slept, and poor stressed out, tired Dan was dragged into the light.

It wasn't all me. An old lady called Judith was found swinging from a beam in her house a week ago. She left a detailed, dated, suicide letter confessing to pushing a man in front of a train. She said he became the focus of her hatred. Her scrawled writing somehow ended up in the newspapers. Her words provoked a debate on isolation and being neighbourly.

The note concluded: 'I'm lonely and scared in this place, and I wanted to be noticed. I don't even think I'm sorry. At least I felt alive. There is nothing after this life as no God would permit such acts. Therefore, I choose oblivion.'

Judith, the birdwatcher, was discovered many weeks after her untimely death. No one missed her. Raymond, her husband, was in bed. His mummified remains were in the only inhabited room upstairs. Social services and the police are investigating.

Whereas before, when I was little more than a child, my recollection of the cruel events was hazy. This time, I recalled nothing. I don't know what I did. However, there were signs. Three times I found my spade covered in fresh mud, and once, there was skin on it. I'd find strange mementoes in my pockets. Weird things like combs and even a tooth once. Twice I had to clean blood splatters from my car.

I forced the being that was Abel away many years ago. I hoped never to see him again. This wretched city dragged him through the veil and set him upon an unsuspecting population who cowered in his fury. The fact others joined in, shows civilisation is just a façade.

I have flashbacks. Are they from my life, or from movies I've watched? There's a memory of a sad and lonely old soldier, images of scared women and isolated graves, and a drunken reveller. Before, there seemed to be rules. No children or pets. The Abel who returned was too long in the gloom. This beast was angry, vengeful, and pitiless. He was a devil to be feared.

I read that the UK has two active serial killers at any one time and over twenty-five in the US. There are always escalating murderers. Any number of violent, ruthless people who kill or destroy for sex, profit or personal gain. Others lose their minds and then commit terrible crimes. I'm not unusual.

Don't tell me you haven't been cut up by another person while driving your car. There will be people who have taken advantage of you over money or time. I'll bet there was a little part of you that wanted revenge. Occasionally, you let your mind wander and imagine the terrible acts you'd do. Then you jolt out of it and, with a shake of your head, carry on your way. When I thought that way, I later found out from the news I did actually do those things.

I have to accept I'm crazy. Well, to me, there's a hint of jollity to crazy. Insane would be more appropriate. I understood at the time when I suggested other people were Abel, that I was distracting them from the truth. I trained myself long ago not to dwell on my actions. I didn't acknowledge my acts. You too may remember fragments when you wake, but soon they are gone from your grasp.

Nowadays, if you want a reminder of what you've done, you can just type unsolved crimes into a search engine. Keeping the odd memento gives you a personal connection but they are dangerous. My brain was so frazzled, I kept forgetting where I'd put them. Imagine my shock when Charlie came in wearing that runner's sunglasses. It's lucky no one suspects what's right in front of them. It was worth it though because every time I opened that chess set, it felt like I was lifting the lid of a cabinet freezer.

As for who chased Olivia that night; I'm afraid I was also responsible. The homeless guy from the park picked up that task for me for surprisingly little. He did say he was looking for a job. It was a final roll of the dice from a desperate man. I wanted her to hate this city as I do. Worryingly, I don't think Abel had anything to do with that decision or the one to hide her underwear.

What about the other crimes I confessed to? Who broke into that woman's apartment and cut her hair? Who took that girl to the woods and fried her alive. Not me, surely? Yet, our scissors went missing at the same time, and I've enjoyed a nice fire since I was a boy. I've never owned a chainsaw or hammer, yet I found a receipt for both, paid in cash.

But what can I do? That chapter is over now. I'm back to being Dan. As we leave the nightmare behind us, it could just be a dream. Summer is here. Today, we start a new journey together. It's a fresh place, and a clean slate. I hear California is beautiful. There will be long, quiet beaches and sun-drenched vineyards. Out the window of the plane, the sky is golden. I wonder, should somebody warn them I'm coming? Let them know that even though he sleeps now, Abel is half of me, and he is alive.

The End.

Dissociative identity disorder (DID)

DID, which used to be known as multiple personality disorder, is a complex psychological condition where a person's identity separates into two or more distinct personalities. It can be caused by many things but often it's due to severe trauma during early childhood. This may be repetitive physical, sexual, or emotional abuse.

Usually, the primary identity is the actual person but they are often passive, guilty, and submissive. Each personality state, or 'alter', may be similar or completely unalike, even to the point of a different voice and mannerisms. They could have a new accent, or even be a different sex or animal. The alters' characteristics contrast with those of the primary identity. Situations such as stress can cause a particular alter to emerge. The various identities might not be aware of each other or if they are, they may deny it. Some refuse to acknowledge their actions even if they're obvious.

Switching can be instant or take minutes, or gradually occur over several days. People with the condition share symptoms as well as the split personality problem. Night terrors, sleepwalking, insomnia, substance abuse, panic attacks, flashbacks, mood swings, anxiety, hallucinations, amnesia, and time loss are common complaints. They may find themselves feeling possessed.

In other cases, the host with the person's real name is oblivious of the existence of the other personalities.

There are no specific medications to treat the condition. Indeed, some are not convinced of its existence. Whatever, it is distressing for individuals with symptoms and those around them. Sadly, over two thirds of people with the disorder have attempted to take their own lives. Perhaps, surprisingly, some studies have shown those with DID often aren't violent. What is true though, is that they may self-medicate, and substance abuse is linked to all types of crime including murder.

The International Society for the Study of Trauma and Dissociation calls for more research and understanding of this little-known condition and is a good first port of call for those wanting more information.

Stress caused the demon inside Dan to take control. I wonder, and worry, how modern life affects people's mental health. Our children are especially vulnerable.

This book started off its life as a simple story about relationships, so I'm not entirely sure what that says about me!

Thank you for reading, I hope you were entertained.

Acknowledgements

As always, many people helped with this book. A special thank you to Richard Burke for his ongoing support. Alex Williams and Marika Dworzak edited and proofread this book on numerous occasions during its many incarnations. I couldn't have done it without you.

I would also like to thank, in no particular order, Yvette Smart, Nicola Holmes, Alex Knell, Mark Blackburn, Kate Symonds, Louise Holmes, Emma De Oliveira, Jo Curtis, Jamie Jones, Steve Mansbridge, Barry Butler, Jono Hill, Caroline Vincent, Ros Rendle, Jim Ody, Yvette Parker-Radford, Nessa Stimson, Sarah Northwood, Jennifer Bradley, Sarah Muxlow, Louise Brown, Teresa Maher, Tina Griffin, Louise Brown, Sarah Hobbs, Justin Whitehouse and Mark Gregson.

And finally, Amanda Rayner, for letting me know what a woman really thinks.

If you enjoyed this, you'll also love Ross Greenwood's *Fifty Years of Fear*.

Serious stories told with a sense of humour.

*

Please leave a review.